THE OUTLAW GOSPEL

- THE KING'S MARK -

BOOK I

EASTON ANDERSON

Published by Franklin Publishers
Printed in the United States of America

For permissions, inquiries, or additional copies, contact:
Franklin Publishers
www.franklinpublishers.com

Table of Contents

Prologue

The midday sun was a red branding iron high in the sky, striking down on my skin, turning it red and blistery. This was made worse by the scorching sand, which felt like hot coals on my bare feet with each step. Above my head flew three harbingers of death, occasionally providing me with a shady respite that lasted a fraction of a second. The air was still and hot. In the distance, a rattlesnake or insect hissed.

All things considered, I was in bad shape, walking in a direction I hoped was right. I didn't care too much about the sun or the sand at the moment. My thoughts and attention were turned to a sharp, throbbing pain in my gut. It took all the strength I had remaining in my left arm to cover a gaping bullet hole somewhere around my liver, which, if I removed my hand, would pour out the blood at a high rate of speed. I had to try and find a shady spot out of the sun so I could bandage myself.

All around was nothing, just an empty wasteland where no man could survive. On the horizon was a small boulder, no taller than a man. If I walked to it, by that time, there could be enough shade for me to recover enough strength to tear a sleeve or pant leg to try and stop my profuse bleeding. I hoped so, anyway.

"Follow Reyes, he said," I wasn't talking to anyone. Perhaps if the birds understood English, they would pity me. "You should get your revenge." I cursed the name of the man who had told me that. "Should've figured you'd be in cahoots with that snake."

My thoughts turned to my mother, to my home. It felt like so long ago, but it hadn't been long. Five months? Six months, maybe? I wasn't too sure at that point. I missed her dearly at that moment, for the first time since she died. I knew that I was gonna join her at that moment. I felt so sure of it, as though the Angel of Death were chasing me like a wild horse. No matter how fast I walked to that stupid rock, to the one thing that had me clinging to life, I felt that it would catch me and trample me under its cold hooves.

I laughed at how stupid I had been. What did I know about killing a man, about vengeance? I was a kid from a big city that had a police department. I hadn't shot a gun before coming out to Folklore. I should've just stayed on my uncle's ranch. That's what mom would've wanted. She wouldn't want me out here playing Lawman and Avenger.

I tried to spit, but my mouth was too dry. I was so thirsty. Maybe there would be some water by that rock? I hated alcohol, but better than water would be whiskey to dull my constant gunshot pain. I'd even drink that Mexican drink; what did they call it? *Mezcal* or something. Anything to get me some relief. Despite my hopelessness, that wild horse with its grim rider called Death never caught up to me. I made it to the rock. There was about a foot or so of shade on one side, but anything was better than nothing. I collapsed into its shadowy embrace, feeling instant relief as I did. It's incredible how something so little can be so great when needed. I sat there for a minute, wishing that my dreams of water had been able to come true, too, but logic told me otherwise.

After several minutes of sitting there, I finally regained enough strength. I grabbed my left shirt sleeve with my right hand and tugged hard, tearing it off at the seam. This would expose my pale arm to the blazing sun, but at least I wouldn't bleed out. I wrapped it around my waist like a girdle.

"Lord," I started to say a prayer, something I'd never done much of in my life. "If you're listening to me, I could really use some water. Also, a horse or a mule wouldn't be so bad either."

I felt exhausted. I looked up at my feathery companions circling above my head. Would they try to eat me if I slept for a bit? Did it really matter? I figured it didn't, if I was just gonna die anyway. My mom was dead; what else did I have left? I thought of my aunt and uncle, but mostly of my kid cousin, Tabitha, crossed my mind. Would those rats kill her, too? She didn't deserve it, not for some stupid ranch in the middle of nowhere. It didn't matter if there was treasure or anything at all. She was just a kid; she didn't deserve to die.

Despite my exhaustion, this thought kept me awake. Kept me from lying down and dying comfortably in the shade. I painfully forced myself to my feet and looked around. There was nothing as far as the eye could see. I sighed and started to climb to the top of the small boulder. Even a few feet could make the difference between seeing some kind of landmark and not seeing anything. My wound stabbed and bled as I climbed, but I made it up eventually. I looked around again. Still nothing. I screamed in frustration, which caused a crow hidden in the brush to jump and fly away.

I hopped off the boulder and sat down in the shade once more. It was no use. The sun was going down. I would have to rest there until the morning.

I didn't sleep much. The setting sun brought cool relief, though the respiteful dusk quickly turned into a freezing night. My joints felt stiff, and my muscles ached. Every shiver hurt as it broke the scab that had started forming around the red circle in my gut. I would've killed someone for a blanket.

By the time the sun came back up, I was just about ready to give up my own ghost. I couldn't believe that I was happy with the blazing fire in the sky that tortured me throughout all of yesterday. With the rising sun, I climbed the boulder once more.

Just as I was about to jump down from the rock, frustrated that nothing had changed between yesterday and today, something caught my eye. A single glare, too far away to see what it was. It could've been literally anything. A mirror on an old, dried-out wagon, a shiny bit of metal on the bit of a horse, or just a somewhat polished rock that happened to catch the sun at the right angle. It didn't matter at that point. I had to follow it. I had no other option, and a chance of something was better than aimlessly wandering.

Climbing down the rock this time was about as difficult as climbing up. The pain felt too much to bear, and it was burning at this point. I started my shamble in that general direction, slowly but surely. I was pretty sure the climb down tore open my scab.

I walked for what felt like hours. The sun got hot again, taunting me, telling me to just lay down and give in. I was just a kid, shot and dying in a foreign land.

I was so distracted by my poor state that I almost missed the very thing that would save my life.

The ground changed suddenly. I wasn't walking on hot, loose sand but instead packed dirt. I saw the very thing that I wanted to see at that moment. There were hoof prints in the dirt. This was a horse trail. I nearly cried tears of joy as I started following the prints. I wasn't going to die.

I can't remember what happened next, but I was somehow lying on the cold ground. I didn't feel pain, so no one had hit me. I'd probably fallen. The ground felt so comfy at that moment, though, so I just closed my eyes for a moment. I promised myself I would get back up after a second, but that second was taking its sweet time.

Chapter 1

El Gaucho, Martín Fierro

About six months earlier

I was tired of train rides. I swore to myself that I wouldn't ever set foot on another train. I was done. Many folks would enjoy traveling by train, but I had decided I was not one of them. This was the final leg of my journey from Port City, Connecticut, to a hoo-dunk town in the middle of nowhere called Folklore. I had a hard time imagining my mother *ever* making this same trip before she'd died, especially not every year since the railroad made it possible to visit her brother. Despite my disdain for train travel, I wished I had gone with her at least once. That's what happens when someone you love dies prematurely; you miss them and regret the time you could've spent with them. Going to my uncle's ranch made me wish I could spend a little bit more time with her.

I was sixteen years old when my mother died suddenly of some disease. She never figured out which one because she was so busy working to support me. In fact, I hardly had any memories of her being around too much until I was eight. She always wanted to send me to college and make me an educated man. Told me she'd always wanted me to be a writer. So, in

1885, when she died, I didn't have any valuable skills besides academics, so I would've been sent to a farm anyway to work as an indentured worker. Luckily, my uncle found out I was alone and paid a train ticket to Folklore. It's hard to feel fortunate about that kind of stuff when you're just a kid, though, especially when it means your whole world is flipped around.

"Hey kid," the train worker said, pushing a cart in the aisle beside me, "We're almost to Folklore. You're the only one getting off here, so we're gonna leave quick. Get your stuff ready."

I nodded, acknowledging him, but I didn't say anything in response. He waited a second but continued, passing out coffee to the other passengers. He'd been on every train I'd been on, so he already knew I didn't have any money to buy coffee or sweets. He didn't even bother to offer it to me, though, which I felt was rude. I didn't feel strongly enough about it to say or do anything.

After getting my leather briefcase from under the seat, I pulled out the only photo of my uncle.

It was a portrait taken from a visit to some city out here in the West. It was the only thing I had left from my mom besides a worn silver necklace she used to wear. The photo wasn't sentimental, but it was the only way I would recognize my Uncle Wesley.

Sure enough, the train hardly stopped in Folklore. The engineer didn't even really stop the engine; he just put on the brakes sufficiently for me to get off. I soon saw why after I got off.

The town was small. Calling it a town is an overstatement. There was a single main street that couldn't have spanned for more than a hundred yards. There were a few minor side streets, but none were wide enough for a stagecoach to fit through. None of the roads were paved; they were just dirt. The train station, if you can even call it that, was a wooden platform built next to the train tracks at the very head of the main street. No ticket booth. No fancy building. A sign beside the platform said train tickets could be bought at the post office.

It started to drizzle.

I looked around the platform, trying to spy my uncle's dirty blonde hair; he had the same hair color as my mom and me. I didn't see him or anyone that looked like him around. In fact, I was the only one near the platform. I wasn't sure what to do when I heard Spanish being spoken from a building near the train platform, a saloon.

"*¿El tren ya llegó?*" The voice yelled loudly, "*¿Por qué no me dijeron, imbeciles?*"

A man stepped out of the saloon doors, unlike any other I had seen until that point. He had long, dark hair and a full, shaggy beard. He wore a wide, flat-brimmed hat and a poncho covering his shoulders. Around his waist, he wore a girdle with a long, ornate dagger sticking out of one side and the handle of a revolver sticking out the other side. He also wore baggy pants and riding boots. He wore a short Spanish saber on his left side, which no one else carried in town.

"Are you Asa Hendricks?" He asked in slightly accented English as he approached me. I was scared to answer. This man looked rough.

"Yessir," I responded quietly.

"You're a spitting image of your mother, you know that?" He said, patting me on the back roughly. He laughed heartily and rubbed my blonde hair, "I am Martín Fierro. I work for your uncle. He sent me to come and get you."

"Come and get me?" I asked, breathing a sigh of relief, "I thought he lived here in town."

"No, *chico*, this is just where the train is. Wes lives probably ten miles from here. What? Did you think his ranch was gonna be here in town?"

"How are we getting there?" I asked, "Is there a coach or wagon prepared nearby?" Martín Fierro let out another hardy laugh. His breath smelled of beer. He rubbed my head roughly again.

"We are gonna ride there, Asa." He told me. I gave him an uncomfortable look.

"I've never ridden a horse before." I admitted, "I am not sure if I will be able to ride there. Could you perhaps go get a wagon? You can call me Ace, by the way."

"*Santa María,* he told me you were green, but I never imagined *this* green. *No te preocupes, chico.* Don't worry. I am one of the most skilled horsemen you'll ever meet. If I can't get you riding, no one can."

His confidence didn't reassure me. He led me down the street to the saloon. There were two horses tied up to a post.

"My horse is called *Magdalena.* She is named after a woman I loved once. She is a Criollo from my home country. That's what we have called the race, anyway. I brought her mother with me when I came here to this country. Her ancestors have been in my family longer than the last name Fierro."

"You sure seem to know a lot about horses, Martín," I said.

"I know everything there is to know. I have been around horses my whole life. Anyways, yours is an old mare called Elenor. She's your uncle's oldest horse. Good stock. A Morgan. She's very calm. Should be easy for you to ride."

I looked at the old mare. She was brown with a dark mane. She was pretty skinny, too, but she didn't look unhealthy. She wore an ancient black leather saddle. She was about as tall as Martín's gray horse, though he was much stockier. Also, his had a very different saddle, one lined with white sheepskin rather than just leather.

"Saddle's old, but it fits her." Martín said, untying the horses, then mounting his horse with ease, "When we get you a new horse, we'll get you a new saddle." He climbed so quickly that I almost couldn't pay attention to how he did it. He must've seen me struggling. "It's easy now. Boot, er... shoe, in your case, in the stirrup, jump up, and swing your other leg over."

To my surprise, it wasn't too tricky. I tried a few times but was able to quickly mount the horse on the third try. Martín nodded and whooped in approval.

"Now, hold on with your knees and grab the reins. For now, you will use the reins to steer, but when you get good, you can direct the horse with your knees. This makes it easier to shoot from the saddle. Good, now to make her get going, tap your heels into her sides."

I did as he indicated, but Elenor, my horse, didn't seem to want to go. I tried a few times, but she still wouldn't budge. Martín wasn't waiting; his horse was already trotting down the path. I jammed my heels into Elenor's sides. Elenor let out a loud neigh and started a swift gallop. I started panicking.

"Martín!" I cried out for help. The man just laughed.

"Hold the stirrups with your feet and yank back on the reins!" He directed. I must've done something wrong because when I yanked back on the horse's reins, Elenor stopped, but I didn't. I flew forward straight into the mud.

"Fierro, who is this kid?" I heard an older gentleman laugh, "He just ate mud like this was his first time riding a horse.

"He is Asa, Wesley's nephew. It actually *is* his first time riding a horse." Martín's fast-approaching voice said. I looked up from what I felt like was my grave. I knew my face was red with embarrassment, but I doubted anyone could see due to the mud that covered me from head to toe.

I felt a strong hand grab my arm and help me up. Fierro helped me wipe the mud from my face and clothes.

"You didn't hold the stirrups." He told me. I scowled at him.

"How am I supposed to hold the stirrups with my feet?" I asked him, frustrated and hurting. "It's easier if you had some riding boots." Martín shrugged. "But *señor* Hendricks didn't give me any cash to buy you anything. He told me to just bring you to the ranch. But you need to dig your feet into the stirrups more if you're gonna stop like that."

Fierro helped me get back into the saddle, and we set off again. I finally got how hard I needed to dig my heels into the horse's sides. Martín said it would be easier to manage the horse's speed once I got some boots with spurs, but for now, I would have to manage with just my heels.

After a while, I felt like I was getting the hang of riding the horse. At least at the trotting pace we were going at. Martín said he'd typically gallop there, but with my inexperience and Elenor's age, he didn't want to risk it.

"So, how long until we are there?" I asked Martín, trying not to sound annoying. I was already tired from the three or so train rides. While this was much different, the sun was hot and already starting to burn my face and heat up my black clothing.

"Not terribly long. We will be there before dinner time. I hear *la señora* Hendricks is gonna cook you a special dinner. If you need to stop and take a break, let me know. We are making good time. You probably ain't used to riding a saddle, so you'll probably be sore after a while."

"Alright, I appreciate that," I said, giving him a nod. "Have you been working for my uncle long?"

"Yes, the better part of eight years. I somehow ended up in Folklore with nothing but my horse, gun, and knife. I needed cash, so I was offering to break horses. Well, your uncle liked me so much that he made me a permanent employee."

"Break horses?" I asked, not sure to what he was referring.

"You know, break horses. Get them used to a rider. Basic riding training. I'm really good at it. Most horsemen here take about two months to break a horse; I can do it in half that time with some tricks from my country."

"Where are you from?" I asked the strange man, "Mexico or Spain?"

"*Ninguno de los dos, chico.*" He put on a solemn face and pulled out his dagger, "Neither. You asking to be killed?" My face turned white, and I felt sick to my stomach. Fierro laughed and put the dagger back in the scabbard in his girdle. "Relax, *boludo*. I'm just messing with you. I am from a country called *Argentina*. It's just about as far south as a man can go."

"By Brazil, then?"

"*Exacto*, but further south."

"Are you a cowboy then? What do they call them? A *vaquero*?"

"Nah, in my country, we are called a different name, *un gaucho*. Very different cultures. We're more skilled, too, compared to all of the *Mexicanos* I've ever met. Don't tell anyone I told you that, though."

"So, how long have you been here?"

"I came to this country when I was about your age, probably. A little older, maybe nineteen? I was stupid. I thought I was going to come here and be a famous gunfighter or treasure hunter. I think I had my head in too many books. My father always told me that I needed to focus more on the horses and the ranch, but you know how kids are, always looking for adventure."

"You're educated then? And rich?"

"My family is rich, but I haven't seen that money since I left Argentina. I guess you could say I am educated. My father was a rancher, and he hired a German to teach us a bunch of things. Reading, mathematics, Latin, Italian, French, German, even fencing. He just didn't teach us English, which is why I don't speak it too good. I learned when I came to this country."

"I never would've guessed," I said thoughtfully.

"Yeah, most people don't. My father was a traditionalist, *aparte de nuestra educación*. We dressed like this. We carry knives. We ate meat and drank *mate*."

"What is *mate*?"

"It is a tea grown in my country. Hard to get here. Very healthy. We call it *la hierba de vida,* the herb of life. I'd offer you some, but my supply ran out years ago, and I haven't been able to get some."

"You live a fascinating life, Martín."

"Nah, I just live my life as it comes. I am a simple man, just trying to make his place in the world." He said, waving my comment off with a hand. "Do you shoot, Asa?"

"No, sir. I've never shot a gun in my life."

"That's about to change," Fierro told me, drawing his revolver from his girdle. He held it by the barrel and passed it over to me. I took the grip and examined it. It was long for a handgun. This was a cavalry revolver, a Colt Dragoon. It had been customized and altered to fire .44 caliber cartridges rather than cap-and-ball. Fierro clearly treasured this gun. It was clean and well taken care of. "Let's stop the horses for a second. Don't point it at anything you don't wanna shoot. To aim, put that post in the front between the sights in the back. Aim at that coyote there."

He pointed a finger down the road to a coyote eating a bird or a small mammal. I held the gun out in front of me and aimed like he said. The gun felt heavier than I imagined, but I got used to the weight.

"Good. Just like that." Fierro said, watching me. I kept my eyes trained on the sights of the gun. "Now, to shoot, pull the hammer back, then squeeze the trigger. Don't pull it or yank it; squeeze, like the squeeze of a hand."

I pulled the hammer back. It let out a loud clicking sound that would become all too familiar to me in the coming years. I had to recenter my sights on the coyote, which didn't turn his attention away from the food. I aimed for a few seconds and fired. The gun cracked, my ears rang, and the coyote yelped. I looked up, but it was running away. I had missed it completely.

"The gun!" Martín yelled. I passed it to him. He took aim, cocked, and fired in less than a second. The coyote dropped, yelping and crying out. Fierro had hit it, but he hadn't killed it. "Come on!" Fierro said, spurring his horse to a slow gallop. I did my best to catch up.

Fierro got off his horse before it even came to a complete stop. I did the same, but not as gracefully. He pulled the dagger from his girdle and passed it to me.

"End its pain, *chico*." He said somberly. I gulped and took the long blade. "Right in the heart, behind the shoulder. Quickly. Don't let it suffer for too long. It's easy to take a shot at a living creature from a distance, but a real killer can end something up close, too."

I looked at him, then at the coyote, whimpering quietly now. Fierro was right; I didn't want it to suffer more. I knelt at its side and plunged the long dagger into its side, exactly where

Fierro told me. The creature closed its eyes and stopped its breathing. It was dead.

I returned the blade to Fierro, who pulled a white handkerchief from his pocket and wiped the blood from the dagger. He sheathed it again and patted my back.

"Good job, *amigo*. Can't have coyotes this close to the ranch. You're gonna have to get used to killing them 'cause that's probably what your uncle is gonna have you do a lot of. We'll work on your aim."

We mounted back up. My mind dwelt on the coyote I'd killed. Killing it made me think of my mother, oddly enough. Had this coyote been a parent to some creature somewhere? It didn't matter. It was dead, and its suffering was over.

Chapter 2
Hendricks' Ranch

"Well, here we are," Fierro said as we trotted past a tall fence gate. Hanging at the top was a long wood plank with the words 'Hendricks' Ranch' painted red. The ranch itself was like its own village. Ranch hands were rushing in and out of the street, doing various jobs and chores. Shacks were on one side, and a building that said 'General Store' was in the center. Women ran in and out of buildings, cooking food or hanging laundry. Children played games like horseshoes or marbles. It was very nearly the size of Folklore itself.

"It's massive," I remarked, trotting past a few workers carrying small hay bales. They looked up at me on my horse, wearing my city clothes, as though I were some sort of diplomat or ambassador from a faraway place. I felt like a stranger. There was a pronounced class difference in the city, but here, black, white, and Mexican all worked alongside one another. The only two who seemed out of place were Fierro and me. Fierro was eccentric and carried a confidence about himself, riding through the ranch grounds. These people respected him. I, of course, didn't fit in because I wasn't one of these people. My face wasn't weathered from the sun, my hands not calloused from years of hard labor. I felt a pit in my stomach, somewhat worried that I would be stuck doing what these men were doing, hauling hay and digging manure. This wasn't what my mother had wanted for me. I had to remind myself that it was good that

I was out here because I would be doing this or worse with no pay if I were still in the city.

"The ranch house is just up the road. You can ride there yourself. I have some other things to attend to. I am sure I will see you again after you're settled in." Fierro said, removing his wide hat from his head. *"¡Chau muchacho, Te veo luego!* See you later!"

With that farewell, Fierro started galloping toward the Foreman's office. I trotted up the road, taking in everything. Despite all the animals and people, for the first time since arriving in Folklore, I realized that this place was beautiful. The grass was green. The mountains were blue in the distance. The air was clear, and the sky was so blue. I felt happy.

I arrived at the ranch house. It was massive. Three stories. A large, square-shaped house. The siding was painted white. It had a large porch on the front that wrapped around it. Elenor walked herself up to a beam next to the patio. I dismounted and tried to tie the reins to the beam. I cursed, realizing Fierro hadn't shown me how to tie a horse up properly.

"Do you need help?" A young girl's voice said behind me. I turned around. There was a girl a few years younger than me. Her brunette hair was braided in two pigtails. Her dress was a light blue and long, stopping just below her mid-calf. She wore a white apron.

"Yeah, that would be nice," I said, rubbing my head. The girl took the reins from me and tied the horse up properly.

"I'm Tabitha." She said, smiling at me. "Elenor was my first horse. I learned to ride with her. She's so nice."

"Asa," I replied, still embarrassed that I couldn't tie the horse up, but this girl could. "Ah, I see... You're my cousin. You look like your ma."

"That's what they tell me." I laughed nervously. Something about this girl was weird. I couldn't exactly put my finger on it, but she was odd.

"Tabitha, there you are!" A woman exclaimed, stepping out the front door. "I've been looking for you everywhere. Did you get those leeks, as I asked? Your cousin will be here any minute, and I need the leeks to finish the– Lord Almighty, Asa, is that you? What happened to your clothes? You're filthy!"

"I sorta got thrown into the mud while trying to ride the horse." I explained, "You must be my Aunt Rachel."

"Oh, you poor child." Aunt Rachel said, hugging my head close to her chest. She was tall, especially for a woman. Or maybe I was just short. I only came up to her chin. Tabitha looked exactly like her. She even wore her long brunette hair in braids like Tabitha had. Rachel looked so tired, though, as though she hadn't slept that night.

"Come on in. Normally, I'd make you take off those clothes, but I can't do that to you right now. Poor thing. I can't imagine the pain you're feeling right now, having lost your mother and all. Food's almost ready; you are probably starving."

She took my hand and nearly dragged me inside. Tabitha followed closely at my heels with that same odd look as though she were thinking about something else.

"Wesley!" Aunt Rachel called once we'd set foot in the house. I heard his steps before I saw him. If I'd thought that my Aunt Rachel was tall, Uncle Wesley was massive. A bear of a man. He looked very different from the old photo I had, too. His hair was long, and he had a thick beard. His eyes lit up when he saw me.

"Asa, my boy!" He roared and smiled, "You've grown so much."

Wesley nearly scooped me up and squeezed me to death with a giant bear hug. "Good to see you too, uncle." I gasped, almost unable to breathe.

I'd never remembered meeting Wesley. He was my mom's younger brother. When she was already an adult, living with my father, Wesley, and their father had come out here to start the ranch. Their father had earned the deed to the property for his valiant service in the War against the Confederates. My mother said Wesley was nearly a bit younger than I was when they left Port City. He'd probably met me as a baby, but I hadn't ever been able to come out with my mother to see him and the ranch, not that it ever before interested me.

"You're skinnier than I expected." Uncle Wesley said, finally letting me down to examine me, "Some of my old clothes will probably fit you, though. And skinniness isn't anything your aunt's cooking can't fix."

"I'll go set the table." Aunt Rachel said, smiling, "Come along, Tabitha."

"Come sit down! I'm sure you're tired from the journey." Wesley demanded, taking me into a parlor. I sat down on a sofa opposite of him.

"Thank you for bringing me out here, sir," I told him. I really was grateful. Living indentured as a state ward had never sounded appealing to me. Even though I would probably never get to go to any college now.

"It's no trouble, my boy," Wesley responded warmly. He removed a wood pipe from his pocket, packed it with tobacco, and lit it up. He took a long drag before breathing out the smoke. "You're family, after all. My sister was very dear to me. I couldn't leave her son with no one. The ride from town went ok?"

"Oh yes, it was fine, except for the part where the horse threw me into the mud."

"*Elenor* made you eat dirt?" He asked, clearly surprised that the old mare had thrown me. "Not exactly. I have never ridden a horse, you see, and I bit off more than I could chew, I'm afraid."

"Well, that's gonna be your first chore." Wesley laughed, "Fierro's gonna help you catch and break a horse. He give you any trouble?"

"Mr. Fierro?" I asked, clarifying, "No, sir. He was actually accommodating."

"Good, good." He said, taking another puff of his pipe, "He's a good man. He is a little peculiar and can be a prankster sometimes, but he knows horses better than anyone I know.

Hard worker, too. That's why I made him the Foreman of the ranch."

"He's the Foreman? I never would've guessed."

"That's because he spends most of his money on whiskey and cards." Wesley joked. I laughed nervously, unsure of how much of what he was saying *actually was* a joke, "He was raised in a pretty traditional way. Real simple man. He is more comfortable among the ranch hands than with rich folk. Don't get me wrong, though; he's one of the most intelligent people I've ever met. When I met Fierro, he'd only been in this country for two years, but he already spoke English better than most of the folk in the county."

That was odd. My uncle said Fierro had only been in this country for two years when he'd met him, but Fierro had told me that he came when he was nineteen…

Aunt Rachel peeked her head into the parlor. "Dinner's almost ready." She told my Uncle, "Why don't you go show Asa where his room is? Get him a change of clothes, and he can wash up before we eat."

"Alright, love," Wesley responded very endearingly. He took one final puff of his pipe and put out the flame before standing up. I followed him up the two flights of stairs into the attic.

"This is where you'll be staying." Wesley said, "I know it's not much, but Rachel said you might enjoy having your own space better than having a room next to ours or Tabitha's. We can move you if you'd like, though."

"No, this is perfect." I responded, smiling, "Thank you so much."

"Life out here ain't easy. And you'll have to work hard, but I am not making you a ranch hand. From today on out, think of yourself as my son. That's why you'll be working with Fierro most of the time. I intend for you to take over as Foreman when Martín decides to leave, so learn the job. We'll call for you when dinner's ready."

Having said that, Uncle Wesley ducked out of the attic room. I decided to have a look around.

The room was large, and it wasn't finished. The walls were wooden planks. If there had been a hole in the wall, I probably could've seen straight through it without a problem. The ceiling was tall, and there were plenty of windows, though, so there wouldn't be any lighting issues.

The furniture in the room could have been more abundant. A bed, a nightstand with a gas lamp, a dresser with a few shelves, a full-length mirror, and an empty bookshelf. The furniture was all brand new despite the lack of décor or fanciness. Even the mattress of the bed.

I peeled off my crusty clothes, taking care not to get dried mud on the floor, and placed them in a laundry hamper near the door. I opened the dresser's drawers until I found some clothes that fit. Sure enough, these clothes did, in fact, appear to be some of my Uncle's old clothes, but I wasn't one to complain. They fit well enough, and I felt as though I would fit in much better wearing these clothes. I looked at myself in the mirror. Despite my lack of boots or a hat, I thought I looked like a real cowboy. The clothing was simple, though, a light blue shirt and brown trousers. Satisfied, I placed my briefcase on the top of the dresser and went downstairs.

Dinner was delicious. Steak, potatoes, and a stew. I had never eaten so good in my life. I also got to know my aunt and uncle a little better.

"So, how did you two meet?" I asked them, between mouthfuls of meat. They looked at each other and smiled.

"It's not much of a story." Wesley smiled, "When my pa and I started this ranch, we didn't have a horse, just a mule. 'Dog,' we called him, I'm not sure why. That mule lived for ten years. He was mean, this mule. Wouldn't let anyone ride him. That didn't stop me from trying, of course."

"One day, when he was around your age, he tried to ride this mule," Aunt Rachel cut him off, continuing the story, "Dog decided he was done with Wesley's antics and kicked him in the leg. Broke it, actually."

"That must've hurt," I remarked. The pair laughed.

"Oh, it did." Wesley explained, "Worst pain I've ever felt."

"Anyway," Rachel continued, "His father, your grandfather, loaded Wesley into a wagon pulled by oxen. They rushed to town as fast as possible to the town doctor, who was my pa."

"Really?" I asked, "Your dad was the town doctor?"

"Still is!" Rachel exclaimed, "I help him every once in a while. I used to be his nurse before I married. While he was at my pa's clinic, he took one look at me and decided that I was gonna be his wife."

"She took all my pain away." Wesley smiled, leaning towards her.

"While he was trying to get my attention, he kept coming in every single time he was in town and kept saying that he had something wrong with him."

"What did your dad do?"

"At first, he would examine him, but after a while, he started to use your uncle for what he called 'clinical trials'. He would give him all manner of mix and potion to see what it would do to him." Rachel explained, laughing hysterically.

"Did anything happen? Was everything ok, I mean?"

"I wouldn't be here if things weren't ok!" My uncle yelled, joking.

"It's true, everything was pretty ok." Aunt Rachel said mischievously, "But my pa *did* discover a couple of herbal cures with your uncle."

"Don't you get started!" Wesley warned her, though he was smiling and holding back laughter. "My pa discovered a cure for the runs, for constipation, and, *really* commonly used among the old folk of the town, my pa discovered a cure for, ahem... erectile dysfunction using your uncle."

I felt my face turn bright red as she said that. My aunt and uncle burst out in laughter. I eventually started to laugh, too. We laughed for a good minute or so until we finally could contain it.

"Anyway..." My Uncle finally continued through his chortles, "The rest is history. I eventually got your aunt's attention, and we got married. We've been happy ever since."

"Well, that's a nice story." I replied, "I hope I can meet a nice girl like that one day."

"There aren't many options here in Folklore," My aunt smiled, "But there are a few good girls around your age. Hard workers, mostly ranchers' daughters. You ought to start thinking about that soon, anyhow, being sixteen and all. I married your Uncle at seventeen."

"I honestly haven't thought too much about it." I told her, "I have been studying most of my life. My mom wanted me to go to college and become a writer."

"That's what you wanted too?" My Uncle asked. I just shrugged. "It didn't sound too bad." I replied, "I always liked books."

"Oh, Tabitha, honey," Rachel said, pulling Tabitha's attention away from her plate. Until now, Tabitha hadn't said a word. She had just been eating quietly. I just figured she was shy. "Did you hear your cousin? He likes books!"

"Oh," Tabitha responded, smiling politely, "I also like to read."

"What are your favorite books?" I asked her.

"I like adventure books. My favorite is *The Adventures of Tom Sawyer*," she told me, but then said something odd: "Your mom died, right?"

"Tabitha!" Rachel yelled in protest. I put my hand up to motion that it was fine.

"She did," I told Tabitha calmly.

"How did she die?"

"She um... she was killed. Someone broke into our house at night and stabbed her. Got away before I could even see who did it."

"Tabby, you need to be more sensitive," Wesley said calmly. He was mad, but it was a calm anger. Anger that you couldn't read by voice, only by body language.

"I didn't know," Tabitha told her father, her tone unchanging.

"Go to your room." Her mother ordered. Without a word, Tabitha scooted out from the table and walked up the stairs.

"I'm sorry about her behavior, Ace," Wesley told me with a sigh. "She's always been… different from other kids. I thought she would grow out of it, but it just feels like it never changes."

"It's fine, really." I told Uncle Wesley, "I am sad about my mom's death, but I really don't mind talking about it. You all are family, after all."

"Why don't you go talk to her, Wes?" Rachel suggested to her husband, "She just doesn't understand what's ok and what's not."

"Why don't I talk to her?" I interrupted, "I'd like to get to know her better anyway."

Both Uncle Wesley and Aunt Rachel approved of this idea. They felt like they wanted me to be a part of the family; I decided I wanted to be like an older brother to Tabitha.

Over the months I was there, I would get to know Tabitha a lot more. She really was a sweet girl. She was certainly different but saw the world differently, too. We talked that night until late about all kinds of things: books, horses, the ranch. She did feel bad for talking about my mom, but she told me it was because she missed her. She would always bring Tabitha new books and candies. I even lent her my brand-new copy of *Tom Sawyer* because a dog had destroyed hers years ago.

It was nice to have someone to talk to about my mom. Someone who didn't see me as a sad kid but as a friend.

Chapter 3
The Peacemaker

The next day, Fierro and I set off early for supplies. Much to my fortune, we took a wagon this time. As much as I wanted to learn horsemanship and riding, I felt sore from the long ride the other day, so it was a relief to ride a wagon rather than on horseback.

"Mind if I smoke?" Fierro asked, pulling out a cigarette. I shook my head. "Not at all," I told him. He put the cigarette in his mouth and lit a match. "Want one?" He mumbled, still holding the cigarette in my mouth.

"No thanks, I've never smoked before."

"Suit yourself." He said, lighting up the cigarette. He took a long drag and puffed out the smoke. He shook the reins, trying to get the horses to speed up a little.

"So what are we getting in town?" I asked Fierro. He smiled and puffed more smoke.

"We are going for some basic supplies." He told me, "Feed for the chickens, some stock the General Store on the Ranch ordered. Wes also told me that we need to get you a gun and some gun leather. Boots and a new hat, too."

"Why do I need a gun?" I asked him. I adjusted the straw hat I now had on my head, "Or a new hat. I feel like this one is fine."

"*Primero*, that hat," He told me, knocking the hat off my head into the back of the wagon, "Is *basura*. No respectable foreman would be caught dead wearing something like that." I retrieved the hat from the back of the wagon, "*Segundo,* if you're ever gonna be the ranch foreman, you need a gun."

"Why?"

"There's a number of reasons. Wolves and coyotes attack the animals often. A foreman is practically the sheriff of the Ranch, too. In my office, there's even a cell for any *sinvergüenza* who tries to steal from the Ranch. Can't enforce the law without guns."

"Guess I never thought about that." I admitted, "What kind of gun am I getting?"

"A revolver. Colt, like mine, but a newer model. Same kind the army is using currently. Not as fancy as mine, but same manufacturer. You'll learn with a handgun first, then we can get you using a rifle or a shotgun. *Aprende lo más dificil primero,* learn the hardest first; that's what my father always said."

"Sounds like he knew what he was talking about."

"Sometimes I find myself thinking that same thing. It *always* bothers me," Martín said, spitting out his cigarette butt into the dirt. "We ain't too far now."

"Is it difficult to be the foreman?" I asked him.

"Nah, it's pretty easy. You're basically in charge of the Ranch, *nada más*. I am responsible for keeping track of the sales, supplies, and staff. Every once in a while, I head to town to see if there's anyone who wants to work. I try to hire cowboys and people who have worked with cows before. It's better if someone else knows them. Just keep an eye out for them; trust your gut. If someone looks rough, they probably are. There are plenty of good folk looking for work always, though."

"I see..."

"Can I ask you a question, Ace?" Fierro turned to me. I nodded. "You ain't interested in being the foreman, are you?"

"Not so much." I admitted, "I always thought I would be something more, you know?" Fierro cocked an eyebrow. "No offense intended, of course. I don't know. Maybe it is, as you said yesterday, about when you left Argentina. You said that you had your head in too many books. Perhaps I am the same way."

Fierro laughed and patted my back roughly. He whipped the reins, urging the horses to continue without getting distracted.

"Listen *muchacho*," Fierro started, smiling an empty smile, "There's a lot worse things you could do in life besides be the foreman. Even the ranch hands and cowboys, the ones who have steady work, even they have it worse than I do. Is this what I always wanted to be doing? No. But Mr. Hendricks is a good man and has given me many opportunities. Pay's real good, too."

"That being said," He continued, "I know your *mamá* wanted more for you. Otherwise, she would've brought you when she visited every year. I say you work hard now, learn the trade of a rancher, but when you hear the call of something else, don't be afraid to follow it."

I nodded my head. Martín was right. If I put my head down and worked hard, I could do whatever I wanted. The West was supposed to be a land of opportunity, and I was an intelligent kid. When the opportunity came, I could take it.

As we pulled into town, things seemed more lively now. It was the rain yesterday that made things seem dead. People were rushing in and out of the street. Men leaning on the wall, smoking and sharing tales. There was loud laughter coming from the inside of the saloon. Official-looking men were directing a few workers, giving them unheard commands.

"Why's everything so busy?" I asked Fierro as we dismounted from the cart.

"They're getting ready for a festival. Boring one, though. The real one is in two months, Fourth of July." He flashed a smile, "That's when I know you Americans like to party."

"I suppose so." I told him, "I haven't kept track of holidays since my mother died." Fierro frowned and nodded.

"Well, I guess we better try and make it a good one." He shrugged and laughed, "You and me will come to town. There ain't too many days that the people of Folklore know how to party, but Independence Day is one of those days."

I followed Martín into the town General Store. It was much larger than the one on the Ranch and had much more stock, too. Fierro went to the desk to speak with the spectacled man there. I took a look around. It seemed like they had everything. Tobacco and sweets, to sugar and flour. They had hats, too. Remembering that Fierro told me I needed a new hat, I decided to look at them.

There were all kinds of hats, different shapes and sizes. My attention gravitated towards a dark gray gambler-style. I wanted to ask Fierro if I could get a jacket to match, but I didn't want to over-impose. It seemed like he would use his own money, not my uncle's, to buy my hat.

With my new boots, spurs, and hat, I now *felt* like a real cowboy. I walked out of the general store as happy as one could be. After helping the store owner load up the wagon with the supplies, Fierro led me to the town gunsmith. Where we acquired my new gun belt, Colt Peacemaker, and some boxes of ammo.

My gun was much different than what Fierro had tucked into his girdle. The gunsmith told me it was stock, exactly how the Sam Colt company sent them. It was fire-blued steel with mahogany grips. It sure wasn't anything fancy, but it was my first gun. It wasn't nearly as long as Fierro's, either. I would spend much more time in the gunsmith throughout my next months in Folklore, learning about the different firearms. It turns out I knew many of them from the stories I had read, but it was nice to finally 'put a face to the name.'

Fierro and I didn't spend more than a few hours in town before it was time to depart. There was more work to do. I was more than satisfied, feeling like some kind of lawman or gunfighter in my new getup. I knew the ride home wouldn't be so long.

"Fierro," I started to ask, wanting to ask him about something he said earlier, "You knew my mom?"

"Of course I did!" He said, flashing a smile, "I worked here for eight years. Your *mamá* came every year for a lot longer than that."

"What did you think of her?"

"Listen, *muchacho,* your *mamá* was as good a woman as any. Better than that. She was *extraordinaria.* She never mentioned me?"

"I'm afraid not. To be honest, she never talked about anything she ever did here. She just talked about my uncle and his family."

"Well, she was fun. She sang and danced. Drank as well as any man. She's the kind of woman who drew everyone close to her. Everyone on the Ranch thought she was wonderful."

I sat back in my seat, surprised and confused. Was he talking about the same woman as I knew?

I never knew her to dance or drink. Was this why she never pushed me to visit the Ranch with her?

"Speaking of Caroline." Fierro spoke up, "I wanted to ask you, but I wasn't sure when. How did she die, if you don't mind me asking?"

"It's fine. She um.. she was murdered." I told him. He stopped what he was doing entirely and looked at me. There was a look of absolute shock on his face.

"Murdered?" He asked, his voice trembling, before rapidly firing questions, "What happened?

Who did it? Did they catch the *idiota*?"

"As far as I know, they didn't catch him." I admitted, "Someone broke into our house one night.

My mom was downstairs; I am not sure why she was there. All I know is that she was murdered. Stabbed to death."

"Well, what else do you remember?"

"Not much. I was asleep when I heard yelling. It sounded like Spanish to me, but I wasn't sure what the man said. I don't think I will ever forget his voice, though."

Fierro cursed in Spanish. He whipped the horses with the reins and lit up another cigarette.

"*No lo puedo creer...*" He muttered, "You tried to find the guy who did it?" I just shook my head.

"There wasn't anything I could do." I told him, "The police told me that the killer probably fled the city shortly after the murder. There just wasn't enough information to ever find him. I think the police said they suspected a famous *bandito* from Mexico who was in town while it happened, but I am not sure. There's no reason that some famous robber would try to rob us."

"Tell you what, *chico*," Fierro started to say, his tone darkening, "If I had been there, things would've turned out very different. Would've beat the *imbecil* to death with my bare hands."

I just nodded, unsure of how to respond to that. I ran through everything in my head, trying to figure out what I could've done differently. I didn't feel like there was anything else to do. I ran downstairs as soon as I heard the yelling. She was already dead, brutally stabbed many times by the time I arrived downstairs. The murderer wasn't there, and there was no indication of where he'd gone off to. The only clue or lead I had was the voice, forever burned into my mind. There were millions of people in the world, though, most of whom I would never hear from.

I pushed these thoughts from my mind, telling myself that there was no possibility in the world of finding my mother's killer. It was foolish of me to think that there was.

"*Che,*" Fierro addressed me in Spanish, interrupting my thoughts and changing the subject, "You wanna stop and practice some shooting? We're making good time. I'm sure your *tío* wouldn't mind. Gotta get you used to that gun, right?"

"Sure!" I responded cheerfully, "That sounds like a good time."

Fierro stopped the cart and let the horses loose for a break. He went over to some large rocks and set up a few empty beer bottles he pulled out of the cart, each at a different length and height.

Satisfied with their placement, he walked back over to me.

"Alright, let me show you how to load the gun," He said, taking my revolver out of my hand, "Open the loading gate like this, then put the cartridge in just like that. Rotate the cylinder until you've loaded them all. Yup, you got it. Now you're ready to shoot. Try that bottle there."

I cocked the hammer back and aimed at the bottle sitting on a rock nearest to us. I aimed for a few seconds and squeezed the trigger. Another miss, same as yesterday.

"No big deal, we got plenty of ammunition." Fierro said, "Don't hold your breath when you aim. Try to shoot during your exhales. And don't tense your back up so much."

"Lot of things to worry about," I remarked, pulling the hammer back again. "You end up not thinking about them after a while."

I aimed once more and did precisely as Martín had said. I squeeze the trigger at the peak of my exhalation. The bottle shattered, sending glass shards flying everywhere.

"¡Eso, muchacho!" Fierro exclaimed, pumping his fist in the air. "Good shot!"

"Thanks!" I stammered out excitedly. "Let me try again."

I pulled the hammer back and raised my gun again. I aimed at the next bottle and fired another shot. It exploded in a hail of glass. Martín whooped and cheered as I fired once more, with the same results.

"You're a dead-eye, kid!" Fierro yelled, "Let's try a game. See that bird there? That hawk?" He pointed with his free hand up in the sky.

"I see it," I replied, pulling my hammer back once more. "I'll give you five dollars if you hit it before I do."

"Deal," I said, taking aim at the hawk. I fired but missed.

"Aim where the bird is going to be, not where it is. That's the key to hitting moving things."

I looked over at Fierro, who hadn't even drawn his gun yet. He just nodded, encouraging me to take the shot. I aimed again, a little way in front of the raptor. I fired. Missed again.

Another gunshot went off right next to me. The hawk went plummeting to the ground, completely out of sight.

"You'll do better next time," Fierro said, laughing. He waved his smoking gun in the air for a bit, then replaced the spent cartridge. He tucked the revolver back into his girdle and went to round up the horses. I reloaded and holstered my new piece and followed him.

When we hitched the horses to the cart and mounted back up, I couldn't help but be confused at what Fierro was doing at my uncle's Ranch. He was a great horseman and a fantastic shot. Not to mention, he carried a saber everywhere, along with his dagger and gun. A man like that really could've been anything. I understood his advice about taking an opportunity when it came, but I just couldn't understand what he had done at the Ranch for eight years. He easily could've made his own fortune doing anything he wanted. And if ranching was something he *wanted* to do, why hadn't he just stayed in Argentina at his father's ranch?

Chapter 4
Wild Mustang

The next few days were difficult. Fierro had put it in his mind that I needed a new horse, that the poor old nag Elenor wouldn't last much longer if I had to push her hard as we would for horsemanship training and herding cattle. Fierro knew what he was talking about, but he wouldn't let me just have one of the spare horses the ranch hands used. "That would be too easy." He told me.

No, he wanted to do things in what he called the "traditional way." In the plains near the ranch, there was a mob of wild Mustangs. Fierro wanted me to go get one and break it myself. I didn't know this then, but Mustangs weren't 'domestic' horses. They were descendants of Spanish horses that had gotten loose hundreds of years ago and spread throughout the West. They are a wild and feral breed.

Certainly not ideal for training a beginner like me. To Martín, though, it was as his father had said: 'Learn the hardest first.'

Fierro taught me to rope horses first. To catch one, I would have to ride up on a horse, rope one, and then pull it back to the pen. We trained in roping and horsemanship a little, just so I could ride and rope simultaneously. I could have been better at it, but Fierro was confident enough that I could do it.

Finally, the day came when we were to go out and get my horse. I woke up early, dressed, and crammed my breakfast down my throat. I said goodbye to my aunt and uncle and rode Elenor down to meet Fierro at the ranch stables.

"You're late." He told me, pulling out his pocket watch. He was leading his horse, Magdalena, and one of the spare ranch horses by the reins.

"I'm not, you liar," I said, laughing. He flashed a smile.

"Late for being early." He admitted. "Get down off the old girl and put her in an empty stall. As good a horse as Elenor is, she ain't fast or strong enough to be chasing mustangs around."

I did as he said, hopping down from Elenor, and I led her to a stall in the stable. I exited the stable and started mounting up the ranch horse that Fierro had brought.

"What are you doing?" He asked, making me stop mounting the horse. "What should I be doing?" I replied with my own question.

"You *should* be getting on Magdalena." He said, "When I got my first Spanish Mustang, my father had me use his horse. You're going to use mine. That way, you can't blame it on the horse if you mess up."

I shrugged and got down from my half-mounted position on the ranch, Morgan. I placed my foot up in Magdalena's stirrup and swung my other leg over her back and into the other stirrup. I adjusted myself comfortably on the sheepskin seat. The strange saddle Fierro always used didn't have a horn for me to rest my rope on, so I spun it around the handle of a hunting knife Uncle Wesley had given me. I felt Magdalena tense up under my unfamiliar weight. Fierro patted her on the nose for a second.

"*Está bien, bebe.*" He whispered to the mare, "*No pasa nada, todo bien.*" This calmed the Criollo a little as Fierro mounted the other horse.

"Take it easy at first." He told me, "Riding a horse is a partnership, not like riding a train. If you don't trust Maggie, she ain't gonna trust you."

He spurred his horse into a trot. Nervously, I kicked Magdalena with my spurs too. I swear, I saw her roll her eyes like a human as she trotted forward, following her master. The whole time, I felt like she *allowed* me to ride her because of Fierro, not because she wanted to. We spurred the horses when we left the ranch, riding in a steady cantor.

We rode for a little while. Fierro told me that he'd seen the mustangs around a spot by the river, so that's where we'd look first. We rode for about an hour before we saw them.

They were beautiful creatures. Wild and free. Doing as they pleased and going where they pleased. If that wasn't the spirit of this country, I didn't know what was. Fierro stopped the Morgan, and I rode up alongside him.

"I will never get tired of seeing this. *Jamás.*" Fierro said, admiring the creatures. "Tell you what, Ace, when I see these animals living like this, that's when I feel like God is real." I nodded in agreement.

"They are beautiful, that's for sure. Never seen anything like this."

"Well, I hope you're ready. My best advice is to pick one and stay with that one. Pick one of the younger ones, a year or so old. They're gonna run when we approach, so you gotta stay alongside. If you can get it with your rope, I'll get it with mine to keep it in one spot while you try and mount it."

"Mount it?" I asked, surprised, "You never mentioned I'd have to mount it."

"Gotta show it who's the boss." Fierro smiled devilishly. "Probably you ain't gonna be able to ride it back, but don't fall off. If you fall off before it calms down, you ain't gonna have the respect of that animal ever. Just grab the mane in both hands and push your feet up on the shoulders. It's gonna try and buck you off."

I wasn't so sure of this anymore, but it felt too late to back out. I examined the Mustangs, trying to figure out which one I wanted. I eventually singled one out: a brown-painted male with a black and white mane. It looked excellent and healthy; I could picture myself on its back.

Without another word, I spurred Magdalena into a gallop towards the horse. This was the only time during my whole ride with her that I didn't feel she was reluctant to give me a ride. I felt her excitement as the other horses took notice and started to bolt. It took my chosen stallion a moment to notice us approaching, but it was too late by the time he did. I swung my rope through the air, tossing the loop around the colt's neck. He neighed loudly in protest, rearing back on two legs. No sooner than I had lassoed the horse, a second rope came from the other side. Fierro expertly rounded his horse to the front of the Mustang, pulling it back to its forelegs with great strength.

I didn't waste any time. I dismounted, nearly jumping from Magdalena's back. I reeled myself in close to the Mustang, keeping my rope taught. The stallion bucked and kicked, but I was fast on my feet. My heart was pumping adrenaline through my veins, increasing my speed, strength, and reflexes. I had never felt so alive.

I closed in on the wild colt's side and grabbed a handful of mane with my free hand. I threw myself on his back, wrapping the remainder of my rope around his neck and pulling back.

"*¡Eso chico!*" Fierro yelled, encouraging me to stay on, "*¡Quedáte alli!*" I didn't understand precisely what he was saying, but his tone was a language itself.

The Mustang bucked, snapped its mouth at me, and kicked. I jerked, pulled, and punched. I pressed my boots into his powerful shoulders, trying to stay level and stay on the horse. Fierro galloped his horse back and forth, jerking the young colt in different directions and trying to tire it out. The horse fought hard, but in the end, we won.

As fast as the stallion had started bucking and kicking, he stopped, blowing hot air through its large nostrils. Fierro whooped and yelled in Spanish, celebrating that we had calmed the horse. I untied my rope around his neck, patted his back firmly, and dismounted. We'd broken his wild spirit.

Magdalena trotted back over, allowing me to dismount and get on her back. Fierro still had his rope around the colt's neck. I rode up next to him.

"Muy bien, chico." He complimented, "You're not bad at this. Let's take this hotshot back to the ranch. We can corral him and start training with a saddle, the hard part of getting a wild horse. What will you call him?"

I pondered for a moment, unsure. Up until that point, I hadn't ever thought of a name for a horse. Dogs, sure. Even names for cats, but never a horse.

"What does 'Fierro' mean in Spanish?" I asked him. He flashed his devilish smile. "Only fair that I name him after you since you helped me get him."

"It ain't modern Spanish." He told me, laughing. "It's an old dialect from Spain. It means 'Iron'."

"Iron it is, then." I smiled myself, looking back at the stallion. I knew he was just swinging his head because he was exhausted, but it looked like he was nodding in approval.

The ride back to the ranch felt like a quick one. Fierro led Iron to a small corral behind the foreman's office. This was the one that was used for breaking horses. We would give Iron a break for the rest of the day and do other chores around the ranch. Fierro only told me at the end of the day, when I was tired and dirty, that I would have to spend the next few nights in the small stable with Iron. It was so the animal would trust me more, he said.

The first night with Iron was awful. He kept awake, whining and neighing all night. I hardly slept at all. The next few nights were better as Iron came to trust me more, but I missed my bed and Aunt Rachel's hot breakfasts.

Training was difficult at first, too. Fierro had me measure Iron for a saddle, halter, and bit.

When those were made, I had to put them on myself, which Iron wasn't a fan of. He fought me every chance he got. Fierro told me that's what I deserved for choosing a stallion. How was I supposed to know that the mares were calmer?

Eventually, Iron got used to his kit, and it was time to learn to ride. This was surprisingly the easiest part. Fierro was right about everything. Riding a horse was a partnership, and Iron had come to trust me over the month. He *allowed* me to ride him cause he knew me. As much as I had enjoyed learning to ride with Elenor, I hadn't felt a genuine bond with her. With Iron, things were completely different. He was *my* horse. He knew me, and I, him. By the end of the month, Iron was completely trained and obedient to me.

Uncle Wesley was impressed that Fierro and I could train such a creature so fast. He knew that Fierro was good at breaking horses, but to break a wild Mustang colt so quickly was utterly unheard of. And now that Iron was ready to work, Fierro was ready to start taking me on the range to let the cows graze. This became my job now.

"You ready for Fourth of July?" Fierro asked one day while we were out. "It's almost the Fourth of July?" I responded with my own question.

"You have a horse brain now?" Fierro joked, laughing loudly, "Yeah. Remember, I told you that we were gonna head into town to party?" I nodded and rubbed the sweat from my forehead.

"I remember." I smiled, "What're you planning on doing?"

"Folklore always sets up nice for the Fourth," Fierro explained, lighting a cigarette. As always, he silently offered me one, but I refused once more, "There will be carnival games, dancing, music, cards, and *una abundancia* of alcohol."

"So what? You're gonna drink and play cards?"

"*We* are, *muchacho; we* are going to drink and play cards."

"Never drank before. I've only played poker a handful of times with the ranch hands."

"There's a first time for everything, *amigo*." Fierro laughed. Our joking around was cut short by a loud 'moo' of the cows, followed by some men shouting.

"Over there," Fierro said seriously, pointing toward a few men roping up some of the cattle from horseback. Some were dismounting to try and push the cattle towards the horses; some had on forest green bandanas. *"Ladrones."*

Fierro acted first, pulling his shotgun from a leather holster tied to his saddle. He spurred Magdalena into a swift gallop toward the rustlers. I followed close behind, fumbling my peacemaker from the holster on my side.

As we neared the rustlers, Fierro unloaded both of the shotgun barrels into one of them. The others cursed, realizing what was happening, and some drew their weapons.

Fierro quickly loaded two more shells into the shotgun. In one motion, he closed the breech and fired a shell at one of the riders and another at one of the ones on the ground. There was more confusion, and horses bucked and reared, throwing their riders. Iron tensed up underneath me as I raised my revolver at the closest one to me.

I squeezed the trigger, but nothing happened. I cursed as I opened the loading gate to check if my gun was loaded. I heard a gunshot, and a bullet whizzed past my head. Iron was frightened by the noise and threw me off his back into the dirt. It hurt and knocked the wind out of me, but it also made me realize what I'd done wrong: I hadn't pulled the hammer back before trying to fire the gun.

By this time, Fierro had discarded the shotgun and now rode with a pistol in one hand, saber in the other, weaving his horse in and out of the group, shooting one rustler, and cutting down another.

One of the rustlers ran up to me. I aimed my gun at him, this time remembering to pull back the hammer. The click of my hammer frightened him so much that he dropped his pistol. I was about to squeeze the trigger but couldn't do it for some reason.

It was as though my finger had stopped working. I wanted to shoot, to defend myself, but my body wouldn't let me take a life.

"Surrender." I ordered, mustering up as much authority as I possibly could, "Or I'll shoot you dead." The rustler laughed and smiled evilly.

"You're just a kid." He said, picking up his gun. He aimed it at me. "You ain't gonna shoot."

Just as I felt that the man was going to shoot, there was a flash of steel as the hand holding the gun fell to the ground. Fierro dismounted his horse before the man could react to the pain of losing a limb. He hit the rustler in the face with a strong fist, knocking him to the ground.

"My hand!" screamed and cursed the last rustler, "It's gone, my hand!"

"*¡Calláte!*" Fierro roared in a tone I didn't recognize. He hit the man again, "You're with a gang?" He asked in the same growling tone. The rustler was busy crying about his hand, not answering the gaucho's question. Fierro punched him again, knocking blood and teeth everywhere.

"N-no..." Stammered out the barely conscious robber, "We were just a few cowboys looking to make a quick buck. We didn't mean nothin' by it, sir."

"*¡Calláte vos!*" Yelled Fierro. In all my life, there would be quite a few times that I saw men degenerate into animals, more than a man should see. This, however, was the first time. Fierro was someone I liked, someone I admired. He beat that man over and over again till he didn't have teeth. Till he couldn't breathe through a swollen and broken jaw. Till his face was red and blue. When Fierro turned to me, I felt genuine fear. This wasn't someone I recognized. His eyes were those of a wild beast. His hair was unruly, and he panted like a dog. There was a darkness on his face that I never would've seen from Fierro. He was out for blood.

"M-Martín?" I stuttered, "Everything ok?" Fierro shook his head back and forth as though he were trying to shake off a bug.

"Yes, Asa." He said, recomposing himself, "I am fine. Are you ok? That was a pretty hard fall you took."

I cocked an eyebrow. I slowly lowered the hammer on my peacemaker and nervously holstered it. I got back up to my feet, looking around. Fierro had easily killed fifteen men by himself. I wasn't sure what to say.

"Let's try and find my horse." I finally sighed, trying to change the subject, "He couldn't have gone far."

"You look around." Fierro told me, placing his hat on his head and brushing down his hair with his hand, "I'll throw *estos imbeciles* in the river. Get them off your uncle's property."

"You do that..." I said, trying not to sound nervous. A wave of relief rushed over me as I got away from Martín. Even though I had almost lost my life there, I only thought of the animal that Martín Fierro had become for a minute there. I was scared of him.

I found Iron standing at the top of the hill where we had first seen the cattle rustlers. I patted him on the nose. He breathed out a hot breath from his nostrils as though he were apologizing for throwing me off back there during the fight.

"It's ok, boy." I rubbed his face between his eyes, "Believe me, I ain't even thinking about that right now."

Chapter 5
Brawl in Folklore

Throughout the next few days, I struggled to talk to Martín. He was acting normal, but seeing a man you think you know act like that is jarring. I tried to operate regularly, but I couldn't help it. When he asked about it, I just told him that I was missing my mom a little extra these days. He understood that and gave me a little distance, though he insisted that I go to Folklore with him for Independence Day. I obliged him, and the day before the Fourth, I finally felt like things were normal around him. I just tried to push all that from my mind.

When the Fourth finally came, we got up early and got started on all our chores. We fed our horses, got all the cows assigned to ranch hands to take to pasture, and ensured the Ranch's general store had their stock set straight. It was about noon when we left, he on Magdalena and me on Iron.

"You're really gonna love this," Fierro said excitedly once we were on the road. "Lotta folk come from all over the county. *Y, ¿Quien sabe?* Maybe you'll fall for one of the local farmer's daughters." We both laughed "I don't know." I told him honestly, "There haven't been many girls I've been interested in."

"Listen, *muchacho*," He said, "If you like *hombres*, that's ok with me, but the locals ain't too kind to that."

"Nah, it ain't like that." I assured him, "I don't know what it is. I like women, that's for sure. I just feel I ain't met someone

I could see myself with, that's all." Martín laughed and lit up a cigarette.

"That's ok, *chico*. Ain't too many women who can really catch my attention, neither. When you get to my age, you care less, though. I have enjoyed the company of many women, but ain't too many I'd want to settle down with, if you know what I mean."

I thought for a moment and swatted a fly buzzing around my head. "Maybe I'm just too young."

"I'll tell you this, Ace." Fierro said thoughtfully, "I've seen you grow a lot in the past few months. You're starting to be a real cowboy now. I might be able to retire as foreman sooner than I thought."

"You really think so?"

"*¡Claro que sí!* You're even starting to talk the part. I don't think that little kid I met coming off the train would've ever used the word 'ain't,' let alone be able to do what you've done. Just look at this horse you're riding now! Wilder than any I've seen, but *you* broke him."

"I had some good help," I admitted humbly.

"I didn't help. I just supervised. If you weren't replacing me as foreman, I'd invite you to come to Argentina once I leave the Ranch and return home." He and I both laughed.

"Is that what you'll do once you leave?" I asked, changing the subject. "Return to your home?"

"*Quizás.* Maybe I will. It'd be nice to see if any of my relatives are still alive, but maybe I'll go start my own ranch. *¿Quien sabe?*"

Good conversation always makes for a faster trip, and that wasn't any less true here. Before I knew it, we arrived in Folklore. There were carnival games, people dancing in the street, and musicians playing various instruments.

As we passed, two girls about my age looked at me and smiled. I wasn't sure what to do, so I tilted my hat at them. They blushed and giggled. Martín laughed.

"*Che*, what was it that you said about women?" He teased me, "*Algo como* 'there haven't been many girls' that you've been interested in?"

"Shut up. *Calláte.*" I said, riding to his side and shoving him with one arm.

"*Ay imirá quien aprende tan rapido!* Look who's learning Spanish fast!" He laughed harder. "On top of that, talking like a real Argentine. Soon we'll be '*Los gauchos Martín y Asa.*' You crack me up, kid."

"Where should we start?" I asked, trying to change the subject.

"The saloon," He replied, flashing his devilish smile, "All good *fiestas* start and end in the saloon."

We walked our horses to the other side of town, near where Fierro and I had first met. We both dismounted and tied our steeds to the horse beam outside next to a few other horses. Both of the horses leaned down to drink water from the trough. I patted Iron on the neck and followed Martín into the saloon.

The saloon was especially lively today. Even though it was early, people were already inside, drinking and reveling, red-faced and happy. Fierro approached the bar, motioning for me to sit next to him.

"Howdy Martín, how are you tonight?" The barkeep said. He was a short man with a bald head and a long mustache. He seemed to know Fierro very well.

"Depends on how the drinks are!" Martín responded with a smile. The barkeep laughed. "Strong as ever." He told Fierro before quieting his voice to a whisper, "I saved something *real* good for you. Who's the kid?"

Fierro patted me on the back before taking his hat off and placing it on the bar. I followed suit, trying to figure out how to behave in a saloon.

"Remember Caroline, Wesley Hendrick's sister? This is her son, Asa." Fierro answered him. "Really?" The bartender asked, looking at me for a few seconds, "I see the resemblance. What happened to your ma, boy? Haven't seen her in a while."

"She died," I said with a frown.

"Brutally murdered." Fierro added dramatically, "Kid had to move out here to live with the Hendricks family. I've been showing him the ropes."

"Sorry to hear that, son." The barkeep said with a frown, "Caroline was a real nice woman. She and Fierro used to spend a lot here whenever she was in town." The barkeep took a bottle of whiskey from under the bar and poured three shooters. He pushed one in front of Fierro, one to me, and picked the other one up. "This one's on the house for Caroline."

"That's a woman worth drinking for." Fierro flashed a smile and raised the shot glass, "*¡Salud!*"

"*¡Salud!*" The barkeep repeated in broken Spanish. I muttered the same, and the two poured back their shots. I hesitated a second, then did the same. The drink was spicy and vaguely cinnamon-tasting. It also tasted like oak. It burned my mouth and then my throat as I swallowed. I coughed and hacked, Fierro laughed, and the barkeep looked concerned. I felt like vomiting but held it in.

"I take it that the kid's never drank before." The barkeep asked Fierro, who could not answer due to his laughter. "Let me get some water."

He went away a second and brought back a glass of water. I gulped the whole thing down quickly and lost my desire to throw up.

"Thanks," I said, still red-faced.

"Better give the kid something not as strong," Fierro said, calming his laughter. "All of his drinks tonight, I'm buying." The barkeep didn't say no to that. He went to attend to other guests. "*Madre mía, muchacho,* I haven't had a laugh like that in a long time."

I stared at Fierro. He and the bartender had been discussing something Fierro hadn't mentioned in front of me until now, at least not in great detail.

"Fierro," I started to ask, in a severe tone, "How well did you know my mother? You knew her, of course. I already heard that, but the bartender just now made it seem like you were good friends."

"We *were* good friends, *chico*, that's no secret."

"She never mentioned you." I told him, starting to get mad, "Not even once."

"Well, I can count on two hands how many times she mentioned you." He retorted.

"No, Fierro, you don't get it. She *never* mentioned you. The first time I heard about you was when I met you. You talk about my mom, and the woman you talk about is completely different from the one I knew."

"Tell you what, Ace." Fierro responded with a devilish look in his eyes, "I'll tell you what I know about your mom, but you have to drink with me. Shot for shot, drink for drink. I'll let you slide with some lighter stuff than that, but I am not drunk enough to talk about Caroline right now."

"Deal," I said, shaking his extended hand. I had to know more about who my mother was because she was a completely different person in Folklore than back home. "For every drink I take with you, I can ask questions about my mom."

"Jacob!" Martín called out to the bartender. After a few seconds, he returned to us, holding a bottle of brandy. He poured me a whiskey tumbler of the stuff and a second for Martín of the whiskey we had taken. We both downed the glasses. While still lousy tasting, the brandy was much lighter and easier to swallow than the whiskey. I at least didn't start hacking and throwing up.

"What do you want to know, kid?" Martín asked, turning towards me.

"Why did she come here, to Folklore? I thought she was just visiting her brother."

"That was probably it, originally." He admitted, "But when I met her, she would come to Folklore for stress relief. Drinking, dancing, playing cards. That kind of stuff."

"So you were with her a lot?"

"Of course! We did enjoy the same activities, after all. And, if you haven't noticed, there's only one saloon here in town. I'd wager that half the people here drank with your *mamá* at least once." As I was about to ask another question, Fierro raised a finger. "We need another drink."

As though he were summoned by Fierro just saying that phrase, Jacob, the barkeep, appeared and poured us another drink each. After a third '*salud*,' each of us finished our drinks.

My mind raced, trying to think of another question to ask, and the alcohol didn't help. Fierro laughed at my drunken state and took another drink without me.

"Tell you what, *chico*," He said, drunkenly standing up, "You think of a question, and come find me. I'm gonna go play cards. Enjoy yourself. Socialize and dance."

I was about to protest, but it was as though Fierro had just disappeared, leaving me sitting alone in my drunken stupor. I stood up from my seat, nearly falling down as I did. I felt warm, so I stepped outside. Sun was setting, and I sat down on the steps. I felt so awful, and I promised myself I would never drink again.

A soft hand touched my shoulder. I nearly drew my pistol in surprise but was stunned when a pretty girl with red, curly hair sat next to me.

"Do you mind if I sit?" She asked politely.

"It's a free country." I tried to say it nicely, but it just sounded rude: "I apologize. That came out wrong. I ain't never been drunk before."

The girl giggled and put a hand on my shoulder. She was dressed like a proper lady, unlike the girls in the bar or the streets, who were dressed much more casually.

"That's quite alright." She said, covering her mouth as she laughed. She smelled sweet, like lilacs.

"Where you from?" I asked, hating myself for being drunk, "Besides here. You have an accent, that's all."

"Well, I've lived here most of my life, but my family is originally from England. My father bought a parcel of land here and ended up starting quite the farm. You aren't going to ask my name?"

"Oh, how rude of me," I admitted, rubbing the back of my head with one hand. I hated how dreadful I sounded drunk. This girl probably thought I was some cowboy or ranch hand. I noticed my hat was gone. Where had I left my hat? "I'm Asa Hendricks, what's your name?"

"Elizabeth Caldwell." She said, offering me a hand. I shook it, only realizing afterward that I was supposed to kiss it like a true gentleman.

"Look, Elizabeth, I ain't normally like this." I told her, fumbling around with my tongue as though English were a language I only kind of spoke, "But I have never drunk before, and I wasn't sure what to expect. On any other occasion, you'd probably consider me a gentleman."

"Oh my, how wonderful." She laughed at me, "Here I was thinking I was talking to a cowpoke. I know who you are, Mr. Hendricks. I think everyone knows your family around here."

"That a good thing or a bad one, Ms. Caldwell?" I asked, nearing my face to hers. She smiled at me warmly.

"I would say that is an excellent thing at the moment." She said, coming closer to me. Her breath smelled of wine, and I was sure she was probably a little drunk, too. I kissed her. For the first time, I kissed a girl. It was lovely; her lips were soft and sweet; they tasted of wine and sherry. I felt my heart jump, even though I knew this was probably because we were both drunk.

"Hey, cowboy!" A man with an accent similar to Elizabeth's yelled aggressively behind us. I pulled away from her and turned to meet the man. He was older, probably in his mid-twenties, with the same red hair and a mustache. "Get your grubby paws off, my sister, before I kick your teeth in."

I should've just let it go. I was never confrontational before, always trying to avoid conflict. I don't know what changed this night, but I guessed it had something to do with the bottle. I thought something stupid to say, and for whatever reason, rather than holding my tongue, the words just came out.

"That's your sister?" I asked, smiling cruelly, "You adopted then? Cause I don't know how anything as ugly as you could be related by blood to Ms. Caldwell."

The next thing I remember was Elizabeth's brother on me. He grabbed me by the caller and threw me into the dirt. He jumped on top of me and punched me several times in the face. I poked his eye with a thumb and headbutted him in the nose. He reared back, giving me time to escape and get back to my feet. Right on time, too, as three more similar-looking boys, all different ages, joined in the fight. I was outnumbered.

"*¡Allí voy, muchacho!*" A familiar voice called from inside the bar. Martín Fierro, drunken and disheveled, rushed out of the saloon. He quickly sent a pointed toe of one of his boots into the groin of the oldest brother, sending him to the ground, then grabbed the youngest in a headlock, rubbing his knuckles aggressively into the kid's scalp. I used Fierro's distraction to send a wide punch right at my original attacker's jaw.

The fourth one grabbed me by my shirt collar and tossed me back, knocking me into a wall. He ran at me and tried to punch me, but I dodged it, forcing him to hit the wall instead. He fell back, clutching his injured fist, so I punched him in the gut, knocking the wind out of him. The original attacker and the oldest were up now, the oldest and youngest both hitting Fierro around and the other two grabbing me and taking turns punching my gut. A crowd had gathered. Some were trying to get the town sheriff to stop us, and others were betting on who would win.

I jumped up with both feet and kicked the one punching me in the gut with both boots, sending him flying back and crashing into the youngest. This kick sent me and the one holding me, the mustache brother, backward over a railing. Both of us sprawled onto a wooden porch, but I recovered faster, standing on top of the downed brother with one boot and beating him with both fists. One brother, the oldest, grabbed me and yanked my back over the railing, sending me tumbling onto the ground. Fierro was grappling with the one I'd sent his way, rolling around on the ground and trading strikes. The youngest and oldest started to kick me on the ground.

I tried to stand up, using my momentum to trip the legs out from under the youngest. I clapped the oldest with both hands on his ears, sending him stumbling backward, clutching both sides of his head. I rushed to Fierro, kicking his attacker in the back of the knees. Fierro grabbed his shirt and I the back of his pants, and we tossed him to the side. The other three were up now, surrounding Fierro and I. We were prepared to start fighting again when a gunshot scattered the crowd and stopped the fight.

A stranger on a black warhorse held a smoking revolver in the air.

"What on earth is going on here?" The stranger yelled, "I'm certain that this sure ain't what the founding fathers intended when they declared war on the British or was it?"

The four Caldwell brothers had already fled the scene, fearing this stranger would catch them or, worse, shoot them. Just Fierro and I stood there with several members of the public who had regathered after the stranger fired a shot.

"You see, *señor,*" Fierro started to say as he rubbed a bruise on his face, "Those four men we were fighting were British themselves. I would say that is *exactamente* what the founding fathers wanted."

The stranger put away his gun and dismounted his horse, leading it by the reins over to us. "You don't sound too American yourself, *amigo*." The stranger said, looking Fierro in the eyes, "Your name ain't Luis Reyes, is it?"

"No, *señor*." Fierro said, flashing his signature devilish smile, "*Yo soy el gaucho, Martín Fierro, a su servicio.*"

"I don't speak much Spanish, but I appreciate your introduction." The stranger said, shaking Martín's hand, "Matthew Selleck. I'm here looking for Mr. Reyes. He's wanted in several states, as well as federally. Most recently, he committed a few particularly barbaric crimes in Port City." Even my drunken ears perked up at hearing that. Was Reyes the bandit whom the police said murdered my mom?

"You're a bounty hunter then? What makes you think Reyes is here in Folklore? It's a small town." Fierro continued the conversation, not even blinking at the fact that Reyes may have killed my mother.

"Not quite," Selleck said, opening his tan canvas duster. A silver badge on his shirt said 'UNITED STATES MARSHAL.' "I 'intercepted' one of Reyes' messengers. When interrogated, the man said Reyes was headed towards here. The scumbag didn't know why, though."

"Ah, I see..." Fierro nodded, "Well, *señor* Selleck, it is getting late. You did save our butts there just now; why don't you come to stay the night at our ranch?"

"Much obliged." Selleck nodded, mounting his horse again. "Was gonna stay at the inn here in town, but I'm sure Ophelia here will appreciate your ranch much more."

Fierro and I mounted up, and the three of us set off for the Ranch.

Chapter 6
Matthew Selleck, Lawman

The following day was business as usual after the scolding I got from my aunt and uncle about last night's fight. Apparently, the Caldwell boys were 'respectable folk' even though it sure didn't seem that way the night before. But there's a reason they say that drinking is of the devil. There was no way anyone involved in last night's fight was sober.

I met Fierro as usual, and we went to take the cows to pasture. To my disappointment, Mr. Selleck had apparently risen before the sun. He was searching for Reyes before I could even talk to him about it. I had to know more. Just the fact that Reyes had been there in Port City and was now here in Folklore somewhere was a sign to me that he had, in fact, killed my mother. I just had to talk to Selleck about it.

"What do you think about Mr. Selleck?" I asked Fierro as we watched the cattle graze from atop of our usual.

"Pretty exciting, huh?" Fierro said, lighting up, "Not every day we get a real US Marshal in our little town, ¿verdad? Even more exciting was to have him in my own home last night. He told me some pretty interesting stories."

"Do you think the man he's looking for, Luis Reyes, killed my mother?" I didn't beat around the bush. I hadn't slept at all last night, thinking about that very thing. The blood drained from Fierro's face.

"I think... *pues, es posible.*" He told me with a sigh, "I don't want to get your hopes up, Ace. I would like to avenge her, too, but I don't know if it was Reyes who killed your *mamá.*"

"Did you talk to Mr. Selleck last night?"

"Yes, I did. I tried to pry some information from him discreetly. I asked about the crimes that Reyes was wanted for, and he *is* wanted on multiple counts of murder, but *señor* Selleck didn't give any specific details. Perhaps if you ask him personally, try and appeal to his emotions, he'd be more loose-lipped."

I nodded my head slowly. Fierro was probably right not to get my hopes up. Port City was massive. If I just assumed that Reyes killed her, I would probably be wrong. I needed to hear his voice.

"I do have one lead." Fierro told me, interrupting my thoughts, "It is kind of a long shot. You remember those guys we fought the other day? The cattle rustlers?"

My mind flashed back to that dreadful day when I saw a side of Martín Fierro that was completely uncharacteristic of him.

"I remember," I responded without another word.

"Well, some of those guys wore green bandanas. This ain't necessarily a sign, but Selleck did mention that Reyes' gang uses a green bandana to mark their members."

"Why would any gang do that?" I asked, vaguely remembering the green bandanas. "Also, you asked one of them if they were in a gang, and he told you no."

"It's for fights. To distinguish who is on their side and who isn't during a battle. I went through it in my head." Fierro told me, poking a temple with his finger, "The one I interrogated didn't have a bandana. It's likely that most of them were with Reyes, and some of them probably didn't know anything about it. If Reyes *is* here, he's likely trying to keep a low profile. There's no reason to come to Folklore unless it's to hide. Even the bank don't have too much money in it. Your uncle probably has the most cash in the whole county."

I nodded. It all made sense. From what I could remember, the ones who wore the green bandanas *did* seem more vicious and organized like they'd done that same crime before, whereas the ones who didn't seemed like newbies.

I rubbed the back of my neck. It ached terribly. Fierro laughed as he saw me.

"Yeah, a fight like last night will do that to you." He told me, "For whatever reason, every single time I get into a brawl, my neck hurts the next day, no matter how many times I get hit or not."

"That was the first fight I'd ever been in," I admitted.

"I can tell." Fierro laughed, "Otherwise, you wouldn't have picked the Caldwell boys. *Esos muchachos son fuertes.* They're strong. I've seen the oldest one throw a full-size hay bale above his head."

"I didn't try to pick a fight with them; it just kind of... happened."

Fierro narrowed his eyes. He could sense that I wasn't telling the whole truth, which was obvious. I spoke again before he could say anything.

"Alright... alright... I ended up kissing Elizabeth Caldwell last night." Fierro shoved me playfully.

"Salí de acá, ¡me estás mentiendo!"

"No, sir!" I smiled, defending against his playful accusations, "She and I kissed on the porch of the saloon."

"¡Donjuan! You dog!" Fierro exclaimed, smiling and laughing. "Just yesterday, you told me that you didn't find any girl fascinating."

"I'm not sure if I do yet." I joked, "We were both drunk last night. I'd have to make sure she's beautiful sober, too. If she ain't, well, I might as well run off with Reyes."

"She is, *te prometo.*" Fierro assured me, "Very young for me, but for you, *¡perfecta!*"

"Good. I'd like to see her again."

"You should!" Fierro checked his pocket watch, "Today is Sunday? Probably, she goes to church with her mother and sisters. None of the Caldwell men are religious, so you ain't gonna see her brothers. If you leave now, full gallop, you could get there before they get out. Especially with Iron's speed."

"What about you and the cows?" I asked half-heartedly.

"*Chico,*" Fierro started to scold me, "What did I tell you about taking opportunities when they come? Don't hesitate, just go!"

"Thanks, Martín," I told him, already mounting up on Iron. He waved me off, slapping the rear end of my horse to get him going fast.

I rode hard, and I rode fast. This little trip turned out to be a good test of how much my riding had improved since my arrival nearly three months ago. I turned corners perfectly and trusted Iron completely.

And things were as Fierro had said. I pulled up to town, and the church bells started ringing, letting everyone out of church. Iron skidded to a sudden stop across the road from the church. I dismounted and tied him up quickly, then leaned against the wall, trying to act as though I had been there doing something, not waiting for Elizabeth to leave the church building.

Eventually, I saw her gorgeous red locks exit the church. I smiled and waved nonchalantly, trying to look as cool as possible. She noticed me and shot me a wide smile. Elizabeth was walking out of the church with her mother, who had the same fire-red hair. She said something I couldn't make out to the older woman and then scurried my way.

"Miss Caldwell." I said, tilting my hat towards her, "How are you doing this lovely Sunday morning?"

"Well, well," she replied, taken aback by my politeness; she did a small courtesy, "It turns out you *are* a gentleman after all, *Mister* Hendricks."

I nodded slightly and stood up straight. I pushed myself off the wall I was leaning on and walked over to her. Her lilac perfume hadn't been an illusion of my inebriated mind. She smelled nice and flowery.

"I thought that church was now, to be frank." I lied, "I didn't realize my watch was wrong." Elizabeth smiled more and rolled her eyes playfully.

"No offense intended, *Mister* Hendricks," She emphasized the 'Mister' once again, teasing me about my manners, "But I don't believe you are a churchgoing man. You certainly don't fight like one." My face turned red, but I tried to laugh it off.

"Alright, alright, you caught me. I wanted to see you. And please, you can just call me Ace."

"That is fine by me, as long as you call me Eliza." She nodded, "I had hoped my brothers hadn't scared you off. They can be a bit... protective."

"That's an understatement," I said, pointing at a cut on my brow.

"I'm terribly sorry about that." She apologized, "I suppose, as payment for the sins of my brothers last night, I will have to let you see me again."

"Tomorrow is my day off." I blurted out, quicker than I wanted to. Luckily, it seems like she found my enthusiasm charming.

"I suppose I can make arrangements to meet you." She said, twirling a curl in her fingers, "But it will have to be in secret. I may have to *sneak out* so my brothers don't find out."

"I can keep my mouth shut."

"Oh, I believe you, Ace."

"Let's say, around noon?" I asked.

"It's a date." Eliza smiled, hurrying back to her mother, who waved and smiled at me. I felt my face turn pink. Once they had loaded into their wagon and ridden out of sight, I mounted up Iron and started to trot out of there.

A few miles down the road towards the Ranch, I found a black horse standing by the side of the road. This was Matthew Selleck's horse, Ophelia. I stopped Iron next to the mare and dismounted. His horse was here, but where was Selleck?

I moved up a hill to get a better lay of the land; perhaps I could see Selleck from up there. I left Iron by Ophelia and trudged up the nearest hill. Imagine my surprise when I arrived at the top only to find out I wasn't the only one with the same idea. Selleck was lying in the grass at the top of the hill, looking through a pair of binoculars.

Selleck must've heard me because he drew his Schofield revolver and aimed it at me before I could react.

"Oh, it's just you." He said, putting the gun back into its holster and looking through his binoculars again, "The Hendricks kid. What's your name again, partner?"

"It's Asa," I told him, a little offended that he didn't know my name after the ride to the Ranch yesterday.

Go home, Asa." He said coldly, not turning from his binoculars. I lay down in the grass next to him, trying to see what he was looking at through his binoculars. "You deaf or just dumb, kid?"

"Neither," I told him angrily. "I want to help you look for Reyes."

"For Heaven's sake, kid, just listen to me. This isn't a game. You aren't gonna be a hero; you're just gonna get in the way."

"No, you listen to me." I put my foot down. This sudden bravado must gotten at least a little respect from Selleck because he looked away from his binoculars. "Reyes killed my mother. I am sure of it. He was in Port City at the same time that she was murdered. I don't have any proof, but I heard someone yelling in Spanish that night. I still have the voice in my head. If I can just *hear* Reyes, I can tell you if it's him or not."

Selleck narrowed his eyes, staring through me. He was trying to figure out if I was telling him some tall tale just so I could play bounty hunter.

"Alright, kid. I'll let you tag along for now." He told me, passing the binoculars my way. "The moment things get hairy, you need to run." I took the binoculars and looked through them, trying to figure out what Selleck was looking at.

"You see that horse trail a little ways down from the horizon?" Selleck asked.

"Yessir."

"Good. That trail is the only one I've found that isn't on any maps I've seen of the area. In my experience, that usually means that robbers and bandits made and use the trail. Keep watch on that trail. I'm gonna go relieve myself and eat some jerky in my saddle bag. Yell if you see anyone on that trail."

I heard Selleck go down from the hilltop, but I didn't look away. I thought about where a trail like that would go. Fierro and I had ridden many of these horse trails over the last few months, so I had a pretty good layout of the county in my head. If I was right, that trail would end up at Hendricks Ranch, or at least near it. It was on the property for sure, assuming it continued in that direction for some distance.

After about twenty or thirty minutes of watching, a lone rider appeared from behind a hill, headed on the trail toward the horizon.

"Selleck!" I yelled, trying to get his attention. In a second, he was up the hill on horseback. More impressive than his swiftness was his skill. He was pulling Iron by the reins alongside his own horse. He released the painted Mustang's reins near where I stood. I didn't say a word; I mounted as fast as possible and rocketed off behind Selleck and Ophelia.

This was the first time that I'd gone off-trail with Iron. I felt lucky he had been a feral horse before because he was very much at home on these open plains. However, the ride was still rough, and I could barely keep up with Selleck on his midnight-black Arabian. It got more manageable when we started to follow the horse trail, galloping quickly to catch up to the rider.

"If you get a shot," Selleck yelled back at me, "Shoot the horse. Take the scumbag alive if you can. Hogtie him and put him on your horse."

Selleck was the most skilled rider I had ever seen besides Fierro. He handled the Arabian mare with grace and skill. Selleck also had a Winchester lever rifle, steel-plated, which he held in his right hand. With his left, he held the reins. Ophelia was just as impressive a horse as he was a rider. She was at full gallop and didn't slow at all. Her solid black coat shimmered. Her mane and tail were long. If I were Iron or any other colt, I probably would've fallen in love with that horse. Assuming that horses fell in love, that is.

The only problem came when the trail broke off into a fork. Selleck didn't slow or stop; he went right on the trail and pointed his rifle to the left, a clear indication for me to head left. I didn't hesitate, and Iron didn't break stride. We rode on to the left fork, horse and rider as one.

We followed the horse trail into a forest, which I was sure was a part of the woodland near my uncle's property. I started to catch a glimpse of a horse in the distance, and I spurred Iron, pushing him to go faster.

Finally, I saw the lone rider in the distance. He noticed me, too, and spurred his horse to a gallop. I couldn't see his features, just a pair of worn jeans, a brown jacket, and, most importantly, a green bandana.

Chapter 7
Luis Reyes

I knew that I couldn't keep up this pace for much longer. Iron wasn't used to running this hard and could only keep up this speed for a short time. I took a deep breath, knowing what I had to do. I promised myself that I wouldn't freeze this time. This was for Mom.

I drew my peacemaker from its holster, pulled the hammer back, and took aim. I aimed right at the rear of the horse. I wasn't sure if my bullet would kill it from this angle, but injuring it would slow it down or, in the best-case scenario, surprise it and force it to completely throw the rider.

I fired this time. I didn't freeze. The horse shook in fear and pain as the bullet hit. It let out a horrible screeching sound and tripped over its own legs, sending its rider tumbling out of his seat. The horse stood up after a minute and limped off as fast as it could off the trail and disappeared into the woods.

I forced Iron to skid to a stop and dismounted as quickly as I could, keeping my pistol trained on the rider, who was still lying on the ground. He was breathing, though. I readied my rope in my free hand. I wasn't sure how to hogtie anyone, but I would try my best. I neared the rider when suddenly he sprang to life, surprising me and knocking me back onto my rear.

"What kind of animal shoots a horse at full gallop, *¡idiota!*" A hoarse, rough-sounding voice said. This was what I was waiting for. This was the voice that plagued my dreams.

"Don't go for your gun, Reyes!" I commanded, fueled by rage. I pulled myself as quickly as possible back to my feet before the outlaw could notice, "I swear I'll shoot you dead."

This was the first time I had ever gotten a good look. Reyes had a short mustache and goatee. His long, shaggy hair was tied in a rough-looking ponytail behind his neck. His clothes were unkempt. He didn't look like anything special. Certainly not like a criminal wanted dead or alive. Until you saw his eyes, that was. His eyes were piercing green, noticeable even against the dark olive complexion he had after years in the sun. They were the eyes of an animal.

"You're just a kid," Reyes said, smirking. He didn't reach for his gun. "Thought you were that Marshal I heard came to town."

"Keep them hands up," I told him. He did as I said. "You don't know me, do you?"

"Should I?" He asked, laughing.

I had my gun trained on him, but he didn't seem to care at all. "You killed my mother."

"Ah, I see now. You want revenge." He rolled his eyes.

"That, or justice," I remarked.

Reyes just laughed harder. "You ain't no killer, kid." He said before pouncing suddenly. He grabbed my gun, holding the hammer down before I could cock it again. "You shoulda just shot me when you had the chance!"

Reyes and I fought over the gun for a little while. I'd kick him; he'd send a knee into my gut. I soon realized that I wouldn't win this wrestle for my gun. I pulled his hands toward my face and bit down hard. He yelled and cursed but let go. I grabbed his iron from his belt, too. Rather than try to shoot him again and risk his speed beating out my desperation, I ran over to Iron. I shoved the peacemaker and his revolver into my saddlebag and gave Iron a good smack on the rear. The horse released a loud neigh and ran off, leaving me alone with Reyes.

"You're dumber than you look, kid!" Reyes said, grabbing me by my collar. Despite his small stature, he was ferociously strong. More robust than any of Eliza's brothers had been. He tossed me into the air like a rag-doll. I hit the ground hard, landing on my chest. I gasped for air before Reyes grabbed the back of my shirt and slammed me into a tree. I couldn't win fairly; I needed to even the odds. I grabbed a handful of dirt as I went down again and threw it in his eyes as he pulled me again.

Reyes stumbled backward, cursing and swearing. I pulled my hunting knife and swung it at him. The sharp blade went through his shirt and sliced his chest rather viciously. He swung wildly at me but still couldn't see. I tried to cut his neck, but he managed to dodge it barely, though the blade did catch his cheek. My next slash wasn't so lucky. Reyes avoided it, finally getting all the dirt out of his eyes.

He bashed my wrist and elbow, sending the knife flying off to who-knows-where. Reyes wrung my neck with two deadly hands and lifted me into the air, strangling me. I knew the fight was over. I flailed uselessly, trying to land a punch or kick, but I couldn't. He was going to kill me.

I never thought that bandits would be the thing that saved me, but Reyes stopped choking me when more bandits in green bandanas rode up. He dropped me then and there and approached the nearest one.

"Gun." He commanded the man furiously. I coughed and wheezed, thankful to be able to breathe again. My respite didn't last, though. Reyes grabbed my hair and jerked my head back. He put the twin barrels of a short, sawn-off shotgun to my head.

"Give me one good reason why I shouldn't blow your brains out right now, *necio!*." He threatened. I couldn't speak still, but I just looked at Reyes with hate in my eyes. If he let me live, I would hunt him to the ends of the earth.

"I'll give you one, Reyes." The man whom he'd taken the gun from said, "That Marshal probably heard the gunshot and is headed this way right now. If he gets here, we're done."

Reyes hesitated for a moment but knew his man was right. He threw my head back into the dirt and mounted up on the flank of one of his gang members' horses.

"If you follow me, kid," He threatened, growling, "I will fill you with holes. Stay away."

Reyes and the gang members rode away. I had to get the last words in. I mustered my remaining bravery, confidence, and energy and stood up to yell.

"Reyes!" I yelled after them. He turned his head, "My name is Asa. I'm coming for you!"

"*Buena suerte, Asa.*" I heard Reyes respond before they were out of earshot. He had just told me 'good luck.'

After they were gone, I collapsed into the dust and just lay there momentarily. I was tired. I had almost lost my life. I wasn't good enough to avenge my mom. I promised myself that I would be the next time I saw Reyes. I promised myself and my mom, wherever she was now, that I would kill Luis Reyes.

A few minutes passed before I heard hooves approaching from the opposite direction of the way Reyes had disappeared. I sat up, turning to look at Matthew Selleck galloping my way, once again leading Iron as well. He slowed to a trot, then stopped when he got close enough.

"You look worse for wear." He remarked, offering me a helping hand. I took it, and he helped me to my feet.

"It was him," I told Selleck. "The rider was Reyes."

"No kidding? How're you still alive then?"

I walked over to my saddle bag, pulling the two pistols out. I shoved my peacemaker back into the holster and offered the other to Selleck. He slowly took it and examined it.

"Smith & Wesson, model three." Selleck thought aloud as he looked at the revolver. "A Schofield, not too different from mine. Unlike mine, this chambered in .44-40. Nickel-plated.

Pearl Grip... and I count... thirty notches, made using a knife along the bottom of the grip. Thirty kills. Yep, this is Reyes' gun, alright."

"I told you, it was him." I insisted, leaning on my horse. I felt like I was going to pass out.

Selleck started to mount up again. "Don't bother chasing them." I said, pulling myself slowly onto my horse, "They're gonna be long gone by the time we get to their camp."

"I'm not going to chase." He told me, "But their camp could still have important clues. You coming?" I just nodded; my throat was too sore to continue to speak.

We rode at a steady trot, following the trail and giving our tired horses a chance to catch their breath. Eventually, Selleck and I arrived at a clearing next to the river. We dismounted, allowing the horses a chance to drink from the cool stream.

'This is probably two, three miles maximum away from my uncle's ranch." I said after taking my own sip from the cool water. Selleck nodded.

"These woods are a good spot to hide. It'd be real hard for someone to accidentally find this spot." Selleck began to look around, "Seems like they were packing up to leave already. There isn't much left over, which suggests that they didn't leave in too much of a hurry. They probably had everything packed up before your confrontation with Reyes."

I took my own look around the campsite. I dug through the coals of the fire, looking for anything useful. There were some burned scraps of paper, but only one was legible.

"This half-burned scrap says 'Hangman's Canyon,'" I remarked, showing Selleck the paper. He frowned.

"There doesn't seem too much else to go on." He told me, "I suppose I'll head towards that place tomorrow, 'Hangman's Canyon.' There's a small canyon near a rock formation that goes by that name. I saw it on a map the other day. It's in the New Mexico Territory. I'm worried that it could say anything about Hangman's Canyon, not necessarily that they have any sort of camp or hideout there. *But* it *is* close to the border. Could be a good stop for Reyes if he's trying to go back to Mexico, which is what I would do with a 'dead or alive' bounty in the US."

"Let me come with you." I insisted, practically begging. He scowled at me.

"Look, you seem like a good kid, "He started, "but you almost got killed today. I'm not going to risk that again. Reyes is way too dangerous."

"I'm tired of people treating me like this!" I yelled in frustration, "All my life, people have told me what to do and where to go. I didn't even want to come to this stupid town, but I didn't have a choice. My mom *died,* Selleck. Brutally murdered by the same man who nearly killed me today. You say it's too dangerous, fine. But I am going after him either way. You can either let me help, train me to fight, or I can go after him myself and get killed. But one way or another, I am making my own choice for the first time in my life. I am choosing to go after Reyes."

Selleck was silent for a long time, deep in thought. Finally, he sighed. He walked several paces away from me and squared up, holding his hand by his gun.

"Stand and draw." He ordered coldly. "A duel?" I asked nervously.

"Yup. Draw your gun."

I squared up to him as well. My heart pounded. Was Selleck serious? After a moment of standing there, I tried to draw my pistol. I hadn't even cleared leather before Selleck pulled his gun and shot in my direction. I was dead; I knew I was. He'd killed me.

I waited to fall to the ground. I waited for a burning, sharp pain that never came. No pain ever came. I dropped my gun back into the holster and checked my chest for wounds. I didn't have any. No blood spilled besides the wounds Reyes had given me during our brawl. Selleck blew his smoking barrel and holstered the iron. He pointed behind me. There was a bullet hole smoking in the tree. Selleck had purposely shot there instead of me.

"You can't even draw your gun well." Selleck said, proving his point, "You think you can fight an outlaw like Reyes?"

"You can teach me." I continued to insist, "In the past three months, I've learned to ride and break horses. To rope cattle. To live out on the open range. I *can learn* to fight, too. Just give me a chance."

Selleck narrowed his eyes, peering into my very being once again. He must've been good at reading people because he just gave me a sigh.

'Alright, kid." He finally conceded, "You can come with. I want you to know that I won't be taking any responsibility if you end up getting shot. I don't want any family members coming after me when you're six feet under."

"Thank you, sir." I said, relieved that he was finally seeing things my way, "I promise, I will make sure that all my relatives know that."

"Go home now. Pack your saddle bags. I need to send a letter tomorrow to the pencil-pushers. We will leave after the post office agrees to send the letter."

I had forgotten all about my exhaustion. I would tell Fierro and write a letter to my aunt and uncle. Fierro would understand, with all of his talk about opportunity. My aunt and uncle, not so much. It was better to say goodbye without actually seeing them. My heart did drop a little when I thought about Eliza, though. If we were leaving tomorrow, that meant I wouldn't be able to see her. She would be devastated or, at the very least, upset. She probably wouldn't ever want to see me again.

It doesn't matter now. I reminded myself. *I have to get Reyes. I have to avenge my mom.*

Chapter 8
A Letter Goodbye

The sun was starting to set when I arrived at the Ranch. I saw that Magdalena was in her corral, which meant Fierro was probably in his house. I rode up to the small building, which wasn't much more than a cabin, and tied my horse to one of the posts of Fierro's small porch. I walked up the stairs, feeling exhausted from my fight with Reyes. I knocked on the door a few times and waited.

"*Chico, ¿qué hacés acá?*" Fierro asked, opening the door, "What are you doing here? You never came back to the Ranch, so I figured you were busy with the Caldwell girl. I honestly didn't think I'd see you until tomorrow morning."

"Martín, it *was* Reyes. He killed my mother." I told him, completely ignoring my question.

Fierro looked outside, scanning for eavesdroppers or spies, and ushered me inside his house. I realized that this was the first time I'd ever seen the inside of his home. It was quaint but not poor at all. The main room was both the parlor and the kitchen. There were a few worn armchairs, several cow skin rugs covered the floor, and a large stone fireplace warmed and lit the room. In the kitchen, there was a small wooden table with two chairs and an iron stove. There was a back door which led to the back of the house. The bedroom was separated from the main room by a small doorway, but there wasn't a door, just a cow skin hanging in the doorway as a curtain. Fierro motioned for me to sit in one of the armchairs. I did as indicated.

Fierro left to the kitchen and came back with a pitcher of hot water and a strange cup with a steel straw. The cup was filled to the brim with what looked like herbs.

"This ain't *la yerba mate.*" Fierro said, filling and passing the cup to me, "It's just normal tea leaves, but this is how we take *mates* in my country." I took the cup and started to drink it slowly. Sure enough, it tasted like tea. "I told you about *mate*, didn't I?"

"You did," I affirmed, taking another sip from the straw.

"It's so expensive to get here." He explained, "It sounds strange, but I miss it dearly. The first thing I'm gonna do once I get rich is get some."

"You'll have to invite me," I told him, passing the cup back to him. He filled it and started drinking from the straw himself.

"I will, Asa. *Mate* is best drank *con amigos.*" He said, taking another sip, "Tell me, *muchacho*, what happened today with Reyes? Start from when you left me."

"It started after I met with Elizabeth Caldwell. I was riding home when I saw Mr. Selleck's horse. Turns out Selleck was trying to track Reyes or his gang. I convinced him to let me help out."

"How did you do that? Selleck ain't exactly been open about his investigation."

"I just told him what I knew. About my mom, and that I would be able to identify Reyes by his voice."

I explained everything that happened there to Fierro. I told him everything, from the intense chase we gave the lone rider to my brawl with Reyes, not sparing any details. I told him of the campsite and how Selleck said I could accompany him.

Fierro had finished the small cup of tea a long time ago but had yet to refill it. He just frowned and stood up. He placed another log on the dying flame.

"You're not honestly thinking about going with him, are you?" He finally asked grimly. "I am," I answered. "I have to get Reyes for all he's done to my mom."

"It's just vengeance you want, *chico.*" Fierro tried to explain, using that same tone that adults always use when they think they're right, "Killing Reyes ain't gonna bring Caroline back. Believe me, if it were, I would kill him in a heartbeat. But it ain't. Just stay here and let Selleck handle it."

"You think I don't know that?" I asked him sharply, "This ain't about that. Yeah, I do want to get vengeance for my mom, but you know how many people Reyes has killed? At least thirty, according to Selleck. That's *thirty* people who are probably in my situation, who lost their mom or dad, brother or sister. You knew my mom, perhaps even better than I did. She wouldn't have wanted that for nobody, and you know it. If I want to find peace for her death, I *need* to take down Reyes, whether that's by arresting him or killing him."

Fierro frowned and stared into the fire for a moment. He turned to me. There was a sad look in his eyes, one that I didn't understand.

"What then?" He asked. I tilted my head, confused at his question. "What happens after you kill Reyes? There are still bad people in the world. People still making others orphans and widows. You can't stop them all. What are you gonna do after you kill Reyes and see there's still evil in the world? You gonna go to Hell and kill the Devil himself?"

"If that's what it takes..." I muttered. "I've spent a lot of time thinking over these past few months. I've learned a lot from you. You talked to me about opportunity. You said that my mom wanted more from me, that when life called, I shouldn't be afraid to take a chance." He nodded slowly, "This *is* an opportunity calling, Martín. I can feel it. I don't just want to be a foreman on a ranch my whole life. I want to do good in the world. Sure, I can't go kill Lucifer, but if I can prevent one devil, one bad man, from doing more bad things, then I've done all I need to. If I do nothing, then I might as well let them kill my mom over and over again. If I could've prevented her from dying, I would've. This is a chance to stop someone else from suffering what she did."

Once again, Fierro was silent. He sat down and rubbed his beard slowly. Finally, he nodded and lit a cigarette.

"It ain't that simple, kid, but you're right about one thing for sure: Your mom did want more for you. And you're probably right about this being the call of something more, as I told you all those months ago. Alright, *muchacho*, you've convinced me. You should go get your revenge. What can I do to help you get ready for tomorrow?"

"Some supplies would be helpful," I told him, trying not to sound too excited. Fierro was allowing me to go! The one person I didn't feel right about leaving without permission, Martín Fierro, was letting me go hunt Reyes with Selleck, "Dried meat, ammunition, other provisions."

"Leave your horse here tonight. I can pack your saddle bags. I'll take Iron in my corral tonight and get him ready before you leave tomorrow morning. I'll also meet with Selleck to see if there's anything else you need. And here, take this." Fierro reached into his pocket and pulled out a roll of cash. He threw it over to me. It landed in my lap, "That's one hundred dollars. Don't waste it. It's for emergencies. Take my watch, too."

I stood up from my chair and pocketed the cash. Fierro took out his pocket watch and handed it my way. I took it. I am sure Fierro was expecting me to leave, but I ran over and hugged him. He was taken aback and surprised at my hug but slowly wrapped his arms around me.

"Thanks, Martín, for everything," I said, holding back tears. "I know I never told you this, but in these past few months, you've been the closest thing I've ever had to a father."

"*Ay, muchacho, no digas eso.*" Fierro told me, "You don't have to say that. I ain't nothing; I just tried to teach you what I know."

"I gotta go now." I finally said, breaking the embrace. "Selleck said he'd get me up early in the morning before my uncle wakes up. I have to write a few letters."

"Que Dios te cuida, muchacho." "God be with you as well, Martín."

That being said, I left the cabin. As instructed, I left Iron tied to the porch of Fierro's home and went on foot up the hill towards the ranch house. I met Selleck as he passed to go to Fierro's house, where he'd been staying the nights, and confirmed that he would wake me early tomorrow.

I arrived at the house and went upstairs right away. From my briefcase, I pulled out my fountain pen, a gift from my mom on my sixteenth birthday, and some sheets of paper and began to write.

"Dear Uncle Wesley and Aunt Rachel," I started the letter. I felt like I hadn't written in forever. My hand ached as I wrote the script on the page, but my handwriting was still as clean as always.

"By the time you read this, I will be long gone. There's much to explain, and I hope this letter will suffice. I wish I could've explained in person, but I couldn't risk anyone trying to stop me. I shall try to explain everything here, but if you have any further questions, you may direct them to Mr. Fierro. He is the only one who knows I am leaving.

"As you know, two days ago, a United States Marshal by the name of Matthew Selleck arrived in the county. You and Mr. Fierro have both been kind enough to allow him to stay here on the Ranch. During his stay here, Mr. Selleck has been conducting an investigation into one Luis Reyes, a criminal wanted by the Government, 'Dead or Alive.' You both may not know that since Mr. Selleck's arrival, I have been carrying out my own investigation into Mr. Reyes.

"After a confrontation with Mr. Reyes, I have concluded that he is the man who murdered my mother many months ago. While I appreciate all that you both have done for me, taking me into your home and treating me as your own son, I cannot nor will not rest until I see justice for my mother's death. I don't expect you to understand, nor do I expect you to be ok with my decision, but I have made up my mind.

"After speaking with Mr. Selleck about this matter, as well as Mr. Fierro, I have made the decision to journey with Mr. Selleck in pursuit of Luis Reyes. You may think of me as a vengeful child, but I feel in my heart a need to do what I believe is the correct and good thing; I deem it necessary that I must stop Luis Reyes by any means necessary, even if I must kill him. He has murdered, in cold blood, at least thirty people, including my mother. If I don't go with Mr. Selleck, I feel the blood of those thirty and any others whom Mr. Reyes slays in the future will be on my hands.

"Give my regards to Tabitha. She was like my little sister while I was here, and I treasure our friendship. She may keep my copy of *Tom Sawyer*. It was a gift from my mother eight years ago, but now I want Tabby to keep it. Please do not think less of me. I wouldn't be going if I didn't feel this burning in my heart. I hope to see you all again someday, sooner rather than later.

"Sincerely, your nephew, Asa Hendricks," I signed, closing the letter. I took a deep breath and placed it in an envelope. I wrote a second letter to Eliza, trying my best to explain my situation and apologize. This letter was much shorter. I felt sorry for her, but I felt strongly in my heart that I had no other choice. At the end of the letter, I told her I would write to her again when I got the chance.

Hopefully, she would be ok with that.

With the two letters written, I put out the gas lamp and went to bed. I knew that I would have difficulty sleeping that night. I felt excited, as though a whole new world was calling out to me from tomorrow. I was going on an adventure, like the books I had read. For the first time since my mother's death, I felt like my life meant something.

Chapter 9
Justicia

The following day, I was awoken by a light tapping on one of my windows. It wasn't rhythmic. I lit my oil lamp and went to the window to peer through. I saw Mr. Selleck on the ground with Ophelia and Iron. He'd been tossing pebbles at the attic windows. The sun wasn't up, but Fierro's watch said it was half-passed four. I wound the silver watch up quickly, ensuring I could accurately tell the time for the rest of the day. I quickly donned my clothes, hat, gun belt, and boots and sneaked down the wooden stairs as quietly as possible. I pulled from my satchel the first letter, addressed to my aunt and uncle, and placed it neatly on the kitchen table. I opened the door quietly and went out of the ranch house.

Selleck greeted me on horseback with a tin cup full of hot coffee. I mounted Iron and took the cup from him.

"Get used to that as your breakfast." He said, "On the road, we save all the food we can get our hands on for other meals. Breakfast is just hot coffee if we can start a fire." We started to ride off in a steady trot. "There's been some mornings where we couldn't start a fire, and I just had to eat the coffee grounds."

"Sounds rough," I replied, sipping the hot drink.

"That's your life until we get Reyes," Selleck said coldly. "You smoke?"

"No."

"Me neither." He admitted, "Don't know why Mr. Fierro said to offer you this then." He held out a cigarette, the same brand that Fierro smoked constantly. For the first time since I'd met him, I took Fierro's cigarette. I laughed lightly.

"Inside joke, I suppose," I told Selleck. I placed the cigarette in my satchel, in the same pocket as the hundred dollars Fierro had given me last night.

We trotted silently until the edge of the ranch, then picked up the pace until we got to town. The ride was quiet. Things were peaceful at this early in the morning. We arrived in town at around six A.M., where Selleck slowed his pace down to trot next to me.

"Take this report to the post office." He told me, handing me a sealed envelope. I took it, and then he gave me a few nickels for postage costs, "I'll grab some supplies from the general store, and we'll get out of here."

I rode Iron over to the post office and dismounted. I looked at the change Selleck had given me.

Fifteen cents. That would be enough to send his letter to where it was addressed, but it probably wouldn't be sufficient to send mine to Eliza.

I walked into the post office and was greeted by the Postmaster, an older man with a balding head, a mustache, and semi-circle spectacles.

"Morning, sir." I replied, trying to sound mature, "Marshal Selleck needs this letter sent out." I gave the letter over the counter. The Postmaster took it and looked down at it through his glasses.

"OK, one sheet of paper. This will be 15 cents to send to Washington, D.C." He said, reading the prices from his book. I passed him the nickels. "Anything else I can do for you?"

"I need a favor, if you will, sir." I told him, "Could you give this letter to Ms. Elizabeth Caldwell? She's supposed to meet me in front of the general store across the street, but I am going out of town with Marshal Selleck. I don't have any change, but I have money."

"Don't worry about it, Asa." The Postmaster said with a smile. "I remember what it's like to be young. I'll get your letter to Ms. Caldwell."

"Much obliged, sir." I thanked him. I said farewell to the old man and went across the street to meet back up with Selleck. As I approached the General Store, Selleck exited with a gunnysack full of supplies. I was about to help him, but he threw me a bundle of something. I unfurled the bundle. It was the dark gray canvas jacket that I had seen months earlier at the store when Fierro and I went to buy my hat and boots.

"What's this for?" I asked Selleck as he loaded our saddlebags with the various supplies he'd bought.

"Trail dust and sun are hard on the skin." He answered, "You'll need a coat to protect you."

"Thank you, sir," I said, putting the coat on. I still knew the price of the coat; it was thirty dollars. Selleck had just spent thirty dollars to get me a coat.

We mounted up and headed out on the trail. We were going fast, galloping the horses down the road. Not quite at full speed, but Selleck told me that we needed to try and catch up with Reyes before he could get to Mexico.

We rode all day, every day for four days. The only time we stopped was when we camped or found some water the horses could drink. Even if we wanted to catch Reyes and his gang, Selleck said we couldn't capture him if our horses dropped dead. Despite this, however, we still pushed the horses hard, going about fifty or sixty miles daily.

"Where are you from, Mr. Selleck?" I asked him when we were stopped once to water the horses.

"Don't call me Mr. Selleck." He told me, "Mr. Selleck was my father. It's just Selleck." I nodded and apologized, "I'm from a town up in the north; it's called Detroit. Haven't been there since the war, though."

"Have you always wanted to be a lawman?"

"Have you always wanted to be a nosey blabbermouth?" Selleck snapped coldly. I frowned at him. Ophelia let out a loud neigh as though she were scolding him. "I know, girl! I know!" He responded. "Sorry kid, I just... well, I've never been good with kids."

"I'm hardly a kid!" I objected.

"How old are you?"

"I'm sixteen. I'll be seventeen soon, though!"

"It doesn't matter how old you are." Selleck told me, "You still act like a kid. When I was your age, I was already on my own."

"Like I'm not on my own? My mom died. I ain't never met my dad 'cause he didn't want me. You met me with Martín and my aunt and uncle, but I wasn't with them long. If that ain't 'on my own' enough to be grown up for you, I don't know what is!"

Selleck didn't have anything to say to that. He was surprised that I was able to stand up to him yet again. He didn't have any response. He just nodded.

"Alright, Ace." He told me, standing up from where he was sitting, "Fine. I won't treat you like a kid anymore." He called Ophelia over and mounted up. I did the same, and we started off.

The rest of the day, Selleck rode in silence. He didn't seem mad, but rather, he had a pensive, stern look about him. He didn't speak all night, either. The only time he spoke the rest of the ride was to tell me we had crossed state lines into New Mexico Territory. We were apparently getting pretty close to Hangman's Rock. Selleck said we had about one more day of riding. We set up camp that night near a tiny stream.

"Ace." Selleck addressed me once we had set up the fire. He didn't take his eyes off the dancing orange and yellow light. "I owe you an apology as well as an explanation."

"What do you mean?" I asked him.

"I've been treating you like a kid this whole time. There's a reason for that." He explained, still not removing his eyes from the fire. "I had a wife once. And a son." He continued in a monotone voice, "Thought I could keep my job with US Marshal Service while having a family. After the war ended, the Union liked the way I operated, so I was hired as a US Marshal while I was pretty young. I think I was twenty-two. They'd send me all over the states like they do now still. I am really good at what I do. I actually met my wife on one of these trips.

"As I said, I was good at it. The best, even. I've always been somewhat of a 'problem solver.' If the Marshals need someone caught or killed, someone high-risk or especially dangerous, they send me."

"That's why you're going after Reyes." I nodded.

"Yeah, exactly. Reyes isn't the first of his ilk, and he won't be the last for sure. I made good money as the Government's attack dog. But money doesn't matter. Not anymore, at least."

"What do you mean?"

"I mean just that. When I was out on a mission, a bandit gang attacked my home, led by a man called 'La Bestia' on account of his savagery. It means 'the Beast' in Spanish."

"I'm aware."

"Well, I don't need to tell you in detail what the Beast did to them, my wife and son. That was nine or ten years ago. My son, Josiah, would be your age now. Being around you reminds me of him. You're similar to how he was, or at least, how I imagined he'd be. That's why I've been giving you such a hard time. I apologize."

There was silence for a long time, nothing but the crackling of the flames and the screeching of bats. One of the horses pawed the ground with a hoof.

"I had no idea," I told him, finally breaking the silence.

"No, of course not." He replied grimly, "How could you have known?"

"I forgive you. And I understand why you've been treating me this way. I promise, once we get Reyes, I'll go off and leave you alone."

"That's not what I'm trying to get at." He protested, "I'm just trying to say I'm sorry for the way I've been acting. It's not right. You're a good kid. And you're brave. I mean, who else would have the courage to go hand-to-hand with Luis Reyes? I think you want to do the right thing, and that reminds me of Josiah, but it also reminds me of myself. What I'm trying to say is that you should come with me once this is all said and done. I'm headed to Washington, D.C., after all this. You should come with me, and I can teach you to become a Marshal."

It was my turn to be surprised. This was something I didn't suspect from him.

"You don't have to respond right now." He continued, "We haven't even got Reyes yet. Just think about it. You don't have anyone to go back to in all reality. It would be a better use of your courage than being a foreman on a Ranch in Folklore. You got heart, kid; you just need the skills."

"I appreciate the offer, Selleck." I finally told him, "I ain't sure what I want from life yet besides getting Reyes, so I need to give it some thought, but I definitely will consider it."

"That's fine. It's a standing offer." He said, standing up, "It's getting late. We gotta get up early in the morning to ride to the next town. It's called 'Justicia'. From Justicia, we can get to Hangman's Canyon." Selleck kicked a little dust on the fire and went to his tent. I went to mine and fell asleep faster than I thought I would.

The following morning went by fast. We rose with the sun, got coffee ready, packed up camp quickly, and then set off to the town of Justicia, about a twenty-mile ride. It was rough terrain and hot, so we took it relatively easy, arriving in Justicia by about two in the afternoon.

Justicia was a desert town, by all descriptions. Apparently, there had been a mining boom here, silver. There wasn't any more silver, though. Justicia wasn't a ghost town but was well on its way to being one in a decade. We tied our horses up at the saloon and walked our way over to the Sheriff's office.

"Can I help you, gentlemen?" The Sheriff, an older man with a bald head and thick beard, asked. He wore a tin star on his vest that said nothing except the word 'Sheriff.'

"Yessir," Selleck told him. "Name's Selleck. I'm a US Marshal." Selleck opened his coat and showed his badge. "My partner here is Hendricks. We understand that a suspect named Luis Reyes may be holed up here, near Hangman's Canyon."

The Sheriff put down his newspaper and looked out the window to see if anyone else was listening.

"Sheriff Amadeus Greene." He introduced himself before continuing. "You heard right. Word is that Reyes arrived at a hideout nearby this morning. He's holed up with a local gang led by a man called Edgars. I wasn't planning on doing anything 'cause I ain't got the manpower to deal with two gangs, but *if* you two marshals are here, well, that changes things. Evens the odds a little. I got a deputy watching their hideout. If we gather a posse and head up there, we might be able to take out Luis Reyes and the Edgars' Gang."

"You're speaking my language, Sheriff Greene," Selleck said. We followed Sheriff Greene out.

He called out to one of his deputies, sleeping in the shade.

"Go gather the others." He told him. "These are Marshals. We're going to take care of the Edgars' Gang, once and for all.

Sheriff Greene mounted up. Selleck and I ran over you our horses and mounted up as well. We rode back to the Sheriff's Office, where the other deputies gathered.

"Listen, kid." Selleck told me quietly as we closed in on the Sheriff's Office, "I don't want you getting close. Take my rifle and just snipe. You got a lot to learn before I will have you getting up close and personal."

"Like what?" I asked, taking the Winchester as he passed me it.

"Like, don't put your gun in your saddlebag and scare off your horse! You got lucky last time, but Reyes would've finished you if his gang hadn't shown up and talked some sense into him."

We waited for the rest of the posse to gather. The Sheriff gave his little speech to his deputies, and we set off towards Hangman's Canyon.

Chapter 10
Battle at Hangman's Canyon

My heart pounded as we closed in on Hangman's Canyon. We had about twenty men, including myself and Selleck. This didn't feel like before when I was chasing Reyes down a horse trail. This felt like I was heading into a battle.

This feeling faded when we slowed the horses as we got near. The Sheriff held his hands to his mouth and blew, making a noise that sounded somewhat like a bird. A man popped his head out of the bushes and ran down the hill to us.

"Sheriff!" He said, panting as he got closer. "They're still there! Those guys from this morning, too! The ones with the green bandanas."

"Good job, Mr. Johnson." The Sheriff regarded the man. "Go take this Marshal here, with the rifle," He motioned to me, "And get him up on the canyon wall to a spot with a good aim on their camp. Take my rifle, too." The Sheriff took his own rifle, a Springfield, from his shoulder and passed it to the deputy.

When he had the rifle, he jumped on my horse's back. Iron didn't seem too pleased about the second rider, but when you can't talk, you really don't have much say in what happens. We started to ride up the hill, away from the trail.

"So you's a real Marshal, eh mister!" The Deputy, Mr. Johnson, exclaimed, "I never met a real marshal before." This man probably had as many years of education as he did teeth. He was fighting on my side, though, so I tried not to judge him so harshly.

"More like a Marshal-Apprentice," I told him.

"A Marshal what?"

"Um... a Marshal-in-training. I'm just learning."

"Oh, I understand." He nodded his head, "Must be pretty exciting. Fighting crime and all that."

"Well, you're doing the same thing I am," I told him. He nodded.

"Yeah, but I only do this sometimes. My real job is a farmer. How old is you?"

"I'm nearly seventeen," I answered.

"Wow... seventeen and a marshal. My li'l girl is almost your age. She's fifteen, I think."

"Well, let's get this done and get you back to her."

We rode for about twenty minutes longer. We were on the top of a mesa now. It was flat, save a long gash in the land, as though some giant had taken an axe to the giant stone.

"Stop right there, next to that tree." Mr. Johnson told me, pointing at the lone tree. It was completely dead, but it would be sufficient to tie Iron to. "We don't wanna get too close now, not with the horse."

"Yes, I suppose you're right." I agreed, "It ain't gonna help our men on the ground if they spot my horse from the camp.

We tied up the horse and then walked over to the canyon's edge, where we lay on the very edge.

This was the very end of the canyon, a great place for all manner of scum to hide.

The miscreants had built their own village in the pocket of the canyon. There was all manner of men walking around. Some wore green bandanas. I felt worried for a minute. This seemed too far of a distance to fire Selleck's Winchester accurately. The Springfield that the Sheriff had given to Johnson would probably be fine, but the Winchester just wasn't a sniper rifle.

I pushed this thought from my mind. The range was the least of my worries. Apart from that, we would be shooting down at the two gangs, which probably increased my accuracy. I continued to examine the camp. There were two trails carved into the circular bowl, one leading all the way up to us and another to the opposite side of the canyon. I had to make sure to watch those trails. Besides the fact that one led up to us, either one was a good escape route for Reyes or anyone else who wanted to flee.

"If they try to escape on horseback up those two trails," I told Deputy Johnson, pointing out the two trails with my left hand, "Don't bother shooting the riders. Shoot the horses. That Springfield will be enough to kill or maim any of the horses."

"You got it, Marshal!" He said, saluting me with his right hand.

We waited for the others. Selleck, the Sheriff, and the other deputies would enter the bowl via the canyon's mouth and demand that they surrender. They were probably gonna get the first shot in, but that's the way that Sheriff Greene wanted to do things. Selleck wasn't going to try to undermine the Sheriff. If fighting started, Johnson and I were on overwatch. Having snipers from up here wasn't a poor plan, especially since we identified the two escape routes.

Finally, after about ten minutes of waiting in the hot sun, the riders appeared around the bend of the canyon.

"Listen up, Edgars and Reyes and others!" I heard Sheriff Greene shout. "If you surrender to us, then we won't kill any of you, and you will get a fair trial. Marshal Selleck here will even take some of you with him to be tried. If you don't surrender, we will fight you, and we will kill you."

Silence. Were the bandits really going to surrender?

Shots rang out. The ground team cursed and hopped off of the horses. They all tried to take cover and return fire.

"What do we do?" Johnson asked me, clearly frightened. "Shoot them!" I yelled, pulling the lever of the Winchester down. I fired a shot and repeated. Johnson began firing, too, the big boom of the old Springfield attracting attention towards us.

Some of the bandits started firing at us. Bullets bounced and ricocheted off the canyon wall, but there was no way that any of them would hit us from the angle they were at. They'd need a rifle with a scope or a Gatling gun. Perhaps a cannon.

As far as I could tell, I hadn't hit anyone. My fears about the rifle range had, in fact, been based on reality. That was accompanied by the reality that I hadn't ever shot it before. I kept shooting, though. The ground team was starting to move forward. We were fighting the bandits back!

As I predicted, however, many of the bandits started fleeing on horseback up those trails I had warned Johnson about.

"Johnson!" I yelled, trying to get his attention, "The horses! Shoot the horses!"

Johnson cursed, but he followed my directions. We began raining fire down on the horses, fleeing up the trail across from us. Some of the riders were thrown from the horses and trampled by another horse. Some of the riders fell with their horses, tumbling off the cliffs. We were so focused on the trail across from us that we'd ignored the trail that led up to us.

I realized we messed up when I heard a revolver shoot right next to me, followed by Deputy Johnson coughing and gurgling his own blood. He'd been shot in the throat or lungs.

Just in time to avoid another shot, I jumped to my feet and ran backwards. I pushed the lever of the Winchester again to cycle another round. The attacker, one of Reyes' gang, cried out, covering his face. Unfortunately, the rifle was empty. It clicked but didn't fire a bullet. Reyes' thug laughed and aimed his revolver for another shot. I ran away from the cliff edge to the right and pulled my peacemaker. I narrowly avoided another shot.

I fired a shot, nailing his horse in the head. The beast came down, causing the thug to miss a third shot and toss his pistol over the cliff edge. He jumped to his feet and rushed me. I didn't have a choice. I aimed and fired one shot from my revolver, followed by another, then finally a third. He laid face first in the dust, blood pooling on either side of him. He was completely dead. I had just killed someone, on purpose, for the first time. I'd shot him dead.

I stared at the body for a minute. My adrenaline made the blood rush to my head. I understood for the first time why Fierro had turned into some sort of animal when we fought those cattle rustlers. That felt like a lifetime ago. My heart jumped and celebrated as though it were saying, 'Whoopee! We did it!' before the dread set in. I didn't even know this man's name. Did he have a family? I felt disgusted with myself.

I pushed this thought from my head. Deputy Johnson hadn't been dead yet, at least not when I jumped up. I rushed over to his body and felt for his pulse, but I couldn't find it. This made me angry. I ran over and kicked the body of the man I'd killed. I screamed and cursed him. I felt frustrated. I didn't know this man, but I *did* know Deputy Johnson, at least enough to mourn him. I knew he had a family and a fifteen-year-old daughter. I knew he had a farm and was here because he wanted to do the right thing. It no longer mattered if this man who I'd killed had a family. It didn't matter how many kids he had or how much his wife needed him if he even had one.

He'd taken a father and husband from other people. He was the same as Reyes. A devil, one who only stole from the world. As far as I was concerned, this guy didn't deserve to live. I felt worse about killing his horse than I did about killing him. I spat on his corpse and left it to be eaten by the vultures.

The battle was over. That much was for sure. We had won, but at a significant cost. I bandaged Johnson's wound so he wouldn't bleed all over me and packed him on Iron's back. I walked the horse down the treacherous path until I met Selleck and the Sheriff at the bottom of the bowl.

"Johnson was a good man." Sheriff Greene said upon seeing the corpse, "Real shame. It's gonna hurt to have to tell his family. I hope you at least put a bullet in the guy that did this, Marshal."

"I put three." I told the Sheriff, spitting just having to talk about that scum, "He's on the top of the cliff there, baking in the sun."

"As he should be." Sheriff Green replied, "I appreciate the both of you, Marshals. We got Edgars, shot 'im dead. None of the gang will ever be back to the county, either, after the bloodbath we caused today. Who knows? I might be able to retire without seeing further violence."

Selleck rode up to us, carrying a man, tied and gagged, on the back of his horse.

"That Reyes?" The Sheriff asked, exchanging his gaze between both of us. I rode up next to Selleck and looked at the man tied up.

"Sure ain't," I told him, grimly.

"Doesn't matter," Selleck said, wiping some blood off his face with a handkerchief. It didn't appear to be his own. "Reyes fled, probably to Mexico. We should be able to get some answers out of this one. He got trampled by a horse on his way out, but he'll survive. At least until we can get him some medical attention. He'll probably know where Reyes is headed."

"Good enough." The Sheriff said, mounting his own horse, which also carried a dead body. It wasn't a deputy, so I assumed it was Edgars. Sheriff Greene was bringing him back to town to make a big show out of it. Tell any potential ne'er-do-wells that Justicia wasn't the place to carry out illicit activities.

All in all, though, Sheriff Greene had lost three good men, including Johnson. That was hard on the old man. He didn't show much emotion but clearly knew these three men and their families. We carried the three dearly departed deputies on our horses to be returned to their loved ones and buried appropriately.

"You ok, kid?" Selleck asked me. I was riding at the rear of our black parade back to Justicia Selleck, the master at reading people, had fallen back to talk to me. We now rode side-by-side.

I'll be ok." I sighed, "I ain't never killed nobody before."

"Understandable. It's not like you've had a lot of opportunities."

"One time, when Fierro and I were watching, the cattle rustlers came, trying to make off with some of the herd. Some of them were even Reyes' gang. I tried to fight, but I couldn't. In the end, Fierro killed them all."

"So what?"

"I ain't sure what my point is." I admitted, "But I can't stop thinking about it." Selleck just nodded, listening to my every word. "I can't understand why God puts bad people in the world and just lets them have their way, killing and stealing."

"I'm no preacher," Selleck told me, "But God is something that I held onto during the war with the Confederates. I was eighteen. One of my war buddies told me that God puts bad people in the world to give good people a chance to stand up."

"Sounds like a wise fellow. What happened to him? A preacher now, right?

"He was shot the next day. Died a horrible, painful death in a trench. Learned one thing that day, and it's still something I don't understand. Bad things mostly only happen to good people."

"I'll second that." I responded, "My mom was my world. Best lady I ever knew. She died a horrible death, too."

"That's why I decided to become a lawman." Selleck continued, "I was tired of bad things only happening to good people. I decided that as long as I live and breathe, I'm gonna make bad things happen to bad people, too. If dark and evil men are gonna act like devils and things of nightmares, I was going to be the thing lurking in the shadows for them."

I just nodded, unsure how to respond. Selleck shrugged. The rest of the ride to Justicia was silent.

Chapter 11
The Return

When we arrived back in town, we were greeted like heroes. The men, women, and children of Justicia stood in the road and cheered. We'd done it. We'd killed John Edgars, the villain of the whole county. You would've thought it was Satan himself we killed, the way these people cheered. Sure, a few people were crying over their lost husbands and fathers, but overall, sentiments among the townspeople were good.

"Ride with me to the town doctor," Selleck told me. We continued on past the greeting party.

Selleck still had the unconscious gangster on his horse, "You feel good about all this?"

"You'd think we're heroes," I said grimly. "I don't feel like a hero. I feel like I could've done more to stop three good men from dying."

"That's how it feels every time a good man dies unnecessarily." Selleck answered, "There's never enough that you can do. I'm used to good men dying, but I am disappointed that Reyes got away. He's the reason we went out there, after all, which makes him the reason those three deputies met their untimely end. I just hope this guy can tell us where Reyes might be headed." He motioned to the unconscious man tied to the back of the horse. "Help me out with getting him into the clinic, will you?"

Selleck and I dismounted our horses, and I helped him carry the injured man into the clinic. He groaned as we moved him, but he didn't wake up. The town doctor was a very normal-looking man for a dying town. I expected him to be more eccentric, but that wasn't the case. He was probably in his mid-forties, his brown hair neatly trimmed and his face clean-shaven. He instructed us to lay the prisoner out on a bed so that he could examine him.

"Head down to the Saloon, Asa," Selleck told me once we had brought the prisoner in. He gave me about ten dollars, too. "Get us a room with two beds and get yourself a hot meal. Try and get some shuteye once the sun goes down. I'll send for you after about six hours so you can take a turn at watch."

"What do you mean?"

"I mean," he started to clarify, "That one of us needs to sit on this scum while the Doc is treating him. We can't have him wake up and escape on us. Another worry is that some vigilante might come after him, trying to get revenge for one of the poor lost deputies. Can't have that either."

"Ok, that makes sense." I nodded my head. "See you in a little while then." He responded with a grunt, and I left the doctor's office.

I mounted back up and walked my horse over to the Saloon. There was quite a ruckus coming from inside as a party had begun. I groaned and dismounted. I tied my horse up and shook the dust off my coat. Finally, I went inside the Saloon.

"Well, howdy there, Mr. Marshal." The bartender greeted me with a smile, "What can I do ya for?"

"I need a room for me and my partner," I told the man. Passing him the ten-dollar bill. "A hot meal wouldn't be bad neither. Keep the change, too. Marshal Selleck will probably want something to eat later, too, if you can keep that ready for him."

"Can I get you anything to drink? Whiskey, perhaps?"

"You got water?"

"I do, but I'm afraid it ain't too clean. You're better off drinking a beer."

"What about tonic?"

"Like a gin-n-tonic?"

"Yeah, but hold the gin."

He gave me a strange look but soon brought the tonic water. I sipped it until the man could get my meal, a nice hot rabbit stew with a few vegetables. I'm sure it was nothing too gourmet, but it beat my lunches and dinners of the past few days, which consisted of beef jerky and river water. I finished my meal fast, not realizing how hungry I had been before this. The bartender brought me another tonic, too, which was nice because the stew had been really salty.

"You're one of the marshals who killed John Edgars?" A woman's voice said behind me. I turned my head to look. She was probably ten years older than me. Pretty, but nothing to write home about.

"I am," I told her. I really wasn't interested in talking to anyone, though. I was tired, and I wanted to go to bed. Today had been difficult, and I wasn't interested in conversation.

The woman sat by me and smiled. She tried to grab my arm, but I jerked it back before she could.

"Don't be like that, Mr. Marshal." She protested, smiling and trying again, "I just figured you could use some company."

"I ain't at all interested, lady. I'm gonna finish my drink and go to bed."

"I could come with." She suggested. I scowled at her. I thought about Eliza. Although we hadn't had time to form our relationship, I felt pretty attached to her. She had drawn my attention. This girl wasn't even close to what Eliza was for me. I wasn't interested in her at all.

"Appreciate the offer, but I ain't slept in a bed for a few days now. When I go upstairs, it's to sleep, nothing more."

"Well, maybe I could-" She started to say before getting cut off by a man.

"Sarah, will you please leave Marshal Hendricks alone." Sheriff Greene said gruffly. She looked at him, then left without another word. "Sorry about that, Hendricks." He said to me, taking her seat. "John Edgars has been a plague on this town for a long time now. Everyone is real appreciative of you and Marshal Selleck."

"No need. We didn't come to take down Edgars. I am glad we could help, but our work ain't done yet. Once we can get some info out of that scumbag that Selleck brought in, we'll be out of your hair for good."

"I understand. Buy you a drink?"

"I ain't a drinking man, Sheriff."

"You ain't hardly a man, no offense intended. You're new to this whole marshal gig, ain't you?" I looked at him, narrowing my eyes like Selleck did when he was trying to get a read on someone, "Oh come on now, Marshal, I don't mean nothing by it. You just seem real young to be out doing law enforcement."

"Alright, I see what you're saying. I am, yes." I answered, nodding my head, "What about it?"

"I just... well, I don't know what I am trying to say. I've been at this a long time. I see the same look in Selleck's eyes as I do mine when I look in the mirror. I would hate to see you waste your life and youth faster than most people. This job takes your soul and then some. Don't put it as a priority. I'd hate to see a fine young man like you lose himself because of it."

"I appreciate the advice, Sheriff," I said. He started to get up, but I spoke again. "I'm sure Mr. Selleck would appreciate a drink later if you're still here when he comes back."

"That can be arranged." He said, nodding thoughtfully. "Have a good night, Mr. Hendricks."

I finished my tonic, then went upstairs to the room where the bartender had given me the keys. I stripped my jacket off and lay on the bed for a little while. I sure felt tired, but there was one more thing I wanted to get done before heading off to sleep. I pulled out of my satchel my pen and a piece of paper; I started writing a letter to Eliza.

I told her about the journey and how we'd chased the criminals on horseback. I described the town of Justicia and the surrounding desert. I wrote about the battle between us and the Edgars-Reyes gangs, about how I shot a man dead, and about how I didn't feel bad about it, about how he'd deserved it.

"We'll probably leave Justicia before you receive this letter," I wrote in my final paragraph, "But I shall write to you again before we leave. Perhaps, if you know where we are going, you can send a letter ahead of time so I can receive it when we arrive at the next town."

I wanted to write more but felt tired and needed to figure out what to say. In all reality, I didn't know Eliza that well. I knew that, and she knew that. She probably was still upset that I had left without speaking to her. I still wanted to write her, though. I wanted her to know that I was doing something meaningful for the first time in my life. Perhaps it was hopeless, and I was just stupid, but if there was a chance of fixing things, of making her understand, I wanted to try to take it.

I put the letter in an envelope and placed it neatly on the desk in the room. I would send it at the post office tomorrow, but it was time to rest for now.

Unfortunately, Reyes' pal that we captured didn't wake up for about a week. He'd had an open wound arm that was older than the gunfight at Hangman's Canyon, and it got infected before the fight. After he arrived in Justicia, the infection got much worse. He was delirious and barely conscious, with a high fever. The Doc took good care of him, though, as long as Selleck kept feeding him cash. He told me it was a 'government stipend,' not his own money, so there was no need to worry about the cost.

We took turns watching the scumbag. Every six hours, we would trade off, paying one of the kids in town a quarter at the end of each watch to go fetch the other from the Saloon. After the first few days, a six-hour watch was boring. There were only so many times that I could clean my gun, mess around with my knife, and flip a coin in the air, trying to guess what it would land on. I would write in my spare time. I wrote most of my second letter to Eliza, though I would only be able to finish her letter once I found out where we were headed. I wrote to my aunt and uncle. I even wrote to Fierro. It would be fun to write him a letter in Spanish. I was only halfway through my first paragraph when I realized that I didn't know enough Spanish to finish off a sentence, let alone a whole letter. I didn't scrap it, though; I just decided to tell the truth and continue the letter in English.

Finally, seven days from when we'd arrived in Justicia, in the afternoon, halfway through my watch, the outlaw awoke.

"Ugh..." He groaned, opening his tired, red eyes, "Where am I?"

"Easy now, partner," I said, holding my hand near my gun. I wasn't too worried about him doing anything, but I also wasn't stupid. I whistled to the kids outside. One of them, the youngest, came to the door. I placed a quarter in his palm, "Go get Selleck. Tell him to get down here now."

The kid nodded and ran off with his friends towards the Saloon. I stood next to the prisoner and called for the Doc upstairs, in his living quarters, doing who-knows-what.

"What do you remember?" I asked the sick man, "You got real sick, but you're at the doctor's right now."

"I was in Hangman's Canyon... and... oh no. What happened? Is everyone ok?" He said, trying to sit up. I placed a firm hand on his shoulder, intending to fight him if he tried anything funny.

"I don't know how else to break this to you, pal." I told him, grabbing the grip of my peacemaker, "But you've been arrested. We thought we lost you due to an infection in your leg, but the Doc here in Justicia took real good care of you. If you cooperate with us, we'll make sure that you're saved the rope."

"No... it can't... Reyes will kill me." He said, panicking. I tightened my grip on his shoulder.

Selleck came in, panting from the run over to the clinic.

"He's awake? Did he say anything?" He asked, running over. I felt a wave of relief rush over me now that Selleck was here. He and I together would definitely be able to control the prisoner if things got violent.

"I ain't saying nothin'. I want a law'er now." The prisoner demanded.

"And I want Reyes on a rope now." Selleck spat back quickly, "Looks like we both ain't getting what we want. As far as I know, there aren't any lawyers in Justicia." He went to the other side of the bed and got in the man's face. "I'll tell you the situation, bud. Your buddies killed three of this town's deputies. Good men, loved by all. You are the only person we managed to take alive. The town's out for blood. Us marshals are the only chance you have of making it out of this town with your life, you understand? So if you don't start talking, we are gonna turn you over to the townspeople. The way I hear it, they don't take too kindly to disreputable folk such as yourself on a good day, let alone on a day they lose three good, upstanding citizens. Understand?"

I wasn't sure if Selleck's threats were truthful that we would turn him over to the people if he chose not to cooperate. Still, I did know that Selleck was honest about one thing: the community did not love this man. They probably would've hanged him already from the tree by the entrance of town next to John Edgars' lifeless body if we hadn't been here keeping watch. The rumors about the gunslinging abilities of the two marshals visiting the town had become significantly exaggerated as the days passed, so no one dared to cross us.

The prisoner shook his head rapidly, making sure that Selleck knew he did indeed understand completely.

"Where's your boss going, friend?" I asked the man, butting into the conversation. If Selleck was going to be the bad cop, I would be the good one. I didn't know much about interrogations and the like, but I wasn't completely ignorant either.

The man coughed, his voice hoarse. I gave him a cup of water. He drank it down quickly before answering me.

"Reyes was talkin' 'bout goin' down to a city called Refugio de los Santos. On the border. They have a big bank there; he planned to rob it before returning home to Mexico."

"Where's home for Mr. Reyes?" Selleck asked in a threatening tone.

"It's called... Las Fuentes. Near there. It's a town in Mexico. Maybe a two-week ride from the border? I ain't never been."

The doctor had come down now. Selleck left for a minute and returned with the Sheriff. This trash was his problem now. Selleck didn't seem to care what happened with him now. The Sheriff could hang him for all we cared. I didn't want to stop them either; if they had decided to kill him, let them. We were a step closer to Reyes now.

We left almost immediately. I barely had time to finish my letter and get it sent. Reyes was gonna rob a bank and make for Mexico, and he was already a week ahead of us. We had to ride fast and hard if we even wanted any hope of catching him before the planned robbery.

Chapter 12
Refugio de Los Santos

We decided to get as little sleep as necessary. The only reason we did end up stopping to sleep a little was because the horses needed it. They were probably getting a little cranky, so we ensured they always got plenty of food and water. Selleck even had some sugar cubes in his saddle bag that he shared with them. The coffee would be more bitter, but that was secondary to keeping the horses happy. Besides our lukewarm coffee in the early mornings, we didn't even stop to eat. We just ate as we rode.

We rode like this for two days until the 17th, which happened to be my birthday. I didn't say anything to Selleck. This was my first birthday without my mom, and I didn't want to think about it, to be honest. By sheer coincidence, though, Selleck slowed his horse down to ride next to me.

"I'm starving." He said. "Tired of dried meat. We're making good time. I'm gonna shoot the next buck I see." Selleck was a clever guy, but there's no way he could've known it was my birthday.

We didn't have to wait long. Probably twenty minutes passed before we saw a pack of deer grazing near the trail. Selleck didn't miss a beat. He drew his rifle from his saddle holster and fired a shot off, hardly aiming at all. A young buck from among the group dropped like a sack of potatoes.

Selleck and I galloped over to the dead animal and dismounted our horses.

"You know how to skin and prepare an animal?" He asked, drawing his knife. I shook my head. "I'll teach you. Skins and antlers usually sell for a good price if you're ever tight on cash."

It was messy, but Selleck was skilled. He'd done this plenty of times and simply explained every part of the process. We had probably fifty pounds of meat, a reasonably clean buckskin, and a pair of antlers at the end of it all. The antlers and skin, Selleck tied to Ophelia. He told me to start a fire and set up camp for the night.

The fresh meat tasted great. Selleck had found some wild sage, which was a perfect seasoning for the venison. We ate around ten pounds each. The rest, we hung over the fire to smoke. Leaving thirty or so pounds of good meat would be a waste.

After we finished the meal, we sat around the fire to shoot the bull a little. Selleck was full of all kinds of stories and tales. Tales from the war to tales from all the guys he'd hunted over the years. He was more talkative tonight than on other nights. I wasn't. Selleck noticed this.

"What's on your mind, kid?" He asked, after the third story without any of my comments, "You're being real quiet."

"I didn't wanna tell you. Didn't want you to think I wanted to be dramatic. Today is my birthday."

"Well shoot, good thing we shot this buck then! Certainly isn't cake, but it was certainly delicious! Happy birthday, kid."

"Yeah. It's just weird, you know? My first birthday without my mom, you know?"

"I think I understand," Selleck said, nodding thoughtfully. "I lost my father when I was fourteen. I remember the feeling."

"What about your mom?"

"Never knew her. She died of pneumonia when I was a baby. Had to fend for myself for four years till the war started. Hate to say it, 'cause those were some pretty awful times, but the war saved me from a life of worthlessness."

"What happened to your father?"

Selleck sighed and stared into the flames for a little while.

"My daddy was a money courier." He explained, "He was gone pretty frequently, driving a wagon full of cash between banks. He'd drive everywhere from Illinois to Ohio. I would go with him when the banks were close to Detroit, but that was rare. He actually taught me to shoot just for these trips; nothing crazy ever happened when I was with him, though. But like I was saying, when he was going out of state, I couldn't come. He told me it was too dangerous to go with.

"To make a long story short, bandits attacked the wagon on a trip to Ohio. Killed my daddy because he couldn't open the safe. I spent the next years on the road, hunting that scum down."

"Did you get them?"

"I did. They all had caught cholera and were dying in their camp. I almost felt sorry for them. I put them down and out of their misery. I returned home, and the war started probably six months later. I'd just spent the past four years of my life turning myself into a killer, and so I signed up. Served under Ulysses Grant himself."

"Why are you telling me all this?" I asked, leaning forward and resting my elbows on my knees. "Because I want you to know that I understand, Asa." He explained, "I understand wanting

revenge. That's why I let you come along. You remind me of myself when I was younger. I wouldn't have found peace if I hadn't found the men responsible for my father's death."

"You still ain't found peace, Matthew." I protested, "What about 'La Bestia'?"

"I found peace for a while." He explained, "At least until the Beast and his gang killed my family. Who knows, maybe after I help you find Reyes, you'll help me find the Beast."

"I will try my best, I promise," I told him. It wasn't right for a man to lose his family. I understood that more than anyone. We went to bed after this conversation, leaving the fire lit to smoke the meat. After two days of near-constant riding, it felt good to get some real shuteye.

Unfortunately, our little break couldn't last. With the sun's rising, we were on the road again, riding at full speed. Reyes was probably in Refugio de Los Santos already, so we couldn't afford to waste too much time. We rode all day, stopping only to water and give the horses a rest. We weren't far now, so we decided to ride through the night, much to our horses' dismay. Refugio was a big enough city that they would have actual stables, where the horses could get a well-deserved rest and some good hay.

Sure enough, according to Selleck's predictions, we arrived in Refugio at about eight in the morning. The stable boy was quick and chatty. We found out that the Bank had yet to be robbed. We'd made it on time!

"Alright, kid," Selleck said as we walked down the dusty street, "Let's find the Bank, then you'll find a hotel or saloon nearby. Get a room with a window that we can watch the Bank from. Show them this if they don't want to make special arrangements for us." He unpinned the silver badge from his shirt and handed it to me. "Don't lose it. It isn't yours. You'll have your own once we get over with, and Reyes is six feet under."

I turned the silver star in my hand. It was heavier than I expected. I nodded my head.

"What will you do?" I asked as we neared the center of the town, "Find the sheriff?"

"Keep watch on the bank." He answered, "After you get the room, come back and find me. We can't tell the local authorities about the robbery. We don't want to raise the alarm and cause Reyes to chicken out. If he goes to Mexico, we'll lose him."

"Why? We know where he's going. Las Fuentes, his home town."

"We can't follow him into Mexico, Ace." Selleck said with a scowl, "What does that badge in your hand say? *United States Marshal*. Once he flees the country, he's out of our jurisdiction. They'll arrest us in Mexico if we try to get Reyes there."

"I didn't think of that," I admitted. Selleck just grunted. We walked a little further until we arrived at an old wooden building with the words 'First Bank of Refugio de Los Santos' in faded white paint. Despite saying it was the 'first' Bank, it could've easily said the *only* one because it was. I always wondered why banks in these small cities did that. In somewhere like Port City, where it was a big city, and there were several banks, I understood why they numbered the banks, but here in Refugio, back in Justicia, and even back in Folklore, all those banks were called the 'First Bank.'

Selleck went up to the porch of a store across the street from the Bank and pretended like he was looking at the wares. I went to the hotel next to the store.

The bottom floor of the hotel was just a saloon. The proper term was a lobby bar, but for me, it looked like any saloon I'd ever been to. Cowpokes and *vaqueros* all over, drinking whiskey, beer, and whatever other alcoholic drinks the locale had. A few rough-looking fellows playing cards and a few scantily clad girls wandering around trying to get a quick buck any way they could.

"Could I get a room?" I asked the barman as I sat on one of the stools. I put a five-dollar bill on the counter. "One by the front of the building?" The man looked at me and looked at my cash.

"We ain't got no space," he told me, returning to drying a glass.

"This may change your mind." I showed him the silver badge. He looked at it for a few seconds, then shook his head.

"Still don't got no space, Marshal." He shrugged, "Buncha rough-lookin' fellas rolled in late last night. Took every room I had."

"These 'fellas' wouldn't have happened to have been wearing green bandanas, would they?"

"It's the darndest thing, Marshal, I can't seem to remember."

I pushed the five-dollar bill forward on the counter. He just stared at it. "Remember now?" I asked.

"I don't." He told me, "I *do* remember them askin' me to let 'em know if any lawman came through. I might be able to 'forget' that little detail though..."

I reached into my satchel and pulled twenty dollars out of the hundred that Fierro had given me. I counted them before the barman and placed them on the counter. He took the twenty-five dollars and pocketed them.

"I would still like to know if any of my green bandana friends came here," I told him. He nodded and placed the glass he'd been cleaning on the counter.

"I believe there were about fifteen of 'em. And, just like you said, Marshal, they wore dark green bandanas."

"They up there now?"

"Nope. Left an hour or two before you walked in. They didn't say where they were going, but they gave me enough cash to stay a few days."

"Much obliged, mister," I said before pushing myself off the countertop and back to my feet. I hurried outside and over to Selleck.

"Bad news," I told him. He rolled his eyes and groaned. "What is it?"

"Reyes' men are staying at the hotel. Booked every available room last night."

"Let's go get them then!"

"That's the bad news! They ain't there. Barman said they left an hour or two ago and that they were probably coming back."

"Let's go investigate the rooms, at least."

Selleck and I trudged through the hot, dusty air and back through the half-doors of the saloon.

Without a word, Selleck went up to the barman. "Let me see the keys." He demanded.

"Keys to what, Marshal?" The barman asked, probably expecting another 'tip.'

Selleck grabbed the bartender by the shirt and yanked him over the bar and onto the ground.

Everyone went silent. Selleck held a fist in front of the man's face.

"I ain't got time for games!" He growled, "Do you have spare keys or no?"

"N-no sir!" the bartender answered nervously. Selleck hoisted him back to his feet and shoved him towards the bar.

"C'mon, kid," Selleck ordered. We went up the stairs to the first level of rooms. Selleck drew his revolver, so I nervously drew mine. He twisted the knob of the first door, but it was locked. He kicked it hard. So hard that it came off its hinges. Selleck charged in.

A woman, half-dressed and with wet hair from a bath, started to scream as our two guns scanned the room for any green bandanas. Selleck exited the room without a word, though I did try to apologize to the woman.

We went through every room like this until the last two on the third floor. There wasn't anyone currently occupying the rooms. Still, a few spare green bandanas, dirty clothes, and other personal belongings littered the rooms. Selleck cursed. Sure enough, it was as the barkeep had said: the green bandanas weren't here anymore.

The window in the last room was open, so I looked out. I had a good view of the Bank. I saw a stagecoach with various escorts on horseback roll up to the front of the Bank.

"Hey, Marshals!" A man yelled from below. I turned to look at him from the window. He was dressed similarly to the escorts but wore a black face mask. "Catch!"

A cylindrical object came crashing through the opened window. I spun to look at it for a second before instantly realizing what it was: dynamite.

"Run!" I yelled, shoving Selleck back out of the room. We didn't make it three rooms down from the last when a vast, fiery explosion knocked us both to the floor. I hit the ground headfirst and hard. So hard, in fact, that I lost consciousness.

Chapter 13
The Roaring Fire

When I finally came to my senses, it was because I heard gunshots. It took me a minute to remember what happened: the man, the explosion, and the fire. The hotel was on fire!

I jumped to my feet. A fire burned all around me. I couldn't breathe from the smoke. Where was Selleck? I looked around, and I couldn't find him anywhere. There were still gunshots coming from outside, probably at the bank. I started to limp down the blazing hallway. It was so hot! As I made my way to the stairs, I heard a woman screaming for help in one of the rooms I had passed. I wanted to leave her to her fate, but I couldn't. I felt partially responsible for this.

I swore and started making my way back, coughing up smoke that burned my lungs. I pushed the door open. There was fire and smoke everywhere in this room. I couldn't see anyone.

"Miss?" I yelled, trying to figure out if I had the correct room. There was no indication for a second. Had she already passed?

"I-I'm in here!" I finally heard her yell from inside the room. "Please, you have to help me!"

I held my breath and entered the thick black fog that impeded my vision. I finally arrived on the other side of the room, but there was so much smoke that I couldn't see the woman. I smashed the window with an elbow. Hot air and flames rushed past me as though the inferno itself was trying to escape the room. I yelled and cursed as the hot air cooked my skin.

"Oh, finally! My savior!" The woman said. We could finally see each other now that the smoke was gone. She was covered in black soot and ash. She had a beam lying on top of her. "Please, you have to help me."

I coughed and wheezed instead of giving a response. I stumbled towards the lady and used all my strength to push the beam off.

"Can you walk?" I finally was able to ask through my burning throat.

"I need help. I think my leg might be broken." She told me, crying. "I'm gonna die in here!"

"Don't panic, I'll help you," I said, grabbing her arm. I hoisted her up, and she was able to rest her hurt side on my shoulders. There were more gunshots outside.

"What happened?" She asked me as we made our way down the two upper levels of the hotel.

"There's a bank robbery," I answered. "This was a distraction." As we left the hotel, a man rushed up to us, her husband.

"My love!" he said, hugging her. She hugged him tight before slapping his chest. I fell down, sitting to rest on the hotel's porch steps.

"Where were you?" She asked angrily. "I could've died in there if it weren't for this young man!"

"Thank you so much!" The man said, squatting down next to me. "I can't thank you enough for saving my Delilah." I was coughing so much that I couldn't say much, so I just waved my hand at him.

A rider in a black mask rode up, just my luck. I shoved the man out of the way as he pointed a shotgun at us.

"Here's the other marshal!" He called out, turning his head towards the bank for a moment. I didn't waste any time. I pulled my gun from its holster sloppily and shot. The round struck the man square in the chest and knocked him off his horse. The stallion ran off.

Despite my burning lungs and throat, I had to fight. I stood up and grabbed the discarded coach gun. I opened the breech to check the two barrels. Both shells were entirely intact. I had ignored the constant gunfighting. One of the thugs was fighting an unseen force or forces down the street. He'd taken cover behind an upturned wagon and had his back to me. I blasted him with one barrel of the shotgun, painting the side of the wagon with his ichor. I heard some of the others curse and yell as the shotgun blast rang out through the street.

Unfortunately, I was too late. The stagecoach I'd seen pull up in front of the bank earlier sped out from behind the building now, escorted by four horses. Sitting in the driver's seat was none other than Luis Reyes himself. He made eye contact with me, smiled, and waved as he passed. I was stunned. I tried to shoot the coach with the second barrel of the shotgun, but they were too far down the street now.

I felt a hand grab the back of my coat. I nearly blasted the man, but it was Selleck, pulling me onto the back of a spotted thoroughbred he had commandeered.

We sped down the street and out of town, gaining on Reyes' crew. One of Reyes' escorts fell back to try and fight us, but I shot him dead as a dog. Selleck pulled up alongside the dead man's horse, and I jumped onto it. As fast as the thoroughbred was, we wouldn't be able to catch Reyes if we were both on the same horse.

One of the other escorts fell back, but this time, not to try and fight us. The bandit crashed his horse directly into mine, sending both horses rolling and both riders tumbling to the ground. Selleck stopped the thoroughbred suddenly to make sure I was ok.

"Go!" I yelled at him, "I'm alright! Go get that piece of trash!"

Selleck yelled at the horse, spurring it hard. It reared up and dashed forward, leaving me behind with the criminal who had wrecked into me.

"Surrender now, and we'll take you in without prejudice," I said, forcing myself to my feet with my peacemaker in hand. The man groaned, clearly more injured than I was.

"Drop dead, *basura*!" The man yelled, trying to pull his own gun from the ground. I fired one shot. He groaned as it hit him in his side. Blood pooled from his mouth. This didn't stop him from trying to fight still. He managed to unholster his piece and fire off every round in his revolver.

However, he was too delirious to actually hit anything with any degree of accuracy.

I holstered my gun. This guy was done. I bandaged his wound with his shirt sleeve, but he died a few minutes later in a pool of his own blood. Buzzards were starting to circle him and the dead horses. They'd eat well today. I started the walk back to town. All I could hope for was that Selleck could catch up to Reyes.

The stablehands let me get some sleep in a hay pile. They said they'd wake me when Selleck got there, which didn't take too long, probably an hour or so. He looked sullen, and there was no one, dead or alive, tied up on the back of the horse.

"What happened?" I asked once Selleck got close to the stables. He dismounted and gave the reins to a stablehand. They'd make sure the animal got back to its rightful owner.

"He got away." Selleck spat, "I chased them to the bridge, but once they made it across, there wasn't anything I could do. Reyes is in Mexico. We lost."

"But we *know* where he's likely headed!" I protested. "Las Fuentes! Or the area around the town, at least! Someone in Las Fuentes outta know where it is!"

"That isn't in our jurisdiction, I already told you." He argued, wiping sweat from his brow, "We have no legal power there. Look, let's get some rest, and tonight, we can talk about our next move. I'm beat, and so are you." He pointed to the soot and ash that covered my face and clothes. They needed a good washing, and I probably did too. That much I could agree on.

Although the hotel was half burned down, we didn't struggle to find a place to stay. It turns out we put enough pressure on Reyes and his crew that they couldn't crack the safe; they just took what they could from the cash registers and safety deposit boxes. After we left the scene of the bank, the local sheriff and his deputies were able to ride in and arrest or kill any of the gangsters who got left behind. So even if we were dispirited that we didn't get our hands on Reyes, the people of the town saw this as a win. The Mayor let us stay in his mansion with his servants to wash our clothes, and hot baths were already prepared.

Selleck didn't feel pleased with this since all the servants were black, native, or Mexican. He'd made a comment about trying to fight against racial injustice like this during the war, but I was too tired to pay attention. I knew he was mad, though. Mad like I'd never seen him before. After all was clean, ourselves included, the Mayor offered to feed us dinner. As angry as Matthew Selleck was, he wouldn't just refuse a meal like that.

We sat at the large oak table, waiting for the Mayor's servants to bring us the food. I felt awkward because neither Selleck, who was very obviously angry, nor the Mayor, who very obviously knew that Selleck was angry, weren't talking.

"So, um... Mr. Mayor, what were you doing before becoming mayor?" I asked him, trying to break the awkwardness of the situation. "This ain't exactly a house anyone can afford on a mayoral salary, as far as I know."

"Please, son," He told me with a smile. He spoke with an accent, probably from one of the South-Eastern states. "you can call me Mr. White." He opened his large mouth to talk again.

"That's just rich..." Selleck interrupted, muttering. I was unsure if he intended for others to hear or was just talking to himself. "Mr. 'White' owning slaves of color. What irony."

"Excuse me, Mr. Marshal?" The Mayor stared at Selleck in disbelief at what he'd heard, "I'll have you know, my servants are *employees*. I pay them?"

"*Really?*" Selleck's voice was full of sarcasm, "And just how much *do* you pay them, Mr. White?"

"That's none of your business, *sir.*" Mayor White said, his round face turning red. "You know as well as I do that slavery is illegal."

I shot Selleck a glare. While he was my mentor, and it wasn't my right to question his moral convictions, I didn't want to be rude to a host kind enough to feed and board us. Sure enough, my glare was able to shut him up.

"To answer your question, Mr. Hendricks," The Mayor changed his tone and looked at me, "My family has always had money. They came over from England when this country was still a British colony. They eventually founded a plantation in South Carolina. After the War of Northern Aggression, I sold my plantation for a considerable sum of money and moved out here."

Before anything else could be said, the servants brought the food and wine in. I was thankful. Words like 'War of Northern Aggression' and 'plantation in South Carolina' were sure to bring out a bitter side of someone who had fought for the Union Army to the capacity that Matthew Selleck had.

Just when I thought things would be better, they got worse. One of the servants, a young native boy, was pouring wine for Mayor White and got distracted. I think he was looking at the revolvers Selleck and I carried, as young boys do. He spilled some of the wine on White's pants.

"*Stupid* boy!" White snarled, his voice full of disgust. He got on his feet and slapped the boy immediately. The boy fell to the ground. White went back to the fireplace and grabbed the fire poker. He raised it to hit the boy but was stopped by the cocking of a revolver.

Selleck was on his feet, pointing his revolver at the Mayor! I stared in disbelief at what was going on. Was the Marshal going to kill the Mayor?

"Drop it. Now!" Selleck growled. He didn't yell, but his voice was full of rage. His eyes burned with hatred. His finger was on the trigger. One single squeeze, four pounds of pressure, was all itwould've taken to turn Matthew Selleck into a murderer. The Mayor dropped the fire poker. The boy crawled away.

"You're making a huge mistake, Marshal." The Mayor threatened. His voice was strong, but his body was weak. His knees shook. His hands trembled. Selleck, on the other hand, was the picture of strength and conviction.

"When I was in the war," He started to say, "I killed a lot of folk who thought like you. I've killed a lot of bad men, but your kind are the worst." He spit on the carpet.

"And just what kind of man do you think I am, Mr. Selleck?"

"I know what kind of man you are." He told the man sharply, "I don't think you are; I know you are. You're a coward who bullies those weaker than him. You're a man who thinks he's better than others just cause he was born in better circumstances. I should shoot you dead, right here, right now."

"Do it," White said, trying to sound mean. His voice wavered. "I'm not scared. You fire one shot at me, and I will have you hanged!"

"That's where you're wrong, you fat piece of trash!" Selleck roared like a lion, the first time he'd raised his voice since drawing the gun, "You are scared. You're scared because you know that when you die, God will judge you for what you've done. You're scared to depart from this life cause you know that you've done bad. But you know what, pig?" The Mayor was holding back tears now. The dark stain left from the wine extended down his legs as he pissed himself. The Mayor didn't answer. Selleck raised his voice even louder. "I asked you a question!"

"W-what is it, Marshal?" White stuttered out.

"I ain't afraid to die. I killed a lot of men, but every single one of them deserved it. *Every. Single. One.* When I kill you, if they hang me, I still won't be afraid to die."

With that said, Selleck fired a single shot. I couldn't believe it. The Mayor screeched like an animal and fell to the ground.

"What on earth did you just do?" I yelled, my voice cracking like a young boy. Selleck blew on his gun and placed it back into the holster.

"Nothing." He told me, walking away. "I didn't do anything except put the fear of God into an evil man."

I was stunned until I heard someone crying like a baby. That's when I saw that there was no blood. Selleck had shot and missed the Mayor. He was on the floor in a puddle of his own urine, sobbing like a little baby. All the servants watched in shock and awe. They wouldn't be letting this scum mistreat them again, that's for sure, unless he wanted the whole town to know that he was a crybaby. I followed Selleck out without another word.

"I guess we are just gonna camp tonight," I said, trying to lighten the mood. I got no reply but knew Selleck wasn't mad at me. This was a side of Selleck I'd never seen before, though. He was a man who stood by his convictions and always did what he saw was right in his own eyes. I knew he'd wanted to kill that bully, but he couldn't murder someone in cold blood. He may not have seen it the way I did, but he was a hero in my eyes, like from the books I'd read. He was the exact type of man that I wanted to be.

Chapter 14
A Letter

"You mean we really aren't going after Reyes in Mexico?" I asked, somewhat irritated.

"I wish we could, kid." Selleck responded calmly after he'd finished chewing on a piece of smoked venison, "But it's not allowed. I could lose my job, and we could get arrested."

"You mean like threatening the mayor of Refugio? You wouldn't use your job and get arrested over that?"

He scowled at me.

"That isn't fair. It's different. He was breaking the law. You can't beat your 'servants' like that."

"And so is Reyes. The only thing stopping you is an imaginary line."

Selleck went quiet. I was right, and he knew I was. He had a point, though, and I understood that.

"What if we go as bounty hunters?" I asked, trying to think of an idea.

"Won't work. I am a US Marshal, so my capacity for law enforcement is different. I have protocols to follow. I have to write reports. I have supervisors."

"Well, if you don't go, I will go alone," I told him. He frowned.

"I'm not gonna stop you, kid. But I don't think it's a good idea. Remember what happened last time you fought Reyes? He almost killed you. That was July, remember? A little more than one month ago. I don't want to see you die, kid. You're a good person, and you want to do what's right; I get it.

That's why we need to come up with a different plan."

"I've made up my mind," I informed him, calming myself down. "I'm going to Mexico. What if Reyes never comes back to this country? I just can't take that risk. I know where he's going, so I am going after him. With or without you."

Selleck just shook his head. He couldn't come, but he understood my decision. He took his Winchester repeater from his saddle holster and handed me his bandolier.

"Take this." He gave me the rifle after I had donned the bandolier. "When the time comes, when you see Reyes, don't approach. Don't say anything. Don't do anything except take the shot. Once you've finished your business there and are back in the States, send a letter to Washington. They'll get it to me, then you and I can meet back up, and I really can make you a Marshal. Deal?"

I shook his outstretched hand, holding back tears as I did. "It's a deal," I told him. He nodded his head.

"Good. I'll see you around, kid." He said, mounting his horse, "Don't die, please." He started to trot away.

"Matthew!" I yelled when he was some distance away. I didn't want him to see me cry. He turned his head toward me but kept riding down the road, "Thank you for everything!"

He just raised a hand to say farewell. I waited until he was out of sight. I slung the rifle on my back and mounted Iron.

Before I left town, I decided to stock up on supplies. I spent twenty of Fierro's money on ammunition, canned food, and medical supplies. I wanted to stop at the post office to see if Eliza had written.

Sure enough, she had. I felt my heart fly as the postmaster handed me a letter. Despite the long journey, the letter smelled of lilac. It smelled like Eliza.

I could hardly wait to open it when I left the post office. I found a shady spot to hunker down and opened the white envelope. There was a single page inside.

"My dearest Asa," I read the start of the letter. I was already happy just to read that. Perhaps she wasn't too upset after all. I continued reading.

"I hope this letter finds you well. It sounds like an exciting adventure you've embarked on. Mr. Selleck sounds like an admirable gentleman. I hope he can teach you much about his trade. It seems exciting that he wants to help you become a real marshal once you find this Luis Reyes fellow. I will admit, I was rather upset when I received the first note you left me, but now, time has healed that wound. I hope you find Mr. Reyes soon because your family misses you greatly. The only one from Hendricks Ranch who is as 'normal' as always is Mr. Fierro. Asa, my dear friend, I will always remember you." She had written.

'*Always remember you?*' I thought to myself, *What does that mean? Is she sick with some kind of disease?* I decided to start reading again.

"... remember you. I cherish the few times we shared dearly. You are the first boy I have ever kissed, and that will always be a sweet memory for me, even with the fight you had with my brothers attached to that memory."

"Despite how much I treasure you, I am afraid our love, if you will call it that, for lack of a better term, cannot exist any longer. My father has seen your letters, and, due to what my brothers have told him about you (lies, mostly), my father is furious. He decided I would move to live with my cousin and her husband in a town called Valle Seco in California. At first, I was heartbroken at the thought of being so far from you. Our love was never allowed to bloom, which saddened me."

"However, as time has passed, I have reunited with a well-to-do merchant, a dear childhood friend from my home country whom I have not seen in some time; we have fallen in love despite the fact we have not been reunited for long. He will ask me to marry him soon, as he will leave before the end of the year. He and I will travel to San Francisco to start our family."

"I hope that this news doesn't leave you terribly heartbroken. We never had a chance at love, but I enjoyed the prospect of it. Perhaps in a different life, where the circumstances had been different, we could've seen that flower blossom, but it is not so in this one. I am sorry. I can't be waiting for some adventurer to return home. Please do not hate me. It has nothing to do with you and everything to do with me."

"Sincerely, Ms. Elizabeth Caldwell."

I stared at the letter and reread it. I couldn't believe it. I knew I shouldn't have felt so heartbroken, but I had romanticized Eliza so much that I couldn't help it. Tears streamed down my face for the second time, but I was quiet. I crumpled her letter in my hands and threw it away. I stood up, wiping the tears from my eyes and face. I went over to my horse and mounted up.

"Alright, boy," I told Iron, who had turned his head to look at me, "Let's go to Mexico. Time to go get this murdering piece of trash."

Chapter 15
Vigil in the Wilderness

As I crossed the river into Mexico, the air changed. I couldn't explain it, but it felt like someone was watching me. It wasn't right. I dismissed the feeling, telling myself it was nerves or the psychological fact that I was in another country now.

I rode all day. It was a long ride to Las Fuentes, according to Reyes' buddy that we'd captured in Justicia, so I wasn't going to push Iron harder than I had to. Poor Mustang had already been pressed hard on this journey, but it had done him good. I was beginning to see muscle where it had been previously unseen on my friend. He was starting to look like a warhorse.

I don't know what I expected from Mexico. The terrain looked identical to the land around Refugio de Los Santos. I assumed that's why they called the area the '*New* Mexico Territory' rather than something else. It all looked like Mexico, anyway.

Water felt scarcer here, though. I started going through my canteen more. I even had to start watering Iron from my canteen. When we finally found water, a small creek barely big enough for a minnow, I emptied out some of the bottles of medicine I'd purchased in Refugio to fill with water. I wasn't sure if I would need the medication, but I did know that I would need the water.

By the time I got to the second stream, which was a little bigger, it was already getting dark, so I decided to set up camp.

I ate the last of my smoked venison that night, but I still had plenty of jerky for tomorrow and some canned goods I'd purchased. I decided, after eating, that I'd just rest by the fire for a while and make up stories in my mind, like Selleck and I had done every night.

"¡Buenas noches, señor!" A voice called out from the shadows. I drew my revolver.

"¿Quien es?" I yelled back, trying to muster my best Spanish to figure out who was there. Two men stepped into my firelight. They were both Mexican, with ponchos and short-brimmed sun hats. Both had mustaches, too. They were leading two horses.

"Buenas noches, señor," The other one, who hadn't called out, said, *"¿Está bien si acampamos con usted esta noche?"*

"Um... *lo siento, amigo,"* I apologized, *"Hablo poquito español. ¿Hablan inglés?* You both speak any english?"

"Está bien, gringo," The original one answered, "I speak some English."

"Good, 'cause this was gonna be real awkward if we couldn't communicate," I told him, holstering my gun.

"Is it ok if we camp with you tonight? We don't need food or anything, but there are quite a few

banditos in this part. It's safer to stay in numbers."

"That's fine by me," I said, nodding.

"You're real young." The man commented. The other man, the bigger one, hadn't said anything since we started speaking English. "How old are you?"

"I'm twenty-two." I lied. Just because these men said they had no ill intention didn't mean they were telling the truth. And that meant that I had no reason to tell the truth either. Especially since people would try to take advantage of my youth.

"What are you doing out here by yourself, *gringo?"*

"I'm actually looking for a certain *bandito,* as you called them."

"You're a bounty hunter then? Come all the way to *México* to collect a bounty?"

"I'll collect it wherever it's paying." I told him, narrowing my eyes, trying to get a read on these guys, "If he's wanted in America, he's certainly wanted here."

"What's his name?" The bigger one spoke up, asking in heavily accented English.

"His name's Luis Reyes. He's an escaped convict in the US. I have reason to believe he's come back to Mexico."

The two of them drew their revolvers and pointed them directly at me. I saw this and tried to pull my own gun, but I didn't clear the leather all the way and got hung up on my holster. The bigger one charged me and grabbed my wrist. He smacked my hand with the grip of his revolver, making me drop my gun. He threw it aside. I looked over to my saddle, lying on a rock just out of reach. The Winchester hung on the horn by the sling. Even if I could get away, I wasn't sure if I would be able to get to the repeater before getting shot myself.

"We figured that was you, Marshal." The smaller one said, pulling a green bandana from underneath his poncho. "Reyes told you he would kill you if you kept following him, and you didn't listen. We'll make your death quick if you tell us where the other Marshal is."

"He didn't come with. I ain't a real Marshal; I just was riding with him. He said he wouldn't look for Reyes in Mexico."

"Smart man. Reyes has eyes *everywhere* down here, *gringo*. You're a fool if you could come here and take Reyes. It's too bad you're a liar. The other one was the guy with the rifle, not you. Where is he?"

The big one hit me in the gut, causing me to double over. He grabbed my hair and pulled my head up. He jammed his gun in my face and pulled the hammer back.

"I swear, I'll kill you both!" I yelled at them. The smaller one laughed.

"You, kill *us*? You can't even draw your gun properly. I've seen you shoot, kid. You handle a gun worse than a blind man. We'd have a better chance of getting struck by lightning than struck by your bullet."

The pair started laughing. I tried to think of a plan. I would get away from the big one and get the rifle.

"*Mátalo.*" The smaller one ordered. The big one placed his finger on the trigger of his gun. I closed my eyes, ready to die in the dirt like a dog. I didn't care. My heart was broken, and I was alone in the world. I was a fool to think that I could ever take on Luis Reyes.

A miracle came, though, staying the hand of my executioner. My safety didn't come in the form of lighting, though, as the smaller one predicted, but instead of thunder.

Two shots, fired rapidly and deadly, rang out through the night as thunder. My attackers didn't even have time to breathe their last breaths. They dropped dead with two holes in their head. I fell to the ground, panting. I was still alive!

"Thought I told you not to die, kid." A familiar voice said, standing over me. I jumped to my feet and hugged my savior.

"Matthew," I whispered. He laughed and rubbed my hair roughly.

"Come on now, Ace. I'm not your daddy." He teased. I broke the hug, red-faced. "Help me clean up these bodies, then we can talk a little. Unless you wanna try to move camp at this hour."

We moved the bodies downwind of us, a reasonable distance away, on the backs of Ophelia and Iron. That way, no coyote, or even worse, a wolf, would be near our camp enjoying an easy midnight snack. We just threw the rest of the gore in the creek with the sand it laid on downstream of us. Finally, we sat by the fire like all the nights we'd been riding together before.

"So why'd you come?" I finally asked, breaking the silence.

"For Reyes." He said. "And to protect your hide." He laughed. "I didn't teach you to shoot and draw well enough."

"Teach me." I pleaded. "You just wasted two guys in less than a second. Teach me to do that."

"I will." He assured me. "Tomorrow, though. I have something to tell you first."

"What is it?"

He was silent for a while. Finally, he spoke up.

"You remember what I told you, how my wife and kid were killed by a man called the Beast?" I nodded.

"The Beast led a gang he always ran with. In this gang, there were three founding members. Each one had a nickname. There was 'La Bestia,' the Beast, whom I already told you about. Next was a woman who called herself 'La Viuda,' the Widow. The final one, a real vain fella, called himself 'El Rey,' the King. These three ran around for the better part of eight years. They were practically uncatchable, and no one knew their identities apart from the main three. I don't know how, but in '77, eight years ago, some Marshals found them. They rounded up all the bounty hunters they could muster and a battalion of soldiers and attacked. They killed the entire gang except for the three leaders. One of them got captured. The other two got away. The one they captured was the King. Turns out he took his nickname from his own surname. He was none other than Luis Reyes, the same guy we are chasing."

I was silent. I understood *precisely* why Selleck was looking for Reyes now.

"So you're chasing him, hoping he can tell you who the other two are..." I said finally. He nodded.

"He's my only chance of catching the Beast. That's why I couldn't let you come down here by yourself. I had to find out who the Beast was before Reyes died."

"I promise you, Selleck, I won't kill Reyes until we find who and where the Beast is. We *will* get revenge for your family."

"Appreciate it, kid." Selleck shot me a melancholy smile. He stood up and dusted off his pants. "Let's hit the hay. We have a long ride ahead of us."

Chapter 16
Las Fuentes

The following two weeks made for a challenging ride. We had to ride a lot slower than we wanted. The terrain was rough, and water was scarce. Our saving grace was the fact that we ran into a few farms and ranches on the way. These people were kind and provided us with water when we showed up dying of thirst. I felt terrible for Ophelia with her black coat. She was probably taking the worst of the heat. Despite this, the Arabian showed no indication of weakening. Selleck told me her breed was raised and created in deserts dryer than this one.

The only real good thing that happened was Selleck's gunfighting training. He taught me to draw, aim, and shoot. He taught me to 'fan' the hammer of my single-action peacemaker with my offhand, which would let me rapidly fire the revolver. Learning how a *real* gunslinger shoots a handgun was challenging but fun. It gave us something to do besides just looking at sand and stones when we were giving the horses a break. I knew only two weeks of practice wouldn't turn me into a skilled marksman like Selleck, but it was a start. There was definitely improvement.

Las Fuentes was an old Spanish fort or mission that had been converted into a town probably a hundred years ago. It had stone walls. The buildings were adobe, a type of cement-like building material. Selleck said it kept the insides chilled in the hot sun. I felt its effects when we entered the *Cantina*.

The air-shaded adobe building was twenty degrees cooler than the outside, but it may as well have been fifty. Entering was a relief. Selleck went right up to the counter.

"*Tequila.*" He told the bartender, an elegant and professional-looking man. He shook his head.

"*No hay tequila.*" He answered, "*Solo mezcal blanco y cerveza. Hay agua fria tambien.*"

"Ok..." Selleck nodded. He put two quarters on the counter, "*Dos mezcals, por favor.*"

The bartender took the coins and filled two shooters with a clear spirit. I felt confused.

"I didn't know you spoke Spanish," I said, leaning against the counter. He slid one of the shooters over to me.

"I don't." He said, showing a subtle smile, "I just know how to ask for drinks. Understand quite a bit, sure, but mostly just insults. Drink up."

I hesitated to take the shot, remembering my experience with the Whiskey and Bourbon in Folklore. I didn't have time to refuse, though. Selleck raised his shooter.

"Salud." He said, in a very American accent. He drank it up before I could say anything in protest. I grabbed my shooter and slurped it down.

It tasted smokey; almost good initially, even. But it burned my throat going down. I started coughing. Once more, I promised myself I would never touch alcohol again. The bartender and Selleck started laughing. I felt déjà vu. The bartender went to the back and came back with a full cup of cool water. I couldn't drink it fast enough.

"*Su primero mezcal,*" Selleck told the bartender, waving his thumb in my direction. I shot him a glare.

"That ain't my first drink, and you know it." I objected.

"I can tell that *you* don't speak Spanish." Selleck said, shaking his head, "Cause that's not what I said."

"Ask him for a room. I wanna go lay down." I was red in the face, embarrassed.

"Un cuarto, por favor."

"Cuesta cinco dolares cada noche."

"That's an outrageous price!" Selleck objected, "Five dollars a night? You're kidding me!" The bartender shrugged.

"Sorry." He said. He went to a different customer, probably figuring we didn't have the money to pay.

"Wait, *señor!*" I called to him. He stopped and came back over with an unamused look on his face. *"Veinte dolares. Cuatro noches.* That ok?" The bartender picked up the twenty-dollar bill I had given him, holding it to the light. He put it in his pocket and gave me a key.

"Number four." He said in accented English. He pointed outside at several small adobe sheds with numbers painted on the doors. Those were the rooms.

"Gracias," I told him before turning to Selleck. "See? It ain't hard."

"Not in the mood for sarcasm, kid."

"Take a few more of those shots. What did they call it? Mezcal?"

Selleck furrowed his eyebrows, and I laughed. I drank another glass of water.

"See that guy there?" He asked, pointing to a rough-looking man in the corner, drinking a beer.

He had three handguns on his belt, LeMat revolvers. "He's Mexican, so the pistols aren't from the American Civil War. Probably a bounty hunter."

"What makes you say that though?"

"What makes LeMat's good for killing? It's a pistol with a shotgun barrel underneath the main one. That was the main sidearm of the Confederate Army. I've seen a lot of men get gunned down by one. They're cap-and-ball revolvers, too; they don't use cartridges, so they take longer to reload. That's why he has three."

"What's he doing then?"

"Waiting for a bounty." Selleck pointed over to an empty corkboard hanging on the wall. "Empty board means Reyes is probably in the area."

"How you figure?"

"Nobody wants to cross Reyes," Selleck explained. "He probably came through and recruited all the men with active bounties. They took the posters down because they don't want the local bounty hunters to all die out going after Reyes' gang."

"So what do we do?" I asked, looking around the room to see if there was any other person of interest.

"I'm gonna join that poker game there." He told me, pointing at a few men playing cards. "Gossip has a tendency to be spread over a game of cards. *And* gambling attracts scum like flies to dung. That's our best option right now."

"So what do I do?" I asked, somewhat irritated.

"Stay on the lookout. Pay attention to anyone with a green bandana or any particularly rough individual who isn't already in here waiting for a bounty to be posted."

I tried to stay awake, but the cool air in the hot climate, mixed with the alcohol I took, was a recipe for sleep. I couldn't help but doze off for a moment. I told myself it would be only a moment, at least.

I woke up probably an hour later. The sun was setting. People were yelling nearby.

"*¡Tramposo!*" One of the men yelled, "*¡Eres un tramposo!*"

"A cheater?" I heard Selleck say, "I would never, I swear!"

"*Cállate*, American scum!" The first man yelled again. The clicking of a revolver hammer woke me up completely. Five men had their guns shoved in Selleck's face. He had his drawn and aimed at his accuser. I pulled my pistol and ran over to point it at the same man.

"Nice of you to join in, kid!" Selleck remarked sarcastically.

"*Cállate, gringo.*" The accuser hissed. "Let's settle this like men, hmm?"

"Yeah, I agree," Selleck said nervously. The Mexicans that Selleck had been playing with put their handguns away. The accuser started heading out to the street. Both Selleck and I followed, holstering our weapons.

"Watch me closely," Selleck whispered, teaching me as we walked towards the street. "Duels aren't about who draws first; they're about who can shoot first. This guy isn't a gunslinger. He's gonna draw and aim straight-armed. When his gun clears leather, I want to be firing my first shot. I know how my gun shoots at less than ten yards, so I'm just gonna shoot from the hip, not waste time using the sightposts."

I stopped as Selleck entered the street, prepared to face the man.

The wind blew slowly. There were plenty of people watching now. This was probably something regular in a town as well trafficked as Las Fuentes.

The Mexican spit out his cigarette, pulled his poncho from above his head, and threw it to the ground. He was using an old revolver, a Patterson. Cap-and-ball, like the bounty hunter's LeMats had been. However, his gun wasn't well taken care of like the bounty hunter's. His was rusty and dirty. It was, as Selleck said, he wasn't a gunslinger. He may have been a soldier once but hadn't been in recent years. There had been plenty of wars in Mexico in the past fifty years. He looked furious.

Selleck was calm but determined. His eyes were narrow like a hawk. He pulled back the right side of his duster to reveal his own firearm, the shiny steel Smith & Wesson Model 3, a Schofield, much newer and much better taken care of than his opponent's gun. Chambered in .45 Smith & Wesson. Selleck wore his gun with the grip forward, backward to how most wore theirs. He'd once told me this was called the 'cavalry draw.' It was something he'd picked up from the war. You'd think this would make him slower, but it didn't. He could draw as fast as lightning. Selleck was a man who always sought the best for himself. His shooting style was old, but his gun was new. He took what was good and added it to himself, and the bad he threw out. This gambler had lost the moment the two men stepped out into the street, and the only one who didn't know it was the *Mexicano* himself.

The gambler placed his hand roughly on the grip of his Patterson. He grabbed his holster with his left hand. Selleck let his hand hover above his gun. His finger twitched. Someone coughed. The wind howled lightly through the streets. After a second, the world quieted again, as though the gale wanted to witness this showdown.

The gambler drew, undoubtedly trying to aim down the sights of his old pistol as my mentor had predicted. He never even got close. Selleck twisted his hand and jerked his gun up to his side. Selleck fanned off two shots with his left hand, which had appeared as though it materialized from nothing, both shots finding their mark in the center of the gambler's chest. The gambler gasped, dropped his gun, and fell backward, dead before he hit the ground. Selleck flamboyantly spun the pistol around his hand, then reholstered it without looking. He started walking back to me before we heard a man yelling down the street.

"¡Asesino!" The man called, drawing a peacemaker and running down the street. I started to draw my own gun, but Selleck grabbed my wrist. *"Te voy a arrestar!"*

"Is there a problem, *Sheriff*?" Selleck asked as the man neared. The man pointed his gun at Selleck's. He wore a badge that said '*Aguacil*,' which I figured out quickly was Spanish for Sheriff.

"*Gringo,* you're under arrest for the murder of Juan Solis, the man you just killed!"

"Pardon me, *señor*," Selleck responded calmly, "But that was as fair a duel as I've ever seen. He challenged me and, therefore, killed himself."

The Sheriff put the gun away and pulled Selleck's coat back, revealing his Marshal star. "Just what are you doing here, Marshal?" The Sheriff asked with a scowl.

"Just passing through," Selleck answered.

"I don't think so, *gringo*." The Sheriff spat. "It ain't a coincidence that a U.S. Marshal shows up in Las Fuentes the same week Luis Reyes returns. I'm arresting you for investigation on suspect of impeding justice and vigilantism." The Sheriff pulled out a billy club.

"Wait a minute, Sheriff–" Selleck protested before the Sheriff knocked him in the chin with the club. I stepped up in front of the Sheriff before he could hit him again. I shoved the barrel of my gun into his ribs.

"One more move, and I'll unload every round into you," I growled. The onlookers, who had also witnessed the duel, gasped and started to murmur quietly.

"Are you threatening *un oficial de la ley, muchachito?*" His voice didn't waiver, but he did back up. He grabbed the grip of his gun.

"Asa, stand down!" Selleck barked, standing on his feet. "Forgive the kid, Sheriff. He doesn't know any better. A little slow, if you will. I'll come peacefully, I promise." I put my gun away. Selleck stood up and let the *Aguacil* tie a rope around his wrists. He looked at me, his eyes full of determination. "You can do it, kid." He said, "I know you can."

The crowd soon dispersed after Selleck went with the Sheriff, leaving me alone. Selleck wanted me to go after Reyes by myself. I took a deep breath and finally started walking.

Chapter 17
Into the Wolf's Mouth

I tried to rest that night. I would head down to the Mayor's office tomorrow morning to see if I could convince him to release Selleck after telling him about my plan.

The Mayor of Las Fuentes' office was a large adobe building in the center of town. It was also the tallest building in Las Fuentes, part of the original fort that the city used to be. The inside was more modern than I expected, though. The floors were varnished wood. The furniture was comfortable, and the decorations were tasteful. I went up to the second floor, where the office was located. The secretary, an older Mexican woman, greeted me cheerfully.

"*Buenas* días, muchacho." The old woman's eyes lit up when she saw me. "How can I help you?" Her accent when speaking English was barely noticeable.

"*Buenas* días." I politely replied, "I am here to speak to the *alcalde*. I want to talk to him about the release of my friend, The other *gringo* who was arrested yesterday."

"I am not so sure *el alcalde* has time today..." She replied, digging through her papers.

"Fine. Tell him I want to speak about Luis Reyes too, then." I responded sharply. As soon as I'd mentioned Reyes' name, she looked up at me. She told me to wait a minute, then went back to converse with the Mayor. She came back a moment later, "You can go back."

I thanked the woman and stepped across the creaky wooden floor. I pushed the heavy mahogany door open and stepped through. The Mayor's office had little by way of décor. A large desk with two chairs in front of it and a large armchair where the Mayor was sitting. Behind the man, hanging on the wall, was a painting of an older gentleman with a long mustache dressed in well-decorated military attire. He was probably the President of Mexico.

"*Señor Alcalde,*" I greeted him in the best Spanish I could muster, "*Buenos días.*"

"Please shut the door behind you and have a seat, sir." The Mayor said in perfect English, motioning to the seats in front of the desk. I did as he indicated. "My secretary tells me you are here to discuss Luis Reyes."

"Yes, *señor,*" I assured him. "I want to deliver Reyes to your hands."

"Good." The Mayor said enthusiastically. "Reyes is a blight upon this land. I can't place an official bounty because I suspect the *aguacil* is in his pocket. I despise the man, though; rest assured, *Señor* Hendricks. Reyes represents everything that I have ever fought against." I believed him. His voice was full of disgust for the outlaw. "How much do you want to bring him in?"

"Nothing, sir." I told him plainly, "I have my own grudges against Reyes that don't have nothing to do with your fine town. All I ask is a pardon for my friend, *Señor* Selleck."

"It will be done. You bring me Reyes, and I will release your friend."

"With all due respect, sir, I think you misunderstand." He raised an eyebrow at me, "Mr. Selleck is one of the finest lawmen to ever live. If you want to capture Reyes, I will need him."

"I won't do it. How do I know you won't run off after I release Mr. Selleck?"

"I give you my word that we won't. As I said, we are here for Reyes specifically."

"No deal." The Mayor said, furrowing his eyebrows. "You bring me Reyes, and you will get your friend. I'll even add a few hundred dollars on the top to make the deal sweeter. You may leave now. Reyes is in a place half a day's ride from here called *La Boca del Lobo*. It is no secret."

I opened my mouth to speak again but then stopped. This Mayor was a man of conviction, similar to Selleck. He had been a soldier himself and was a patriot. I knew he would keep his word, but I also knew there was no point in arguing.

I wondered how I would take Reyes and his gang on by myself. I went out of the Mayor's office quietly, deep in thought. I had to come up with a plan. We had killed or captured most of Reyes' gang, but he still probably had enough that I couldn't take them alone. That's when I remembered about the bounty hunter in the *Cantina*.

I went back to the old building. The people were nervous when they saw me. Selleck and I had caused nothing but trouble since we arrived, so I understood the high tensions. The bounty hunter with the three LeMat revolvers was still there, waiting to see if any work would come. I went right up to his table and took a seat.

"*¿Qué quieres, gringo?*" He asked in a rough voice. He was probably asking me what I wanted.

"*Hola.*" I started, sounding completely stupid. "*¿Inglés?*

"*Mi* English *no es* very good." He told me in a heavy accent. I barely understood what he was saying.

"Well, my Spanish ain't either."

"What you want?"

"*¿Es cazadero usted?* I tried asking him in Spanish, "You a bounty hunter?"

"You mean *cazador?*"

"*Sí, cazador de personas.*"

"*Sí amigo, pero se dice cazador de recompensas, no de personas.*" He told me. I heard the word '*sí*' and that was enough for me.

"Luis Reyes," I said, looking him in the eye, "Wanna go get him?"

"*Me gustaría.* You know where he is?"

"A place called *Boca del Lobo*. Do you know it?" I asked. He nodded his head.

"*¿Antes* que *vayamos, cual es tu nombre, caballero?*" He asked me. I cocked an eyebrow, clearly not understanding what he had just asked. "Your name?" He repeated himself in English

"Asa Hendricks. ¿Y *usted?* What's your name?"

"Román Hernandez."

"Good to meet you, S*eñor* Hernandez. *Mucho gusto.*"

"*Igualmente,* Mr. Hendrick." He told me, shaking my hand. I considered correcting him on my name, but it would be more complicated than it was worth. We went outside and mounted up.

Hernandez's horse, or rather pony, was rather funny looking. The mare looked like she had hair covering her face. The scary-looking bounty hunter was much less intimidating on her back. I didn't care too much, though; as long as Hernandez could ride fast and fight hard, who was I to discriminate against his choice of steed?

We rode hard all day until Hernandez said we had arrived at Boca del Lobo. I didn't know what 'Boca del Lobo' meant. I figured I'd know when we reached it, but it was just a large cave. There were horses tied to a post outside.

"Those Reyes' horses?" I asked Hernandez. He shrugged. I dismounted and searched the saddlebag of one of them. Sure enough, I found a green bandana inside. I pulled it out and showed Hernandez.

"Kill them. *Con el fusil.*" Hernandez told me, pointing at the Winchester repeater on my back. I pulled it off and shot each horse in the head, one by one. After a few seconds, all five horses were dead. Hernandez dismounted, drawing two of his LeMats. I reloaded the rifle.

"Let's go get these *imbeciles*," I said, nodding at Hernandez, using the word Fierro always used as an insult. He grunted and nodded.

We entered the cave. Initially, it wasn't huge, perhaps twenty yards long, if that. I can see why Reyes used this as a hideout. It would be tough to get attacked by surprise.

As soon as we exited the cave on the other side, bullets started to rain down on us. Hernandez was hit right away in the shoulder. He yelled, but it sounded more angry than anything. We both blind-fired in all directions and then split up. I took cover behind an old mine cart. The bullets stopped as soon as we were out of the line of fire.

"I told you, kid!" I heard Reyes yell, "If you followed me, I'd kill you. I gave you every chance to walk away; now you're gonna die." I stayed silent for a moment, but I saw Hernandez. He made a signal with his hands, trying to say that he would route them. I wanted to keep them distracted.

"You know I can't just walk away, Reyes," I yelled back finally. "Killed too many people for me to just let it go."

"You got a lot of heart, kid!" Reyes laughed. "Tell you what. I'll give you the chance I've never given anyone I ever killed. You told me back in Folklore that I killed your mom. What did you say your name was, kid? I'll remember you and take a shot of *tequila* in your memory. That's probably more than anyone would ever do for a ranch rat like you!"

"You ain't gonna kill me, Reyes!" I shouted, "We can talk on our way to Las Fuentes when I take you in!"

"Are y'all hearing this kid?" He asked the other thugs, laughing, "Just tell me your name, kid!

Ain't no harm in it, right?"

"If you're not gonna come peacefully, I'm gonna have to put a bullet in you!" He and his thugs laughed.

"My name is Asa. You hear? Remember that *Asa Hendricks* is the man who's gonna kill you!" The laughter stopped instantly. No one dared speak. Even Reyes was as quiet as a ghost's shadow. The silence felt like it lasted for hours. I was wondering if Hernandez had somehow gotten them all with a knife.

"You said *Hendricks?*" Reyes asked, his voice trembling. "I killed your mama *this year?*"

"You did!" I roared. "You killed her, and so I am gonna kill you."

"Kill that rat!" He yelled in a fearful tone. "I want him dead. *Now!*"

The gunfire started again, ricocheting off of the mine cart. I returned fire blindly. "Behind us!" One yelled, "It's the bounty hunter." They all stopped firing at me, but the gunshots didn't stop.

I stood up from my cover and fired a shot in their direction with the Winchester. I hit one of them in the back. He groaned and fell off the ledge they were standing on. The rest cursed and confusedly started firing back and forth between me and Hernandez.

"Enough of this!" I heard Reyes yell. Hernandez and the *Bandito* traded insults in Spanish back and forth. I ran up a pathway carved into the stone. I fired the rifle at another one of the men, spraying gore from his head.

A loud shotgun blast from one of Hernandez's LeMats stopped everyone, including me, dead in their tracks. All at once, the only three members of Reyes' gang living turned and aimed their guns at me. I switched aim between the three of them. Reyes stepped forth, dragging Hernandez' limp body on the stone. He threw Hernandez in the dust between us. A weak groan escaped the poor man's body.

Reyes aimed one of Hernandez's discarded revolvers at the injured man. Blood pooled in the dust underneath his body, but the whimpering from the Bounty Hunter's lips told me he was still alive.

"Drop the rifle, or your buddy gets it!" Reyes threatened. Hernandez lifted his head, pleading with me to comply. I knew that if I dropped the rifle, I was probably dead, but if I didn't, Hernandez's blood would be on my hands. I eventually caved and threw the repeater over to their side. One of Reyes' men leaned forward and retrieved it.

"Nice rifle." The man said, smiling. I spit to my side.

"Don't even bother going for your pistol. I can shoot you any time I want; I am *choosing* to speak with you first." Reyes said, "Let me get this straight." He rubbed his fingers on his temple, "Your name is Asa Hendricks. Your mom isn't *Caroline Hendricks, is she?*"

I couldn't answer. I was shocked. My jaw hit the floor. How could Reyes *possibly* have known my mom? I was under the impression that her murder was a robbery gone wrong. Had there been some more outstanding piece of the puzzle I was missing?

"Answer!" Reyes screamed. His voice was threatening but tinged with panic.

"She is," I said, my eyes narrowing. I saw sweat roll down Reyes' brow. He was *scared*, but of what? Of me?

"I gotta tell you, Ace," Reyes said, laughing nervously, "I was *not* expecting to ever see you again. Not after what I did to Caroline."

"How did you know her?" I asked, trying to keep him talking. I just had to think of a plan. Hernandez was losing blood, fast.

Think, Ace, think!

"You mean to tell me that you were riding around with Fierro the *whole* time you were in Folklore, and he told you *nothing*?"

"What are you talking about? Fierro? How do you know him?"

"Fierro, your mom, and me go *way* back, kid. *Way back.* I knew you as a baby! You should ask her about it once you get to Hell. Tell her I sent *you* there too!"

With that said, he blasted a shot at Hernandez. I was too late to save him, but the fact that Reyes had shot him first may have given me a chance. My mind flashed back to Selleck's duel in Las Fuentes. The world stopped. Everything was silent, save a loud ringing in my ears and the sound of my blood pounding through my head.

I drew my revolver to my hip and fanned the hammer back, firing all six shots as fast as lighting. One made contact with Reyes'. Only one. Only one shot *almost* saved my life. It hit Reyes in the hip. He winced, but the shot wasn't fatal. He aimed the LeMat at me and fired a single shot into my gut. It burned and hurt like someone had shoved a fire inside my belly. I fell backward into the dirt. My vision started to turn dark.

"Crap, kid, that's gonna leave a mark!" Reyes' voice said. He stood over me, looking into my eyes.

I weakly raised my gun at him, pulled the hammer back, and tried to fire, but no shot came out.

I tried this a few times, but my gun was empty. He kicked my hand, which sent my gun skittering across the stone floor.

"I'll admit, Ace," He said smiling, "I *almost* thought you got me." I tried to spit at him but ended up spitting blood on my own face. "I'll tell you what I'm gonna do since you're dying. Can't let you die in peace, can I?" He laughed, "After I leave your corpse in the desert somewhere for the buzzards to eat, I'm gonna head back to Refugio and finish robbing the bank. Then I'll head back to Justicia and kill everyone in town. Finally, I am gonna head back to Folklore so that me and Fierro can rob your uncle blind and steal his wife and little girl. And the worst part is, you *almost* prevented all that. I can respect the fight, though. I won't forget you, at least not anytime soon. Almost died by Caroline Hendrick's son. What a story this will make!"

"I'll... kill you," I muttered. It hurt to talk. I felt like I was losing consciousness. My head hurt. Reyes laughed.

"See you in Hell once I go. Tell Caroline I said hi!"

The last thing I saw was Reyes' boot above my face. Then, everything went dark.

Chapter 18
Leona Montenegro

Leona was a beautiful young woman. She was 18 years old, with long raven hair that reached her lower back. Her hazel eyes were large. She was thin and long-legged. Her Spanish ancestors came here to Mexico a little more recently than many of her peers, the most recent being her maternal grandmother. Because of this, her skin was different than many of her peers, being a creamy white rather than an olive tan. She considered herself a lady rather than a farmer's daughter, much to the disturbance to her younger sister, who did more work around the farm than Leona did. Leona felt that her sister, a rather plain girl in comparison, resented her because she was not the favorite.

Leona probably would've had no lack of suitors in a larger city like the *Capitál* or Ciudad Juarez. She was the image of beauty, especially here in Mexico. But things weren't so here in her small farming community. The men, especially those near her age, valued submissiveness and lack of desire for more extraordinary things than just farming. So, even though Leona was undoubtedly the most beautiful girl in the community, all the boys knew that she had a fiery temper and big dreams. She was untouchable as a potential wife. Leona didn't *just* want to be a mother and farmer's wife. She hated it here. Being her father's favorite daughter, though, she felt she couldn't just up and leave as her sister María could. Not that María ever would, though. Leona just thought that she probably could and wouldn't be missed.

Leona, being that she never had the opportunity to leave their village for long term, taught herself to read. Everything she had learned was self-taught since her father thought a housewife wouldn't need to know about reading or arithmetic. He never stopped her from learning, but he never tried to send her to school or help her. She loved books, especially romance novellas. As she read stories about corsairs coming to land and stealing away a young, beautiful protagonist, she often liked to imagine that was her experience. The buccaneer, at first, would take her as a prisoner, but after a while, the girl's feminine charms would convince the man that she was more than a prisoner. The two would travel the world together. It made Leona's heart swell just thinking about it: a forbidden love, fighting against everyone just to be together.

Leona didn't want to be *just* a housewife. She was worried she would end up that way. Leona wouldn't be able to stand such a life. She wanted adventure, drama, and romance. What romance was there to find in a marriage her father arranged with another farmer or a rancher? Many were content with such a life, but she wasn't. Her father wasn't an evil man and never hit her or her sister. He was always kind and affectionate, but she wasn't happy with farm life.

Her mother was one of those who hadn't been content with a farmer's life either. Leona always wondered why she stayed on the farm. She had been a nurse during the war with France and Spain before Leona was born. Her mother had even told Leona that she had fought a little in a few battles.

Before her mother passed from disease, she had taught Leona everything she knew about medicine and dressing wounds. It was helpful for Leona. She could take care of her father if he was wounded, working harder than he should've. She could also care for the family cow and mule if injured.

The day she finally saw a glimmer of hope, a chance to run away from her small *pueblito*, started like any other. She rose with the sun and brushed her long hair after a bath. She dressed in a simple yet traditional dress and went outside to help her sister with the chores. María had already been working on the tasks for an hour. Still, her father allowed Leona to do her morning routine, saying that she was older and trying to find a husband in order to justify his favoritism.

After feeding the chickens, Leona would take the family mule and walk up around a mile and a half to the market with goods to sell. On rare occasions, her father would allow her to go to Las Fuentes to sell the goods, but he always had to go with her. The road to the local market wasn't dangerous, but *banditos* and *ladrones* would frequently occupy the road to Las Fuentes. As long as she was with her father, a large and tall man, she would be safe. Even if he had to pay a small tribute to them, he was still intimidating enough in size that they didn't dare try anything with Leona.

After arriving at the market, she would do her typical activities. Sit in the shade and read a book, try to sell a few textiles or raw cotton from her family's farm, and she would look at the wares. She especially enjoyed it when the silver and gold merchants came to market. They would often allow her to try on most of their jewelry wares. She couldn't ever afford anything, but it was nice to pretend. Once it was around three o'clock in the afternoon, she would start to head back.

So that's what she was doing at the moment: heading back home. She was humming a tune she had heard at the market, played by an older man with a guitar. She dreamt of balls and dances, of princes and pirates. There were condors on the side of the road, pecking at something that hadn't been there this morning. Some bloodied dead animal, for sure. Leona turned her head in disgust and guided the mule to the other side of the road. She didn't want to look.

She was *almost* past the condors' meal when she heard an awfully human-sounding groan. Did Leona dare look back and see what the birds were pecking at? She was worried about looking. Usually, anything the vultures ate always looked disgusting. But what if it was a person? What if they were still alive?

Leona picked up a good-sized stick from the side of the road and reluctantly made her way over to the condors. She saw blood but not much else. It would have helped if Leona had opened her eyes a little more. She swung the stick wildly at the vultures, screaming at them in Spanish to leave and get away. When they all cleared, she dropped the stick and gasped.

In front of her laid a *gringo*, about her age, blonde-haired and beaten. One of his shirt sleeves was entirely torn off at the seem and tied around him like a bandage. His cream-colored shirt was utterly stained with blood at the torso. His skin was burnt from the sun, his lips dry from dehydration, and his feet sore from the sand. How far had he traveled like this? He opened his eyes for a brief moment to reveal that they were blue. Leona's heart jumped. The American boy moaned and closed his eyes once more. She couldn't just leave him out here. He didn't have boots, a coat, or a hat. His clothes were dirty and tattered, and he probably needed a new bandage for whatever

She pulled the mule over. Thankfully, she had sold all she had brought to the market, so the beast had plenty of space. She hoisted the boy up with all of her strength and put him face down on the mule. He groaned but seemed ok. As painful as it probably was, he would only have to be able to ride like that for a short amount of time.

"Don't die on me, *gringo*," She whispered to the boy's ear in Spanish, unsure if he'd even understand, "You're my only ticket out of this horrible life."

Chapter 19
The Necklace

I woke up feeling groggy. Everything hurt. My skin, my feet, and my gut. The air was cool, and the place that I was in was shady. It took my vision a minute to clear. I tried to remember where I had been before. It all came back to me like a train. Selleck's arrest, Boca del Lobo, the showdown with Reyes, and my journey through the hot desert.

The only thing that I didn't remember was where I was now. As my eyes adjusted, I saw that I was in a small adobe room, lying on a straw mattress. I tried to sit up, but my gut hurt too much. I lifted the shirt I was wearing, a long, burlap shirt as opposed to the cotton one I had been using, to reveal that my gunshot wound had new, clean bandages on it. I peeled the sanitary bandages back. Someone had removed the bullet and stitched up the hole. What had happened?

A door opened suddenly, surprising me. I instinctively reached down to my hip for my gun, but there wasn't anything. I wasn't wearing the belt even. Just a pair of loose-fitting pantaloons.

Through the open portal walked the most beautiful girl I'd ever seen carrying a tray of food.

She was tall and thin. Long black hair waved behind her gracefully. She was surprised to see me awake. Her brownish eyes were tender and lovely to look at.

"Gringo," She said in a siren-sweet voice, *"Estás despierto. ¿Cómo te sientes?"*

I had no clue what she'd said, apart from '*gringo*', a word I'd learned very quickly in my pursuit of Reyes. I wasn't quite what it meant, but it referred to American people; that much was for sure.

"Uh… you speak English?" I asked her. "¿Hablas *inglés?*"

"Not very much." She said, shaking her head. "I read it. Wait."

She left the tray on the night table and quickly left the room. She returned a few seconds later carrying my pen and a pad of paper. The girl handed them to me. She wanted me to write what I was going to say? What kind of person reads English but doesn't speak it?

I thought for a minute. I had a million questions but needed to decide which to write first.

"Where am I?" I scribbled. My hand was weak and trembled, making my handwriting much sloppier. I passed the sheet back to the girl. She read it and reread it, smiling.

"My father's house." She told me. "You're safe. I help you." I took the paper back from the girl.

"You're the one who fixed me up?"

"Yes. I help you. Take bullet out and sew you."

"Muchos gracias," I told her in Spanish. She smiled and laughed lightly, undoubtedly at my poor Spanish. Her teeth were very straight and clean. It surprised me.

I took the paper back. Next question… "How long have I been out?" I wrote to her.

"One week." She told me, raising a finger. "You had fever. I help you."

"¿Tu nombre?" I asked her.

"Leona Montenegro." She responded, pointing at her chest, "And you?"

"Asa. Asa Hendricks."

"Good to meet you."

"You as well, Ms. Montenegro." I smiled at her. I wrote on the paper. "I really owe you, big time, Leona. Anything you want, I will do."

She read it and reread it three different times. She gave me a huge smile and hugged me. What was her deal?

"You can walk?" She asked.

"Help me up," I responded, giving her a hand. She took it and grabbed my shoulder. I stood up slowly. The pain in my gut hurt, but it really felt much better. Once I was on my feet, I stretched my legs and yawned. Leona giggled. I turned red, which drew out an even louder laugh from her. "I feel like I'm starving."

"Eat." She said, holding up some kind of dish. It smelled good and was warm. I wasn't sure how to hold it. It was a dish made with that Mexican flatbread. What did they call it? *'Tortilla?'* Each one was filled with meat and greens. I thanked her and grabbed one. It was delicious.

"Leona!" I told her, "This is so good. You cooked it?" She laughed.

"*Sí.*" She replied. "I cook it for you." She paused, waiting for me to finish my meal. It was the best thing I'd eaten in weeks, so I scarfed it down faster than I should've. Once I had finished, she spoke. "You help me?"

"Of course!" I answered, "Whatever you need, I'll help, yes."

She turned around and dug through a chest. I tucked my shirt into the pantaloons. When she turned back towards me, she held a pair of ornate riding boots. They were very clearly Mexican in design, but who was I to complain? I shoved my feet in. They were a little big, but it would work. She then handed me a plain-colored poncho and my gun belt. No gun, though.

"My gun?" I asked, pantomiming a gun with my thumb and index finger in case she didn't understand. She shook her head.

"No gun. When I find you, no gun."

I nodded, understanding what she'd meant. Reyes or one of his men had taken my guns, boots, hat, and coat when they took me out to the desert.

She took me by the hand and went to the other room. There was a small table where a man and a younger girl were eating. Leona addressed them.

"*Hola papá,*" Leona addressed the man with a kiss on the cheek. He was older, dressed traditionally, and dark from time spent in the sun. I assumed this was her father.

"*¿Se despertó el chico?*" He said, pointing at me. "*¿Cómo se llama? Y, ¿qué le pasó?*"

"What's he saying, Leona?" I shot her a confused look.

"He asks what is your name, and what happened to you?" She answered, smiling at me.

"Uh... *Hola, señor.*" I tried to not sound stupid as I spoke Spanish, "*Mi nombre es* Asa Hendricks." I thought for a minute, trying to think of a way to explain what had happened to me. "I don't know how to say 'some outlaws shot me' in Spanish, Leona. Help me out?"

"*Unos banditos le dispararon en el camino. Le robaron todo.*" She said, turning back to her father.

Her father finished his food, the same type of meal I had just eaten and stood up. He walked over to me and put his hand on my shoulder. He was shorter than I expected.

"*Leona,*" He addressed his daughter, "*Dile que lo sentimos mucho y estamos acá para ayudar.*" I looked over at the girl, waiting for her to try and translate what he'd been saying.

"He say that we feel bad for what happen to you and we help you," Leona said. Her dad just smiled and nodded.

"*Llevale al mercado contigo hoy, Leona.*" He spoke with his daughter once more, "*Te puede ayudar vender y le pagaré.*"

"What'd he say about me?" I asked Leona. She started to giggle until her father shot her a scowl.

"He say that you come with me today. He pay you." She tried to explain.

"Oh no, *señor*," I started to say before turning to Leona, "Tell him that I can't accept any money. You all saved my life."

Leona spoke with her father again, presumably translating what I had said. He responded, but I didn't understand a word. Leona turned back to me.

"He say that he want to help you get back to Las Fuentes. You need money to pay for transportation to your country. He will give you that."

"Much obliged, *señor, muchos gracias*." I tried to thank him. He just smiled and nodded. The girl behind him, the one at the table, stood up. She seemed a few years younger than Leona. She was probably Leona's sister.

"*Papá, ¡dijiste que hoy sería mí turno para ir al mercado!*" I didn't understand what she was saying, but I knew her tone. She was complaining to her father, though I wasn't sure why.

"*¡Cállate, Maria!*" He said harshly to her. "*Leona hizo el desayuno, entonces ella se va al mercado con el chico. Aparte de eso, no vas a tener nada de que hablar con* él. *Ella es más cercana de su edad.*"

The girl grumbled something else and then sat back down, pouting. I looked over at Leona, who just shrugged. Her dad said something else to Leona, then passed her some cash. He went to a backroom, which I assumed was his bedroom, then returned with an old straw hat. He placed it on my head and nodded, seemingly satisfied with my appearance.

"*Gracias, señor*," I told him, but he just smiled and nodded. I wondered if I'd been saying 'thanks' correctly in Spanish.

"Come, Asa. We need to get ready to go." Leona said, grabbing my hand. Her father furrowed his brow when he saw this gesture, but apart from that, his expression didn't change. I took one last look at Leona's sister, Maria, I think her name had been, who was scowling at us. Then we left the diminutive house.

Leona led me to an old barn, where a donkey almost as tall as had been waiting for us. Leona threw a blanket on its back and began loading various textiles and cotton bags on the beast.

"Need me to help with the donkey?" She gave me a confused look, so I repeated in Spanish: "*¿Te ayudo con el burro?*"

"*Es una mula.* A mule." She responded. I just shrugged, "Help would be good." She smiled and blushed, probably thinking I was a true gentleman, as I took the bags from her. My abdomen ached, but I didn't want to show any visible sign of pain or weakness. This was a fine lady, and I didn't want her to think I was any less of a man.

Once everything was loaded, we departed. It was a hot day, and I was grateful that Leona's father had let me use the hat. The clothes I had been given were cotton, so they weren't bad for the sun either. We walked silently for a long time, probably because we were unsure how to communicate so the other would understand. Finally, we came to a dark brown spot in the sand on the side of the road.

"I find you here." She said, pointing at the spot. I hadn't realized initially, but the brown stain in the sand was dried blood. *My* dried blood. I felt a little surprised at the fact that I was still alive. It was a large stain.

"I really appreciate you, Leona." I told her frankly, "You really did save my life."

"Tell me about you." She continued onward, past the blood stain, "Why are you in my country?"

"To be honest, Miss Montenegro," I said as I walked by her side, "I am here with a lawman from the United States."

"Lawman?" She asked, not knowing the word.

"Um... *aguacil,* I think..." I remembered the badge of the Sheriff who had arrested Selleck. I had to leave here soon and head back to get him out.

"Why are you here with him?"

"We are looking for a man, an outlaw or *bandito*," I started, looking at her to make sure she understood, "His name is Luis Reyes. He's a really bad man."

"I know of this man." She nodded, "It is as you say: he is a bad man. Make many people suffer much. And this 'lawman?' Where is he?"

"He's in Las Fuentes," I answered, "In jail there, wrongly arrested."

"So you need to go soon?" She asked. Her tone was light, almost excited, even. Did she want me to leave so bad already?

"Yes." I answered, ignoring the dread I felt at the thought of her wanting me to leave, "I have to get my friend out of jail, then we need to pursue Reyes back to the U.S."

"We are almost there." She changed the subject, pointing at the small, open-air market in the sun. It was smaller than any I had ever seen, and the people were poor, but nevertheless, the market was lively.

Leona smiled, walked right over to a vacant spot in the marketplace, and gave me a bundle from the mule.

"Put this up." She said. I just nodded. She went over to some other girls around our age, leaving me alone with whatever was in the bundle.

After a minute or so of struggle, I discovered that the bundle was some kind of tent or pavilion. It took me even longer to figure out how to set it up. Leona was too distracted with gossip or whatever she'd been discussing with her friends to notice me struggling. I eventually got it, and not too long afterward, Leona 'conveniently' noticed that I had finished.

An old man was the first one to approach the booth. He smiled when he was Leona and looked at me momentarily before returning to speak with her.

"*Leona,*" He addressed her, "*¿Cómo estás, bella?*" She smiled and kissed the older man on the cheek.

"*Bien, señor Guerrero, ¿y usted?*" Her sweet voice brought life to the old man's tired eyes. "*Estoy bien, gracias a Dios,*" He answered her question. While I didn't completely understand what they were discussing, I was sure they were just greeting each other.

"*Y este gringo, ¿quien es? Es tu novio? Muy guapo, eh?*"

Leona turned red in the face and shot me a look. I was still clueless as to what was going on.

She looked back at the aging gentleman and shook her head.

"*No,*" She said, in an assuring voice, "*No es mi novio, ¡lo juro! Solo necesitaba trabajar, nada más.*"

"*Está bien, princesa,*" The old man chuckled, "*No me debo meter en el amor de los jovenes. Dile a tu papá que lo voy a traer más huevos mañana, ¿bien?*"

"*Está bien, señor Guerrero.*" She told the man before he left. She was still red in the face.

"What happened?" I asked, wondering if the old man had been trying to make advances on her.

My blood started to get hot. "What did he say to you? Who was that guy?"

"He is *el señor Guerrero.*" Leona explained, trying to cover her face until the blush disappeared, "He was very close to my mother. He just ask me if you were my *novio*, that is all."

"What does that word mean? *Novio*?"

"I don't know how to explain it." She said, shrugging. I could tell by her tone that she didn't *want* to explain it, so it was probably embarrassing. I decided not to pry any further.

The day went on. I felt utterly useless in selling the goods. No one here spoke any English, so Leona did all the talking. I was there to sit around doing nothing. Leona seemed to enjoy the company, though. She'd told me that she was managing the market booth by herself most of the time when she came here. It was tedious at times when she was by herself, she explained. In the late afternoon, Leona got up and instructed me to follow her.

"Where are we going?" I asked, following behind. She was walking fast, and we still needed to pack up the mule, so I was confident we weren't leaving.

"I need to buy something." She told me, turning back toward me, "Remember that my father gave me money today?"

"I remember?" I told her.

"It is money for our lunch." She explained, not slowing her pace. She was clearly excited about something.

"So we are going to buy food?" I asked. I had been getting a little hungry, so that was good news.

"No, I'm sorry," Leona said, momentarily stopping to look me in the eyes. "I have been saving the money for a long time."

"So what are you going to buy?"

She didn't answer with words but pointed at another market stall, probably fifteen feet in front of us. The Merchant at the stall was essentially the wealthiest person around. His clothes were fine, above the average traditional Mexican attire. In fact, they weren't Mexican in style at all but rather European. He wore a fine three-piece suit that was too hot for this weather.

I didn't pay much attention to him, though. Like Leona's, my eyes were caught by a glimmer of something shiny in the sun: silver. More specifically, silver *jewelry*.

"Ever since I started coming here." She explained, not taking her eyes off a beautiful silver pendant, "I want to buy one from him. I never had money. He only come a few times in a year. I have saved my money for six years to buy one from him."

I was as surprised as I was impressed. Leona seemed like a humble girl, not the kind that wore silver necklaces. Of course, my mother hadn't appeared that way either, but her necklace was one of the only things I still had from her.

When I remembered the necklace, I felt my neck to see if her necklace was still there. It was just a long, simple chain, but it was Mom's. If Reyes had stolen it, that gave me another reason to get him.

Surprisingly, the cold metal chain hung around my neck, below my shirt collar. Reyes and his outlaws probably hadn't seen it when they ransacked my possessions.

Leona approached the Merchant, who spoke Spanish with some kind of accent. I wondered if he spoke English too because his accent didn't sound like Spanish was his first language.

"Excuse me, sir," I said to him. His eyes widened when he saw my pale face.

"A *gringo*?" He asked in an accent that wasn't English either, "Here in this farming community?"

"Doesn't *gringo* mean white person? So that would make you one, too?"

"No sir, it does not." He explained, "I assume you don't speak Spanish well. It refers to Americans."

"Where are you from then, partner?"

"How lovely!" He exclaimed, visibly excited, "A cowboy too!" He tipped his top hat to me. "My name is Herr Johannes Wilhem. The honor to meet you is mine."

"You're German, then?" I asked. He nodded.

"Leona has been coming to me trying to buy this necklace for years." He explained, "*¿Verdad que sí, Leona?*"

"Yes, *señor* Wilhelm. How much is it, again? I have enough this time!"

"Let me see, my dear." Herr Wilhelm asked, leaning his head over the table. She held up a large wad of bills. He took them from her hand and started counting. When he was done, he shook his head, disheartened. "I'm afraid you're short, my dear. *Que faltes un poco, cien, más o menos.*"

"That's how much you told me it was last year!" She protested, holding back tears.

"Prices change, my dear." He told her in a mocking tone. "You can just come back next time."

"It will take a year for me to save one hundred more!" She yelled. A man behind the German Merchant, whom we hadn't noticed, put his hand to his side. The Merchant had armed bodyguards.

"Calm down, Ms. Montenegro." He told her, "Perhaps we can make a trade? Surely you have something that would be equal to one hundred pesos?"

She looked at him. Her eyes were filled with tears. I could tell she'd been waiting a long time.

She shook her head quickly. I'd been in their house. I knew that she didn't have anything. I signed.

"How about this?" I asked, pulling the silver chain from my neck, "This plus the money Leona has?" The Merchant took the necklace and analyzed it carefully. He even tasted it.

"Yes, this is worth *at least* one hundred pesos."

Chapter 20
The Dance

Leona was just about as happy as possible with her new silver pendant. I was a little sad to have lost my mother's chain, but Leona's happiness made me feel that the trade had been worth it. The gorgeous girl skipped and twirled around like a young child. She showed her friends, the other shopkeepers and merchants, and the passersby her new necklace.

She was so overcome with joy that she hadn't even thanked me properly. Not that any thanks were in order in the first place. Leona had saved my life. The very least I could do was help her get the necklace she'd wanted since she was a child.

"Asa, thank you so much!" She eventually said to me, giving me a huge smile. It made my heart melt.

"No thanks is necessary." I told her, "You saved my life, Leona."

"Come," She took me by the hand, "Dance with me!" Sure enough, music had started playing somewhere in the market. She led me swiftly to the source. Once we were there, she took my hands, and we began to dance.

I didn't know the melody. It was some kind of Mexican Folk rhythm. I also wasn't much of a dancer. Mom had taught me a little, telling me that all women wanted a man who was good at dancing, but she hadn't had much time for me to learn how to *really* dance. Leona was the exact opposite. She was beautiful and graceful on her feet. She was sophisticated and aware of the facial expressions she made during the dance. The crowd clapped with the song's beat, and a few more dancers joined in, but all the attention was on Leona, the most beautiful girl in the community. Which, of course, meant all attention was on me, too. The people were surprisingly supportive, though, cheering and clapping at me, trying to help me keep on beat.

"Throw me in the air!" Leona told me. I wasn't sure about that, but she was already too far away to object. Leona danced towards me, jumping when she got close. I tried my best to grab her hips and toss her up like she wanted. Leona pirouetted with the grace of a swan in the air, her loose traditional-style dress flowing beautifully, and landed in front of me. She grabbed my hands and wrapped them around her. I blushed, and the crowd cheered and laughed. They started chanting something.

"What are they saying?" I asked Leona quietly. She smiled. Her cheeks were as pink as mine.

"They are telling you to kiss me." She whispered. She looked at my lips for a second, wondering if I would actually kiss her. I wondered that myself, actually. Eliza had been beautiful, but she was homely compared to Leona. I felt more nervous around her than I had ever felt around any girl.

Finally, Leona got tired of me waiting. She kissed my cheek softly. I turned red, and the small crowd cheered and dispersed. She pulled herself gently from my arms and gave me a huge smile.

The pain in my abdomen started to flare up. I tried to act tough but couldn't any longer. I put my hand on the wound and groaned.

"I am so sorry!" Leona cried, realizing what had happened, "Asa, I completely forgot about your hole!"

"It's fine," I told her, trying not to react too much. "Can you take a look?"

She pulled me over to the well near where we had been dancing, sat me on the bucket, and helped me pull the poncho and shirt off. The bandage, which had been sterile and white before, was now stained crimson. She slowly unwrapped it and examined the wound.

"It looks like you tore the stitches." She said, wiping blood from my torso, "It is my fault. I made you throw me. One moment."

Leona left me to cover my open wound with just my hand. She returned moments later, carrying a bottle of a gold-colored liquid. She put some on a handkerchief and cleaned my wound with it. It stung and smelled honey-like. I could also tell from the smell that it had a *lot* of alcohol.

Once Leona had finished cleaning the wound and removing the broken stitches, she placed the bottle on the ground. She dug through her bag until she pulled out a needle and thread, which she subsequently poured the strong liquor on.

"Here." She told me as she passed the bottle, "Drink." I took one sniff of the stuff and knew that I didn't want to try it. It smelled like the *mezcal* that Selleck had bought me, but sweeter.

"No, thank you," I said as I gave her back the bottle.

"This will hurt very much if you don't drink. It is *tequila*." She said, confused at my refusal.

"I don't drink." I explained to her, "Too many bad experiences. I don't drink at all."

She seemed nervous to start stitching me up again because I hadn't drunk the *tequila*, but I put on a stern face. It *did* hurt quite a bit, actually, but I was in too deep now to change my mind about the alcohol.

"Talk to me, Leona," I told her, wincing with the pain of the needle going in for another stitch. "What about?" She asked, focused on her work.

"What are your dreams?"

She paused, pondering for a moment. Perhaps she was trying to translate what she would say in her head.

"I want to travel." She started again, finishing that stitch, "I would like to see many things."

"What's stopping you?" I asked. She just shrugged.

"Many things."

"Well, maybe after I get Reyes, I can come back and help you get out of here," I said in a trembling voice. Each stitch was excruciating.

"Yes, perhaps." She said, tying the final stitch. She looked up and smiled, "It is finished."

"Thank you, Leona," I told her, looking down at her work. She finished bandaging me and then got up. I put the shirt and poncho back on and followed her.

"Asa," She told me when we were headed back to the market stall, "Don't worry about coming back for me. I already have a plan to escape from this place."

We cleaned up the marketplace stall and headed back towards the Montenegro farm. I felt happy, even after losing my mom's necklace.

The following morning, Leona woke me up early. She gave me breakfast in bed. Nothing incredibly fancy or delicious today, just beans and tortillas. She seemed like she was in a hurry to get out.

"Leona," I asked as she walked around the room, grabbing and shoving things into her bag, "What's going on?"

"Nothing." She answered quickly. She looked at me and threw her hands down in frustration.

Something was going on, but I wasn't sure what it was. "I can't explain it to you. Bad English."

"Ok, well, can I help you in any way?" I asked cautiously.

"Yes. Get all you need together. We need to leave."

I didn't ask more questions. Leona was jumpy already. I didn't want to frustrate her more. I started to pack my few things in my satchel.

"Hurry," Leona said, looking out the door to see if anyone was there.

"Leona, can you please just tell me what is going on?" I whispered. I wasn't sure if we should be sneaking, but I did, just in case.

"I will tell you later." She told me quietly, "Please just follow."

She led me outside to the old wooden barn where we had left the mule yesterday. Once inside, she pulled an old rawhide saddle off a bench and passed it to me.

"You want me to saddle the mule?" I asked, holding the saddle in my hand like an ancient artifact. It looked to be close to one hundred years old.

"Yes." She answered, "Please do it quickly."

I didn't respond. I tossed the blanket from yesterday on the old mule while Leona caressed her head, trying to keep her quiet. What was she planning? Once the blanket was situated, I threw the saddle on the mare's back and cinched up the straps. Leona placed an old bit in the mouth and tossed the reins over its head. She motioned for me to get on. I didn't ask questions; I just launched my leg over the old mare. The effort made my side ache, begging for a rest, but I ignored it.

Leona rushed over to my side and gave me a hand. I grabbed it and helped her over the back of the mule, sitting her right behind me. The mule let out a loud bray. I heard the house door open. Leona wrapped her arms around my waist and squeezed tightly.

"Go!" She hissed quietly. I never questioned her. I dug my heels into the sides of the mule. It started galloping.

"*¡Espera!*" I heard Leona's dad yell, chasing after the galloping mule. I was wondering if I should stop, "*¡Párate, ladrón; traiga mi hija!*"

"Don't stop!" Leona yelled. "We go to Las Fuentes."

I nodded. I wasn't sure what was happening, but I had to get Selleck. I had already been unconscious for a week. Who knows what could've happened in that time?

Eventually, we could slow down the mule now that we had lost our pursuer. I turned to Leona, who had a big smile on her face. I wasn't sure what happened, but I felt Leona had just left her father completely.

"I need answers." I told her, "What on earth just happened back there?" She shrugged and played dumb. I narrowed my eyes at her. "Don't play dumb with me! I know you can understand what I am trying to say."

Leona sighed and put on a sad face. She looked me in the eyes. There were tears in hers. She was about to cry.

"My father..." She started to say, in her heavy accent, "He is bad man. He hit me many times. He hear about our dance yesterday and think that you try to take me. He say that he kill you. I won't let him touch you."

I narrowed my eyes at her. Something was wrong with her story, but I couldn't communicate well enough to interrogate her effectively. I sighed and continued riding. I would sort this out when we arrived at Las Fuentes. There were people who spoke English and Spanish there. Someone could help me sort this out and discover what Leona actually meant. After all, Leona's father hadn't seemed like a bad man. He'd been cordial, even friendly to me in all the interactions I'd had with him.

We rode for a little while. Leona told me what directions to get to Las Fuentes, but she couldn't tell me how far we were. I hoped we would arrive before nightfall. I knew Selleck was being held in rough conditions. I also knew we had to try catching Reyes before he left Mexico. He had told me his plans, thinking that I was dead already. We had to get Reyes before he could get too far ahead of us. He already had a week's headstart.

"Is your hole ok?" She eventually asked, noticing that I was clutching my side a little. It was sore.

"It's alright." I told her, "Hurts, but I'll be fine."

"Stop the mule." She said seriously. I did as she commanded. She hopped off the mount, and I followed. She led me by the hand and sat me down on a rock that was a comfortable height.

"What are you—"I started to say as she took my shirt off. I was embarrassed a little. I hardly knew the girl; here she was, just doing whatever she wanted to me. She unwound the dressing on my wound and examined it closely.

"Stitches didn't tear." She finally said. She pulled a handkerchief from her bag and held it on the wound to clean up the sudden bleeding. "Hold this here." I did as she said. Leona started to dig through her bag a little more.

"You a nurse?" I asked, trying to make conversation. I felt awkward sitting here with my shirt off before her.

"My mother." She answered, not taking her eyes off her bag. "Move your hand." I did as she said. She held an old tobacco tin with some kind of salve inside. She carefully spread the salve on the wound with a finger. Her touch was delicate. It didn't hurt at all. In fact, the salve made the wound feel better. Once she finished that, she started wrapping a clean dressing around my waist.

"What was that you put on it?"

"Is called *savila* here. I don't know what is called in English."

"What's it do?"

"*Prevenir infección*." She answered, finishing the dressing, "How you feel?"

"Not too bad." I said, standing up, "At least not bad for someone who got shot a week ago. We should get riding again." I put the old shirt and poncho back on.

"Las Fuentes is not too far from here." She told me as I helped her mount up. "*Treinta* minutes, maybe?"

"*Treinta*..." I repeated, trying to remember my numbers in Spanish. "That's thirty, right? Ten three times?"

"*Correcto*." She told me as I got up on the mule again. She wrapped her arms around my waist as I kicked the mare again to get moving.

Sure enough, we rode through the gates of Las Fuentes around thirty minutes later. I didn't know exactly what time it was since Reyes' men had stolen my watch, too, but I guessed it was around six or seven P.M.

"I gotta go get my friend." I told her, worried she wouldn't understand, "What will you do?"

"I come with." She shrugged. "I help you."

That wasn't too bad of an idea. I was going to talk to the Mayor again and see if I could convince him to let Selleck out this time. On top of that, the Mayor spoke English and Spanish well, so he could help me figure out what Leona wanted.

We rode off towards the Mayor's office. I wasn't sure what I would say to him, but I had to figure out something good quickly. Matthew Selleck depended on me. My aunt and uncle, too. This wasn't just about revenge anymore. They were in trouble, and they had no idea. I had to stop Reyes and Fierro.

Chapter 21
Another Duel in Las Fuentes

"I'm sorry, *señor* Hendricks, but I will not release *señor* Selleck to you. He has not yet been to trial even." The Mayor of Las Fuentes shook his head. He had a grim expression on his face. He was stressed. Especially after I'd told him that Reyes had gotten away and left me for dead.

"I know that, sir," I argued politely, "but I can't leave here without Mr. Selleck. If I did that, just what kind of friend would I be? If I want to go after Reyes, I need you to release Mr. Selleck first."

Leona sat in the chair next to me. She didn't understand what we were discussing, so she just looked around the room aimlessly. I could tell the Mayor was getting distracted by her. After all, she hadn't been there the last time I'd been in his office.

"If you can pay a fine of two hundred American dollars, I will release *señor* Selleck." The Mayor finally said, throwing his hands down to his sides.

"I can't do that. I told you already Reyes' men took all of my stuff. I've got nothing. I know it's a lot to ask, but please, sir, I am begging you. Throw me a bone here."

The Mayor shook his head. I sighed and turned to Leona. Perhaps someone of the fairer sex could move the Mayor's heart?

"Sir, do you mind if I borrow a piece of paper and a pen?" I asked him. He gave me a confused look but gave me what I asked. I started to write.

"My friend is imprisoned here in Las Fuentes. I need him out before I can head back to my country. Can you help? I'd owe you more than I already do. I need him to get Luis Reyes, the criminal."

Leona took a minute to read it, but after she did, she had a determined look in her eyes. She gave me a nod and looked at the Mayor.

"*Señor Alcalde,*" She started, crossing her legs and placing her hands in her lap, "Usted tiene un lindo cuadro del presidente Porfirio Diaz mirandole."

The Mayor turned to me and furrowed his brow in a confused way. I shrugged. I didn't have any idea what she was saying. I just hoped she didn't say anything wrong to him. In hindsight, I really didn't know Leona. She could've been psychotic, for all I knew.

"*Graicias, señorita...*" The Mayor said in a confused tone.

"*No soy tan educada, pero sé esto: El Presidente Diaz es un hombre muy honorable. Este bandito de que hablan, Luis Reyes, es una mancha en este país. Aún si se encuentra en los estados unidos, esta diciendo a la gente allí que méxico es un país de criminales y sinvergüenzas. El señor presidente no le gustaía eso, ¿o sí?*"

I couldn't understand Leona at all, but she sounded very diplomatic. She must have been making quite the speech. I only understood a little bit. She was talking about the President and how he was an honorable man. I heard her mention Reyes, too, so she must've been trying to make a comparison or something.

"*No... supongo que no...*" The Mayor answered. His tone was thoughtful. He rubbed his chin as he spoke. Leona may have been getting through to him!

"*Yo digo que debe soltar el amigo. Es un hombre importante, y el señor* Hendricks *está convencido que* él *puede vencer Reyes. Piensa en lo que haría el señor presidente. Le aseguro que no van a volver a Las Fuentes. Van a ir y van a capturar Reyes, nada más. Cuando se van de acá, no volverán.*"

The Mayor turned to me with a smile. He shook his head slowly and laughed.

"You were smart to bring this young lady, Hendricks." He told me, "I will release Selleck to you. I am not sure if you understood what she said, but she tells me you will never return to Las Fuentes once you leave. Is that true?"

"If that's the condition for Mr. Selleck's release," I said, squeezing Leona's hand excitedly, "Then I promise we will never come back."

"What assurance do I have?"

I looked the Mayor in the eyes. I narrowed my vision.

"I swear on my sweet mother, whom Reyes murdered. I swear we will not return to Las Fuentes on her soul."

The Mayor momentarily looked me in the eyes, trying to read my thoughts. See if I was lying, perhaps? After that few seconds was up, he nodded his head.

"I believe you." He told me. He then called his secretary in.

"*¿Señor Alcalde?*" The secretary asked, popping her head in the door.

"Go retrieve *señor* Selleck from *la carcel.*" He said, writing a short note, "If *el aguacil* gives you any problems, give him this." He passed the note her way. She came into the room and took it from his hand. "Assure that he has returned all of his possessions, including his gun."

Without another word, the secretary ducked out of the room. The Mayor turned to us, smiling. "Would you like a drink before you leave?" He asked. I shook my head.

"I told myself I wouldn't drink anymore," I told him. He laughed, pulling a tall decanter and a tumbler glass from one of his desk drawers.

"I shall drink for you then, Mr. Hendricks. *¡Salud!*" He took a large gulp of the whiskey and put the glass down softly. "Is there anything else I can do for you, sir?"

"There is, actually," I remarked, rubbing my chin. "Ms. Montenegro here has helped me much. I am just not sure exactly what she wants. I would be very thankful if you could help me figure it out."

"I can try and help you." The Mayor said. He turned to Leona and started talking to her in Spanish. The two spoke back and forth for some time. Despite her limited formal education, Leona must've been well-spoken because she could answer and converse with the Mayor, a very well-educated man. After talking for a while, the Mayor turned back to me.

"It seems *señorita* Montenegro intends to travel with you to the United States." He explained, "She has told me that she wanted to come with you to Las Fuentes so she could trade her mule for a horse and possibly a new gun for you."

"Wait, what?" I asked him. I was baffled. "I don't want to bring back with me some girl I barely know!" The Mayor laughed.

"Apparently, she thinks you don't have a choice." He responded, "She says she saved your life, so you owe her one. And, she says that you owe her for convincing me to release Mr. Selleck. If you believe there is some mistake, you should take that up with her."

I looked at Leona. She stared at me with her huge hazel eyes and sweet smile. Even if I could communicate with her well enough to protest, there's no way I could've said no to a girl like that. I blushed. The Mayor laughed.

Finally, the door opened. Selleck walked in, looking worse for wear. "Hey, kid." He said, giving me a painful smile. I smiled back.

"Looks like we're both worse for wear," I responded. He laughed, "Reyes shot me."

"I was wondering what was taking you so long. Who's the girl."

"Her name is Leona Montenegro. It's a long story, but she's coming with us. I don't have a choice, apparently. Doesn't speak too much English."

"Good enough answer for me. I don't speak enough Spanish to try and object, neither."

The three of us said our farewells to the Mayor and stepped outside. Leona clung to me like a shadow. I couldn't blame her. As bad as I felt at the moment, Leona had cleaned me up and changed my clothes. Selleck was dirty, smelled terrible, and looked like he hadn't seen the sun in the whole week he'd been imprisoned. She was probably a little taken aback by his appearance. He was unshaven, too. He grew facial hair reasonably fast because his mustache was long, and he also had a full beard.

"He's my friend, Leona." I tried to explain to her. "The one you helped free. He's good people."

"Don't worry." Selleck told me, "Your girlfriend will be alright with me once I have a chance to clean up. Let's head back to the hotel. I have around twenty bucks left; we can get a room and a hot meal. Head out early tomorrow morning to the place where Reyes almost killed you."

"We don't have time." I said, shaking my head, "Reyes is headed back to the States as we speak.

He's about one week ahead of us or more."

"What do you mean?"

I explained Reyes' plan to hit everything we'd foiled: the bank, revenge on the people of Justicia, and finally, Folklore.

"Ok." Selleck said exhaustedly, "Let's eat something, at least. I haven't eaten anything decent in a week now. Then we hit the road. Try and see if we can trade the old mule for a horse and get going. Hopefully, we can catch them before they get to Refugio."

We were on our way to the saloon when the Sheriff rode up. He didn't seem happy.

"Hey!" He yelled, dismounting his horse. He seemed mad. "Just who do you think you are, *gringo?*"

"Hang on just one minute!" Selleck raised a hand, trying to diffuse the situation.

"*¡Cállate!*" The Sheriff said, batting Selleck's hand away, "I wasn't talking to you! Reyes shot you, kid! You should be dead, but you come back into my town and think you can tell me what to do?"

"I ain't done nothing that wasn't the right thing!" I argued, reaching for my non-existent gun instinctively.

"Nah, I prefer not to talk." The enraged Sheriff growled. He spit. The saliva landed on my boot.

I scowled at him. "Stand and draw! Save your words and show me your *pistola, idiota!*"

I scoffed and looked at Selleck; he shrugged. Leona was hiding behind me a little, clutching my arm.

"I don't have time for this." I told the Sheriff, "We have to go do *your* job: catch Reyes before he hurts anyone else. I know he paid you off, but that don't mean you gotta stop us."

"If you ain't gonna draw," The Sheriff threatened, "Then I'm gonna arrest you!"

"On what charges?"

He pointed at Leona. She hid behind me even more and gripped my arm tighter.

"Today, a farmer out in the countryside reported some *gringo* cowboy stole his mule and kidnapped his daughter. I betcha that girl is her."

"Don't touch me!" I yelled at the Sheriff as he tried to grab me. He pulled his pistol and poked me in the stomach with it, right on my gunshot wound.

"Fight like a man or die like a dog; the choice is yours."

I looked at Selleck. He gave me a nod of approval and passed me his Schofield. The Sheriff holstered his peacemaker and walked out into the street.

The Schofield didn't fit my holster well, but it worked. The barrel was lengthier, a seven-inch cavalry barrel as opposed to the four-inch my peacemaker had. It was heavier. I tried to get used to the weight in the few seconds before I walked onto the road. My heart pounded. The pain in my wound flared up as though to remind me of the last time I had tried to shoot anyone. I had to remind myself that the Sheriff had jabbed it with the barrel of his revolver and that it wasn't telling me, 'No, you'll be shot again!'

Leona refused to let me go, so Selleck grabbed her and pried her off as gently as he could. "¡*Sueltame!*" She cried out, trying to free herself from the Marshal's grip, "Let go!"

"Relax, girl." He told her calmly, "This is just something the kid's gotta do."

She calmed down a little and pulled herself from his hands. She didn't follow me or try to grab me again. I sighed and shook my head. I was scared, to be honest. My mind flashed back to the fight with Reyes in Boca del Lobo. I tried to push it out, but it kept entering my mind like a fresh burn: constantly stinging, and I could do nothing about it.

I met the Sheriff in the street. His eyes burned with hatred. He wanted to shut me up. I couldn't beat him, at least not while thinking about my fight with Reyes. I had to make him doubt. Maybe I could trick him into running?

"Glad we came out here." I told him, smiling painfully, "That way, all eyes are on us."

"What are you on about, *gringo?*" He snapped. I laughed. It was painful, but I had to make him feel nervous.

"What, with all the people watching, at least half of them gotta understand me!"

"And what do you have to say, hm? Last words? Ain't nothing no cowboy like you can say that is profound."

"Maybe not," I said, smiling devilishly. I tried to picture Fierro's mischievous smile in my head and copy that. Even if he did turn out to be my enemy, if Reyes was telling the truth, he had plenty of charisma and a way of making people think what he wanted. "Of course, they *all* might want to hear what I have to say..."

The *Aguacil* scoffed and put his hands on his hips. He started pacing back and forth. He was getting anxious. My plan was working.

"Alright, *americano*," He roared, "Tell everyone what profound and deep things there are in your small mind!"

"If you insist..." I laughed and raised my head, looking at the crowd gathering, "*Gente* of Las Fuentes, your sheriff here is a traitor, *un traiador!*" The Sheriff started sweating. "He's sold his duty to uphold the law to the fugitive Luis Reyes, *El Rey*. Just look at his new hat and gun! He ain't worthy to be your Sheriff."

"*Cállate gringo...*" The Sheriff growled quietly. He placed a hand on his pistol grip. He was going to draw. I had to time this right...

"Look!" I pointed my left hand at him, "He's getting more mad! He's red in the face. Even if this man kills me, it's your duty as good citizens of this fine country to hang him! He's a traitor to you, to this town, and to your honorable *presidente* and his country!"

The crowd was getting restless now. I knew that at least *some* of them understood what I was saying, and the news was starting to spread. The dirty Sheriff was beginning to shake. His face was a tomato. He was muttering to himself.

"*¡Muerate, gringo estupido!*" He screamed a high-pitched scream and drew his gun. This was what I'd been waiting for.

I pulled Selleck's Schofield out of my holster and raised it up, holding it by my hip, just in time to look down the barrel of the Sheriff's Colt. He pulled the hammer back with his right thumb, but I was faster. I fanned the hammer three times. He managed to get a shot off, but it was too late; all three of my shots had struck his torso. The revolver fired into the ground before him, kicking up the sandy dust. He let out a groan and tried to walk to where no one knew but ended up falling facedown in the sand. I felt my lips turn into a smirk. I spun the gun around my finger once and holstered the weapon. I had won.

The crowd of people stood stunned. No one made a move. Their Sheriff, dirty as he could be, lay dead in the dirt. Finally, Selleck stepped forward, shadowed by Leona.

"Nice shooting, kid," Selleck said, ruffling my hair. I handed him his Schofield. "Go get his gun and hat. You're gonna need them to face Reyes."

We heard horses galloping. Men dressed in military uniforms rode toward us, weapons drawn. They clearly had not yet received the message about the Sheriff being a rat. They were coming for us.

I quickly ran over and snatched the Sheriff's peacemaker and cowboy hat from the dirt. The wind was starting to pick up. I returned to Selleck, who was already retrieving Ophelia and the Mule from the stables. He helped Leona on. I started running over to mount as well.

"Grab the Sheriff's horse!" Selleck barked, "We won't be able to escape with two riders on that mule. He won't need it anymore."

The Sheriff's horse, a pale mare with a grey mane, snorted and huffed as I hopped on but didn't buck. Within the first minute, any resentment she held for me, her master's killer, seemed to have disappeared. That, or she just didn't care too much for the Sheriff.

Once I had mounted and adjusted myself in the saddle, all three of us yelled, whooped, and kicked our mounts to start our escape. I smiled as we left town. I had just won my first duel.

The army, militia, or whoever was chasing us to avenge the slimy *aguacil* didn't give chase for long. Probably since many of the citizens, who knew what was going on regarding the Sheriff's alignment, stopped them and tried to explain the situation. We didn't know. We just ran. We rode till nightfall, where we could set up a meager camp and get some shuteye. We had a *lot* of riding to do if we wanted to catch up to Reyes.

Chapter 22
By the Fireside

The fire was warm. This warmth brought back memories lots of memories over the course of the last six months. The nights out with Martín on the range, traveling with Matthew Selleck, and the burning hotel in Refugio de Los Santos. If all went well in the next few weeks, this adventure would be over and done with.

I looked over at Selleck. The Marshal had bathed and washed his clothes in the river. Leona had a folding tin hand mirror in a bag that she lent Selleck to shave and trim his hair, which he was doing currently. He had only had a little time to collect his things from Las Fuentes, and his shaving kit was one of the ones he'd forgotten. Selleck was using his hunting knife. He hadn't cut himself yet, but the blade was large and unwieldy for a task like shaving one's face, so he would probably miss a few spots. He didn't seem like this was the first time he'd done this, either.

I rubbed my own chin, feeling the short stubble on my face. This was the first time in my life that stubble had really grown. I felt happy. I was becoming a man.

Finally, I looked over at Leona, who was staring at the dancing flames. She was sitting close to me, but we weren't touching. She was mysterious and beautiful. A girl with no formal education who could read English and Spanish and convince the mayor of the city of Las Fuentes to willingly release a man whom he said he wouldn't. For free at that, with no fine paid at all. Just who was she?

She must've felt my staring because she looked up towards me. I quickly tried to look away and act like nothing had happened, but she'd already seen me.

"You need something?" She asked, combing through her long dark hair with her fingers. I turned cherry red.

"No, I was just– well, I was just wondering about yourself." I stuttered. She cocked an eyebrow. "Well, I mean... How old are you?"

"I have Eighteen years." She answered, smiling. Her eyes were trained on me. I felt uncomfortable because I regarded myself as indecent. She'd just seen me kill a man. Granted, I wasn't a murderer, but it still felt... wrong to think that she might be judging me.

"You're a year older than me. I am seventeen." I said, trying to shake the uncomfortable feeling I had.

"You read books?" She asked.

"I do." I told her, "At least I did. I s'pose I ain't read so much as a word since being out on the road." Leona nodded. I wasn't sure how much she understood from what I had said.

She dug through her bag a little bit and, a few seconds later, pulled out a worn leather-bound book. She handed it to me. The cover had the title *The Adventures of Tom Sawyer* engraved in English.

"This is my favorite book." Leona remarked, pointing at the book, "in English." She added. I turned the book over in my hand. It was well-worn, and I could tell it had been read frequently.

"I like this one too." I told her, "I gave my copy to my cousin a few months ago."

"You can keep it if you like."

"Oh no, I don't need to. It's yours." I told her, passing the book back to her. She took it and placed it back in her bag.

"What about your favorite book in Spanish?" I asked. She smiled and dug through her small bag again. She pulled out a second leather-bound tome in the exact same condition first. She'd been carrying around two books in her bag this whole time? It was considerably thicker than the other one. I looked at it. It didn't have the title on the cover, so I opened it to the title page. It read *Don Quijote de la Mancha*. "I've never read it. Is it any good?"

"Very. You need to read it." She answered. I opened the first page, but it was entirely in Spanish.

I shook my head.

"We'll find an English copy," I answered. She just smiled at me. "You know, I always wanted to write books." She cocked her head.

"I wanted to write books." I repeated, pantomiming, writing, "I wanted to be an author."

"Oh! *Un autor.*" She said as she nodded. "You need to! I like it!"

I laughed. Leona looked confused. She was probably wondering why I was laughing. I wasn't sure myself, but I thought her intensity was adorable.

"Perhaps I will." I explained, "Once this is all done with."

She paused. I could see her visibly trying to put sentences together. She looked attractive when deep in thought. I hadn't realized until this conversation just how intelligent Leona was.

"You want to kill Luis Reyes." She stated finally, "Why?"

"He's a bad man." I told her, "Plus, he killed my mom."

"Ah, I see." She clearly understood that. "My mom die too."

"Reyes killed your mom too?"

"No. *Tuberculosis*." She answered. "Eight years ago." I nodded.

"I'm sorry to hear that." I replied, "If I could kill tuberculosis, I would."

It took her a moment to understand or mentally translate it, but Leona laughed quite loudly at my dumb joke. I smiled. She seemed like a perfect woman. Being around her made me forget that around three weeks ago, I had gotten a letter from Eliza telling me she was getting married.

Leona was so loud that she distracted Selleck. He cursed. I turned to him. He'd cut himself with the knife. She quieted and looked at me as though to ask if she were in trouble.

"Everything alright?" I asked Selleck. He just laughed.

"I'm fine." He said, closing the hand mirror. He came over and gave it back to Leona. He sat down on the other side of the fire. "Just cut myself, that's all. Too dark to shave."

"Cleaned up real nice though!" I said, pointing at him, "Didn't he, Leona?" She just nodded. I was curious to know if she understood what I had said.

"Nothing a few good meals can't fix." He smiled, "So, Asa, tell me about your confrontation with Reyes. You mentioned he shot you and told you his plan, but that's all. You didn't tell me anything else. What did you find out from him."

I thought for a minute, trying to remember exactly everything that had happened and in what order.

"Me and the Bounty Hunter from the bar, Hernandez was his name, went up to Reyes' hideout." I started to recap, "We killed their horses parked out front, then went in. Well, they must've heard us cause they started shooting.

"After that, Hernandez tried to route them while I kept Reyes talking. Then I started fighting when Hernandez got behind them. We probably killed five of them or so. Reyes managed to get one of Hernandez's pistols and kill him.

"After he killed Hernandez, I tried to shoot him with my revolver. I fired all six shots and hit him once in the hip. That wasn't enough to stop him, and he shot me and left me in the desert. There, Leona found me, and you know the rest, basically."

"Hip's not a nice place to get shot." Selleck nodded, "Especially if you're planning on riding horseback for the next two weeks. They're probably going slower than normal."

"That means we might catch up." I agreed.

"Yes. Did Reyes say anything to you? Besides his plan?" Selleck continued to pry, "I'll be frank with you, kid: did you ask him about The Beast?"

I thought for a moment about my conversation with Reyes.

"Reyes mentioned that he knew my mother." I admitted, "Her murder wasn't random or accident. He targeted her. Not sure why, but he said Fierro knew."

"Wait," Selleck said, rubbing his ears to ensure he heard me correctly, "Reyes *knows* Fierro and your mom?"

"Not just that, he says he knew them from a long time ago," I added, "If I remember right, his exact words were that they go '*way* back.'"

"You think one of them might be the Beast?" Selleck asked. "More specifically, that *Fierro* might be the Beast?"

I thought for a moment. My mind flashed back to when Fierro had turned into an animal while fighting the cattle rustlers. *That* was absolutely beast-like.

"It's possible." I finally said, thinking, "A few things don't make sense though."

"Like what?"

"My Uncle told me Fierro's only been in the country for ten years." I explained, "You told me that the Beast's gang was active starting around 1870. That's a five-year difference."

"Could be that Fierro lied."

"It's certainly possible. Another issue is that if Reyes is The King and Fierro is The Beast, who is The Widow?"

Selleck was silent, but he looked at me the whole time. He knew exactly what I was thinking because he was thinking it, too.

"There's no way." I told him, my voice cracking, "It ain't possible that she's is The Widow. *My mom* ain't even a widow! My dad left her when he found out she was pregnant."

"It *is* possible." Selleck said grimly, "You know it, and I know it. If Reyes and Fierro knew her, reportedly from 'way back' when, then you *know* it's possible, Ace."

I felt like crying. My mom may have been a bandit? That was unfathomable to me. She was the nicest, sweetest lady I'd ever met. How could she be a murdering bandit?

I was startled when I felt a hand rub my back softly. I looked up. It was Leona. How much of this conversation had she followed? Or did she just see I was sad and was trying to comfort me?

"Look, Ace." Selleck sighed, "I don't want to say it's true. It probably isn't. Especially if Fierro isn't The Beast. I just... I want you to keep it in your thoughts. To prepare yourself. 'Hope for the best, but prepare for the worst.' I think that's how the saying goes."

Selleck was right; it probably wasn't true. There were too many inconsistencies in the story. Reyes probably wasn't even telling the truth. He'd probably just been messing with my head. Still, I couldn't help but remember the fear he'd shown when I mentioned who my mother was.

We went to sleep shortly after that. Didn't have tents anymore, so we just had to sleep on the ground under the open sky. I just hoped it wouldn't rain anytime soon...

I didn't sleep for a long time. I worried that I would dream that my mom *was* The Widow, and then I wouldn't be able to shake the feeling that it was true. I didn't want her to be, and I certainly didn't want Fierro, a man I'd looked up to, to be The Beast. That would mean that Fierro had killed Selleck's family! That didn't sit well with me at all.

Leona, who had decided to sleep next to me, must've noticed I was having trouble sleeping. I hadn't even seen that she was still awake, but the next thing I knew, she rubbed my hair softly and hummed a quiet tune in my ear. Her voice was sweet like honey and lulled me to sleep with ease.

Thanks to her and her gentle song, I didn't dream of my mother or Fierro. I didn't dream at all.

Chapter 23
Refuge for No One

After two weeks of consistent riding, we still hadn't caught up to Reyes. Selleck, as tolerant as he was of Leona's presence, blamed her. She wasn't an experienced rider, so she couldn't gallop as fast as we could. Not that Leona would've been able to, even if she were experienced. The mule she was on couldn't go nearly as fast as our horses. I tried to remind Selleck of that every time he complained about her lack of speed. I was sure she didn't understand every word he said, but she probably did comprehend that he was complaining about her.

It didn't seem to matter too much to her, though. This was all new to her. Specifically as the terrain changed from dry sandy desert to dry *rocky* desert. Although it looked almost the same to me, she always had something to comment on, even if her comments weren't always in English. She'd picked up quite a bit of English in the past few weeks of traveling with us, though, and was now able to communicate much better in English than either of us could in Spanish. That came with already *knowing* how to read in English, though: one can pick up speaking and understanding pretty fast once they associate the letters on the page together with the spoken word.

Plus, I had been reading to her. It happened one day when we were stopped to water the animals. She approached me with *her copy of Tom Sawyer* in hand and asked me to read to her aloud. Leona followed the words intently with her eyes as I read them, listening carefully to how I pronounced each word. She even read along quietly at times.

Leona wasn't the only person practicing something, either. I had to get my gunfighter training in, especially since my new peacemaker was different from my previous one. It was nickel-plated and had a longer barrel. Selleck told me it was a 'gunfighter colt' rather than the 'civilian model' I'd been carrying. He helped me out with practice a lot, too. Selleck had watched my duel with the Las Fuentes' Sheriff *very* closely and was able to tell me *everything* I'd done wrong in great detail. There was enough that he criticized about it that you'd think I had lost the duel!

We were disheartened when we saw Refugio again, though, rather than Reyes. I tried to keep an open mind about it, telling myself we'd passed him without knowing, but I knew the truth: the mule couldn't even go half as fast as our horses. It didn't have to stop for water as frequently as my new mare wanted to, but the mule wasn't fast.

"Let's go into town," Selleck said, riding alongside me, "See if Reyes has robbed the bank. If so, we should make our way back to Justicia."

We left the animals at the stable and walked into the town together.

Everything was in shambles. Buildings were burnt. Horses lay dead on the ground. There were spent bullet casings and shells lying everywhere. To top it all off, a wagon of bodies was being collected. It was obvious that Reyes had been here, and he'd done a number on the people to get revenge on us for stopping him. I felt guilty. There was a great stone in the pit of my stomach. I felt like throwing up. Reyes was a monster.

"Marshals!" A familiar voice cried out in desperation. Both Selleck and I got chills. The Mayor of Refugio ran up to us. "Marshals, am I glad to see you! Thank God you're here."

It was quite the change of pace from when we last saw the Mayor of Refugio. Selleck had threatened his life and scared the life out of him in an attempt to get him to treat his hired help better. We never expected that he would be *glad* to see us.

"Mayor," Selleck said calmly, tipping his hat.

"Oh, it was horrible, Mr. Selleck!" The Mayor exclaimed, "Bandits from Mexico rode into town, killing and burning everyone and everything in their way. They rode straight to the bank and stole *everything!* Our town is ruined! You must get the money back."

"Calm down, mayor." Selleck told the older man, "We're here to help. We are starving, though, from our ride here. Got anywhere to eat that isn't burnt, preferably?"

"I would invite you to my home, but that turned out *so well* last time..." The Mayor said sarcastically, seemingly remembering what had happened a little more than a month ago when Selleck and I were here, "However, there is a restaurant on the other side of town we can go to. The *banditos* stopped and fled once they hit the bank, so everything past it is ok." Leona giggled at the man, laughing at how he said '*banditos.*' He turned red in the face but didn't say anything.

He led us down to the restaurant. They were still open but didn't have any customers, so I am sure they were grateful for a party of four. Once we had sat down and ordered, the Mayor opened his mouth.

"They ran off towards the northwest." He said quickly, "Oh, it was so dreadful, Marshal. I can't explain it. They came and killed and robbed and–"

"We get the idea." Selleck cut the man off, "Where was your Sheriff during all this? You mean to tell me that the Sheriff and his deputies didn't try to stop them at all?"

"Well, the Sheriff... he was indisposed."

"What's that s'posed to mean?"

"He moved out further west. Said it had something to do with him being fired." The Mayor said with a sigh. He was sweating. Something was wrong.

"Now, tell me, why on earth would you go and do a thing like that?" Selleck said, narrowing his eyes at the man.

"Well, there was a good reason!" He replied nervously.

"Why haven't you replaced him either? That doesn't seem right to me."

"I swear, I have tried!"

"In fact, why are you still breathing?" Selleck asked, placing even more pressure on the man, "I say, if a Mayor can't find a replacement Sheriff, it becomes one of his mayoral duties to enforce the law. There's a lot of dead folk out there, Mr. Mayor. I find myself wondering if you weren't fulfilling your mayoral duty of law enforcement. Cause if you were, you should be on that cart of dead men."

The waiter brought us our steaks. Leona started digging in happily, but both Selleck and I were staring at Mayor White as though we were peering into his soul. He nervously shifted his gaze between the two of us as he started to sweat. Finally, he broke down crying. It was not quite as bad as when Selleck had shot at him, but bad enough that people started noticing.

"Oh, Mr. Selleck, you are right about me!" The man sobbed, "I am a coward and a liar. I fired the Sheriff and his deputies because they wouldn't go after *you*. I explained to them what had happened at my mansion the last time you were in town, and they agreed with *you!* I am such a horrible person; I didn't do anything to save the bank! Please, you have to help me!"

Selleck smirked and started cutting his steak. This was the first actual meal that had been presented to him since he was arrested in Las Fuentes. Still, he had waited until we got a confession from Mayor White to start eating. The Mayor was sobbing. Leona and Selleck were eating. I couldn't believe this. I just started laughing.

"Yes, laugh at me!" The Mayor exclaimed between sobs. "Laugh at how pathetic I am!"

"It's fine, Mayor." I finally remarked, taking a bite of my own steak, "We'll try and get your money back." I continued eating.

"Oh, thank you, Mr. Hendricks!" He groveled, "You will make a fine Marshal one day, just like Mr. Selleck!"

Selleck had emptied his plate rapidly. Mayor White had just finished his sentence when Selleck started hitting him with questions again.

"How many of them were there?" He asked, chewing his last bite. "Eyewitness reports say there were between twenty and thirty of them."

"That ain't very helpful, now is it?"

"I'm sorry, but I wasn't there to count them myself." The Mayor apologized. Selleck glared at him.

"You said they went northwest. All on horseback, or did they have a coach like last time?"

"They were all on horseback. That's how they were able to get in and out so fast. No loading of wagons or anything, just all grabbed what they could and left."

"How much did they take?"

"Nearly all of the money! Around probably ten thousand dollars! Or more! Twenty or thirty thousand!"

"That's a lot of money." Selleck sat back in his chair. "How much of it was yours?"

The Mayor went red in the face once more. He looked angry now. He stood up and opened his mouth to yell, but Leona started mimicking his crying from earlier. Embarrassed and beaten, he sat back down.

"How much is yours?" Selleck repeated the question.

"Probably most of it." White finally admitted defeatedly.

"*That's* why you're so earnest to get it back, I see..." Selleck teased the man.

"Please, sir," White begged. "Don't make me get on my hands and knees. I'll admit, you were right about everything. The servants, the Sheriff, even the money. But this town *needs* that money back. It *is* my fault that it was taken so easily. I promise that if you help me return it, I *will* do right by these people."

"Prove it." Selleck challenged.

"How?"

"Pay the check. For our meal."

"Sir, I just had nearly all my money stolen!"

"Sell something if you have to." Selleck leaned forward in his chair. "Your place has some nice furniture. While you're at it, Mr. Hendrick's girlfriend needs a new mount." It was my turn to blush, apparently. "The Mule she's on isn't fast enough. And some new clothes for her and Ace. Mexican traditional ain't exactly their style."

The Mayor shot me a defeated look. I just shrugged and laughed. Leona smiled. Mayor White just nodded finally. He'd do it.

We managed to get some clothing and supplies for the road, too. As comfy as the traditional Mexican clothes Leona had given me were, I was thrilled to be in something a little more to my taste. Leona was as thrilled as anyone could be. I guess it didn't matter where the girl was from, she loved shopping. No one proved that more true than Leona. She wanted to try on all the dresses, but we were crunched for time. She eventually settled on a plain blue prairie dress after I promised to buy her something more fancy later.

Once we were back at the stables, Leona had managed to trade the old mule so that Mr. White could get a discount. She still picked whatever horse she wanted, disregarding the price. She ended up with a spotted Highland Pony colt they had in the stables. It was tall for a pony but still shorter than an average horse. A good size for Leona, though, who was giddy as she could be to have her own horse. Apparently, much to the dismay of the man footing the bill, it was a purebred, too, with papers anDeverything. Some German merchant had traded it for a draft horse after one of his died. I thought the Mayor was going to have a heart attack.

Finally, we hit the road again. Selleck rode point, but I rode alongside Leona to talk with her for a while.

"How do you feel?" I asked once we were out of town. She shot me a *huge* smile.

"Very nice." She told me excitedly. I could tell she was delighted with her new steed and belongings. "Never had my own horse before. And also, I never had a blue dress before."

"You look beautiful," I replied. Leona giggled, and I turned red. "I mean... The dress looks beautiful on you." I was trying to save myself from further embarrassment, but I got even more embarrassed.

"Thank you, Asa." She told me as she fluttered her eyelashes. I felt my face turn into a beet. She laughed more.

"What will you call your horse?" I said, trying to change the subject.

"He will be called... Rocinante." She responded. "Because of Don Quijote's horse."

"What does that mean?" I asked. Leona shrugged. I had a feeling that it wasn't a widespread term.

"You'll have to explain to me the Tale of Don Quijote one of these days."

"I can't." She told me, "Too hard."

"Well, we'll find an English translation. There's probably one out there. I am not sure what to call this one yet." I patted the mare on her neck. She let out a small whinny.

Leona was deep in thought for a moment. She stared at the pale mare for some time. "Call her 'Aunt Polly'." She said, referencing *Tom Sawyer*.

"That's not a bad idea. I'll call her Polly." I gently stroked the horse's mane. "You're not too bad at naming horses, Leona."

Leona laughed. I felt happy to have met her.

"We gotta pick up the pace, lovebirds," Selleck called back to us. Blood rushed to my cheeks, "Kid, you help Leona learn to gallop better. We have a long way to Justicia, and we have to get there before Reyes."

"Hang on!" I yelled up to Selleck. I galloped my horse to ride next to him. "Listen, I know that Justicia is at risk, but Reyes will beat us there."

"How do you figure?" Selleck asked. "We've made good time so far. They beat us to Refugio, but now that your girlfriend has a real horse and boots, we can ride faster. Catch Reyes before he gets to Justicia."

"She's *not* my girlfriend, Selleck." I protested. He shook his head.

"Doesn't matter. I see the way you look at her. You're falling for that girl." He told me. I turned pink once more.

"He beat us by several *days*," I explained, ignoring his comment about Leona. "He's probably almost to or already at Justicia. Even if we ride through the night and all day tomorrow, he will have been through Justicia already. We are just chasing him at this point."

"So what do you wanna do then, Ace?"

"We try to beat him to Folklore. We know he's gonna end up there. I feel bad for Justicia; I do. Folk there were good to us. But all we can do is pray for them at this point. We ain't gonna beat Reyes there. If we want to get Reyes and Fierro, we need to go to Folklore."

Selleck thought for a moment. "Eventually," he sighed.

"You're right, kid." He said painfully, "He's probably at Justicia right now or on his way to Folklore. The road to Folklore is shorter from here than from Justicia. We might beat him or, at the very least, get there before Reyes can cause too much damage. Unfortunately, you're right."

"I feel bad." I told him, "I hate being right about this. Those were good people."

"That's what being a lawman is about, kid," He explained, putting a hand on my shoulder, "You have to make hard decisions sometimes to save more people. Sometimes that includes a sacrifice."

I slowed back down to ride next to Leona. I tried my best to instruct her how to ride a little better, and then we set off towards Folklore.

Chapter 24
The Battle of Folklore

By the time we arrived in Folklore, the sun was setting. We were exhausted. We had been riding nearly non-stop since leaving Refugio, about a week's ride typically. We made it in four days. Selleck had decided that we didn't need to spare the horses. They could rest all they wanted when we got Luis Reyes. All that mattered at this point was stopping him.

Our hopes were that we had arrived at Folklore before Reyes; that way, we could ambush him and his men. Unfortunately, gunshots from the town told us that we had not beaten him. Despite this, the shots also meant we were still on time. We could still stop Reyes and Fierro.

The three of us rode into town and dismounted behind a building on the main street. The Sheriff was taking cover behind an upturned wagon. We didn't see any of his deputies.

"Sheriff!" I called out to him. He was across the street, but there was a break in the gunfire, so he looked over.

"Hendricks?" He said, clearly confused at why I was there. "We're here to help," I told him.

"Thank the Lord because I don't have a single deputy left. They all either died or deserted, the cowards."

"How many are there?" Selleck asked with gun in hand.

"Can't tell. Maybe ten?" The Sheriff said. He peeked over his meager cover, "The rest ran off towards the northeast. Towards Hendricks' Ranch."

"Any way past 'em?" I asked, "I need to save my uncle."

"I'm afraid not, son." Sheriff said, "They've set up a Gatling gun on the road."

"A Gatling gun?" Selleck exclaimed. "That thing'll tear us to shreds!"

"That's what I am trying to take care of."

There was silence for a moment. We heard Reyes' men at the end of the street, wondering if the Sheriff was dead. I swallowed hard.

"Sheriff, I'll distract the Gatling gun." I told him, trying to sound confident, "You route them and attack from another angle."

"No way, kid." He shook his head. "They don't even know you guys have arrived. I'll distract. You get up on the saloon's balcony and hit the Gatling from up there."

"Go, Ace!" Selleck told me, giving me a shove towards the back alley. "I'll stay here and help the Sheriff."

I drew my peacemaker and ran through the alley. I almost didn't see Leona at my heels. I wanted to tell her to stay with Selleck, but the sound of the Gatling gun drew my attention away. It sounded like a thousand stampeding bulls, with hooves of thunder. It made Leona jump and cling to me. She probably didn't know what was happening since there was never mention of a Gatling gun in *Tom Sawyer*. I tried to shove her away, but her grip was tight.

"It's gonna be ok," I whispered to her ear. "I will protect you."

This pacified her a little because I could finally escape her terrified grip. She still followed me, though, but that was fine. At least she wasn't slowing me down.

We went to the back door of the saloon. I almost pushed the door open, but I heard voices yelling inside. What they were saying was drowned out by the constant gunfire, but there were thugs inside the saloon, that was for sure.

I crouched down and pulled my knife. I'd never killed a man with a knife before, but three months ago, I'd never killed anyone at all, so I supposed there was a first for everything. I told Leona to stay put. I didn't know if she'd listen.

I sneaked through the door. It would have made a lot of noise with its usual creaking, but the guns outside drowned it out. The saloon smelled of black powder and whiskey. I only saw one man inside, stamping out a cigarette. He had his back turned to me. This was my chance.

I crept up behind him, reading the knife. I grabbed his shoulder and plunged the blade into his back. He yelped and groaned. I stabbed him again and again. He wouldn't be quiet! Finally, his groans were replaced by the sound of gargling. I must've pierced one of his lungs. I didn't even have time to think about what had happened, though; before I knew it, someone grabbed me on the shoulders and threw me hard against the wall.

Another thug pulled his sidearm and plunged it in my face. I grabbed it hard before he pulled the hammer back, stopping it with my thumb. He tried to jerk free, but my grip held true. I punched his wrist hard with my free hand until the pistol came loose. I yanked it back and threw it up the saloon stairs, keeping the weapon away from him.

No sooner than I'd done that, a bony fist cracked my jaw. I went tumbling to the ground, barely maintaining consciousness. I woke up just in time to feel the large thug's toes slam themselves into my gut. I gasped for air and felt blood in my mouth. The foot recoiled back and kicked again, but I grabbed it this time. He tried to pull his boot away, but I hugged it tightly. The thug bent down and grabbed my shirt. He slammed my head into the plank floor a few times. I felt woozy. I couldn't fight back. He finally grabbed my throat in both hands and squeezed till his knuckles turned white. I didn't have enough consciousness to fight back effectively. I panicked and flailed, trying to hit the large man. I was powerless against him.

Until a thin arm grabbed him around the neck. A second fragile-looking hand came down on his shoulder, plunging my knife into the man's clavicle. He started screaming. The hands let go. He spun around.

I managed to sit up and catch my breath. I heard a woman screeching. The thug threw up his arms in an attempt to defend himself. Blood and skin went flying as Leona slashed down on his arms rapidly. She grabbed his hair and yanked his head down. She stabbed his gut again and again. She pulled the knife out of his abdomen and slammed it into his back until, finally, he fell to the ground.

The knife clattered to the wooden floor, and Leona also went down, covered in blood. She held her legs to her chest and panted rapidly. I crawled over to her, hugging her. She'd just taken a man's life in the most brutal way possible, I might add. She was panicking. I hugged her and rocked her gently until her heart slowed and her breathing calmed.

"You're not hurt?" She finally asked. I shook my head. "No. You saved me, Leona. Thank you."

"Asa..." She whispered, pushing my head away gently. There was blood on her face, but it wasn't hers. I pulled out a handkerchief and cleaned it. She stared at me with her large hazel eyes but said nothing.

"We need to go upstairs." I finally said, remembering the Gatling gun, which had stopped momentarily to reload. Leona just nodded.

I passed her the pistol once we arrived up the saloon stairs. I didn't intend for her to use it, but I told her that if she needed to, she would have to. She was still visibly shaken from the fight but seemed to understand. I wished more than ever that I could comfort the girl. This wasn't what she had in mind when she said she wanted to come with me.

I left her in one of the saloon's upper rooms and had her lock the door behind me. I still had unfinished business.

I ran outside as the Gatling gun started firing again. I was on the balcony of the saloon, and the thugs on the ground hadn't seen me yet. This was a reasonably short shot, only twenty yards, but I wouldn't have any cover once I fired. The Gatling would tear me to shreds if I missed.

I aimed carefully. My heart pounded, and my ears rang. The Gatling was deafening. Finally, I took my shot. It struck its target, the thug's chest peeking over the powerful gun. He fell over backward, pulling the large firearm down with him.

Confusion spread through the rest of the men. There were seven of them left. All of them were down by the wagon where the Gatling had been. They pointed up at the balcony, at me. I cursed and tried to run inside, but a wall of bullets blocked my path. I ran the opposite way. I didn't have anywhere to go but down. I vaulted the railing, swearing as I did. I crashed and rolled onto the ground and into the ditch, right out of the line of fire of the rest of the thugs. I breathed easy for a moment, but only a moment. They weren't thirty yards from me and would be on me in seconds. I had to act fast. I started crawling through the grass like a snake, trying to reach the road behind them. If I could do that, I could catch them by surprise and... then what? I only had five rounds left in my revolver, and there were seven of them. Even if I was fast and accurate enough to take one down with each round, there would still be two left.

I had forgotten about Selleck and the Sheriff, who, once the Gatling gunman was taken out, had started pressing forward. They were in range now and began opening fire once I felt that all was lost. I jumped up from the grass and saw them engaged in a firefight with the seven thugs.

I charged the one nearest to me, who was taking cover behind the wall of the saloon. The unsightly man saw me and turned to meet my fire, but my gun was already cocked and trained. I fired one round into his chest. He slid down against the wall, leaving a trail of red fluid behind him. I pushed his body aside with a boot and took his place. It was over for the last six. We had them surrounded.

They didn't surrender, though. I saw one fall after another. One of them had a Springfield rifle and fired toward someone I couldn't see. I heard a man cry out and fall after the shot. I fired two shots at the Springfield thug. Both hit him in the side, and he dropped dead. The last three turned towards me. They had forgotten about me. I shot one in the head, and the other two fell from bullets that rained on them from down the street. All of Reyes' men in Folklore were dead.

We had won the Battle of Folklore. There wasn't time to celebrate, though. I heard a man yell, the Sheriff.

"Hendricks!" He cried out loudly. I holstered my gun and rounded the corner. The Sheriff was crouching over Selleck. Matthew Selleck was the man who had been shot!

"Selleck!" I screamed in horror. I sprinted over as fast as I could, sliding in the dirt on my knees when I got close.

"It's bad." The Sheriff explained. He had his bloody hands pressed on Selleck's thigh. "He's been shot in the leg. Could be femoral artery. We need the doctor, now!"

"Go get him!" I barked. He moved his hands, and scarlet ichor sprayed out of the wound. I shoved my own hands down hard on it.

"Kid." Selleck groaned out painfully. "You better not be crying."

"In your dreams, old man!" I tried to play along. "This is just a flesh wound."

"I don't know about that." He started to close his eyes. "Feeling *real* light-headed right now."

"Never mind that, old timer!" I yelled, trying to remain calm. Leona ran over from the inside of the saloon and helped me put pressure on the wound, "You ain't gonna die."

"When did you become a doctor?" Selleck remarked, putting on a painful smile.

"Leona's basically a doctor," I told him. I turned my head to match her eyes, "Tell him he's gonna be fine, Leona!"

She stared at me with her mouth open. What was she supposed to do or say? She just shrugged without a word.

"Don't bully your girlfriend, kid." Selleck barked, "Talk to me about something, Ace."

"Um… What's your big dream, Selleck?" I asked him, trying to keep him awake. He pondered the question momentarily.

"I always wanted to see the world." He told me after thinking for a moment. "This country is beautiful, but I can't help but think there is more to see elsewhere, too."

"Where do you want to go?" I asked, "We can save up cash and go when you retire. Just the three of us."

Selleck thought for a moment. I adjusted my hands, trying to cause him a little pain to see if he was still awake.

"Australia." He said weakly, "I'd like to go to Australia."

"Ain't that a country full of criminals?" I teased.

"No better place for a lawman, right?" He laughed, "I've heard that Australia's not like anywhere else in the world, that God got tired of making everything the same by the time he got around to making Australia, so he made everything different. All kinds of crazy animals down there, kid. At least that's what they tell me."

"We'll go then!" I told him, holding back tears, "You can tell me about all the animals and things that are strange there later."

Finally, the Sheriff ran over with the doctor.

"Yeah, we should go," Selleck said, laughing weakly. The Doc ran over. "He's lost a lot of blood," I told him. "Still has the bullet in him, too."

"This isn't good." Doc said, examining the leg, "I can't do this by myself, but my daughter, your aunt, Asa, is still at Hendricks' ranch. I need a nurse."

"I will help." Leona finally said. She had a look of determination in her eyes. "Is she a nurse?" Doc asked me.

"Not exactly, but she's as good as you'll get now." I explained, "She dug a bullet out of me a few weeks ago."

"Fine, she'll do. Go save my daughter, Asa."

I looked up at Leona. I didn't want to leave Selleck but trusted her with his life. She was already busy at work with the doctor.

"Leona," I whispered. She looked up at me. I didn't know what to say, so I kissed her on the cheek. She turned pink but smiled slightly. I couldn't help but return it with a huge smile of my own.

"Come back to me when you kill Reyes." She whispered. She looked sad, and separating from her for the first time since I'd met her hurt my heart like it was breaking in two.

"Let's go, Ace!" The Sheriff said, pulling my shoulder. I took one last look at Leona, just in case it would be my last, then mounted Polly and started the ride to Hendricks' Ranch with the Sheriff.

Chapter 25
Ambush on the Road

The night was starting to fall as the Sheriff and I mounted up. Leona was busy helping the doctor attend to Selleck, but I felt her looking at me as we started the ride to the Ranch. I hadn't realized this before, but she and I had grown *very* close over the past few weeks. We hadn't separated until now, at least not since I met her. Like a shadow, she was always by my side, hanging over my shoulder quietly. I never felt annoyed by it, though. I'd never gotten much attention from girls before, so Leona's constant presence was welcome.

Leona always made me happy. She always asked me to read to her so that she could learn more English. She always sang and hummed to me when I couldn't sleep, and always slept next to me, just talking and learning. I had learned a lot about her, even though we weren't able to communicate very well. I'd discovered that she loved to read, that she was smart, that she was a good talker, and that she had a perfect memory. Leona could remember anything she had seen or read.

To sum things up, I felt connected to Leona in a way I had never felt with anyone before. She was kind, brave, and had a sense of righteousness that made Selleck seem like an evil man.

At this point, leaving her felt like I was abandoning a part of myself. I wanted to be with her always. Selleck always teased me about her, but now I knew he was right; perhaps I was in love with Leona. I promised myself I would do right by her and stay alive for her. She'd saved my life, so I would repay her by continually trying to do my best.

Right now, though, the task at hand was Reyes. The Sheriff and I galloped down the road in the dark. The horses were sweating. Polly, the poor horse, had just gotten done traveling such a long distance that I thought she would give out on me or throw me. I was riding her to death.

"Just a little more, girl," I promised her, stroking her mane gently.

That's when I heard it. A single gunshot rang out, then a second and a third. Blood erupted in front of me like a volcano. A horrible screech filled the air. Had I just been shot?

The next thing I knew, I was on the ground. The wind was knocked out of me. I felt my chest for gunshot wounds, but there were none. An almost human-like moan and whimper sounded out. The pale mare, Polly, lay on the ground, wheezing, panting, and kicking her legs. She was still trying to run and force herself to get up. Although we hadn't been together long, she was loyal as any horse, probably more so.

I scrambled through the dust over to her. I touched her face. She screeched and whinnied in pain. I pulled my knife. I couldn't let the poor girl suffer anymore.

"I'm sorry, Polly," I whispered in her ear as I plunged the knife into her powerful neck, ending her misery quickly. I felt tears burn my eyes. That's when more gunshots rang out. There was so much smoke and dust that I couldn't see anything. I heard the Sheriff curse and swear. He fired his revolver back at the unseen enemy.

I was tired of this nonsense. I drew my gun and let out a loud war cry.

"I will kill you all!" I roared, charging up the hill to the grove where the gunfire came from. Bullets erupted and ricocheted all around me, but I didn't care. One grazed my cheekbone, but it was already too late. There were four men in the trees with rifles. I took aim and fired. The one I'd been aiming at started tumbling down the hill. I blasted another and a third. The fourth started running. I gave chase.

"Leave me alone!" He cried as we ran through the woods.

"You should'a left *me* alone, you rat!" I roared like a wild animal.

I picked up a discarded gun, a Remington Rolling Block, and chased the man. Once I had a shot with the rifle, I took it. The bullet tore through his shoulder viciously and sent him to the ground. I ran at him. He rolled himself over and took aim at me with his pistol. I shot my revolver from the hip, blasting a hole right through his forearm.

"I'm getting *real* tired of you idiots," I growled. He started sobbing.

"Please don't kill me, mister." He begged, "I d-didn't want to, but they made me!"

I grabbed the man by his shirt and hoisted him to his feet. I slammed his back into a tree and pointed the barrel of my gun at his chin. In the moonlight, I finally got a good look at him. He was just a boy, no older than sixteen. What was he doing working for Reyes?

"You didn't want to, hm?" I grumbled, knocking his chin with my handgun. "Well, you should've thought of that!"

"Please, mister!" He cried, clasping his hands together, "I just want to go home! See my mama. Please, if you let me go, I will leave and never come back. I'll be done, I promise!"

I clenched my jaw, gritting my teeth together. I tried to convince myself that I hated this kid. He seemed so terrified. It reminded me of myself when I saw Fierro become a wild animal, just as I was doing now.

I tightened my grip on his shirt and gun. I wanted to kill him so badly, I told myself. It would be so easy to spatter his pathetic brains everywhere. I was gonna do it, I tried to convince myself.

Fierro kept coming back to mind. Selleck too. I remembered when Selleck had terrified Mayor White in his mansion. He could've killed him, but he didn't. Who did I want to be like?

Did I want people to fear me, like Fierro, or did I want people to respect me like they did Selleck? This was the turning point. I knew it.

I pulled the hammer back on my gun, ready to send a bullet into his head. He cried out, but I couldn't hear it over the blood rushing through my ears. I wanted to kill him so bad, but I couldn't. My finger, as though it had a mind of its own, wouldn't pull the trigger. This kid didn't have anything to do with my fight with Reyes. I knew that.

I yanked his green bandana from his neck. He stared at me in surprise. I tossed him to the ground. He grunted but couldn't believe it. I had spared him. The part of me that wanted to be a hero wouldn't let me kill this kid. It wasn't in my nature, and my own body was defying my will because of that.

"Go home, kid." I told him as I started to reload my gun, "Reyes and his men are gonna die tonight. Don't let yourself be a victim of this war. Go to your mama. Tell her you're sorry and live out the rest of your days in peace."

The kid was silent. I started to walk away. I heard him sobbing now, this time from relief. "Thank you, mister." He shouted as I started to exit the forest, "I'm going home. I promise."

I sighed. The Sheriff was waiting on his horse. Poor Polly lay on the ground motionless. I shook my head and leaned down to close her eyes. I whispered an apology to her before turning to the Sheriff.

"Must've been a good horse." He remarked, throwing a cigarette into the dust.

"Shouldn't have worked her so hard." I said, ignoring his comment, "She didn't deserve this death."

"No horse does." He commented, "They say God gave men rule over all the beasts of the field, except for the horses. They had their freedom but gave themselves up to men."

"Let's get going." I mounted up behind him. His horse huffed as though to say goodbye to a comrade in arms.

I couldn't help but feel relieved, though. Up until now, everyone I'd killed had been a sinful person. Up until now, everyone whom I'd had the opportunity to kill either deserved it or was trying to kill me. I hadn't killed that boy, though. I hadn't made myself into a murderer.

We rode silently the rest of the way to the Ranch. I prayed we'd get there in time. As we neared the Ranch, the black sky glowed with an orange light. My heart started to sink.

Chapter 26
Hell on Earth, Part One

When we arrived at the ranch, you could've told me that the Sheriff and I had ridden into Hell, and I would've believed you. I didn't see a difference.

Everything was on fire. The barns, the houses, the sheds, and the foreman's office. Ash was in the air, and smoke filled the night. The cattle and horses screeched and brayed as they were burned alive. Worse yet were the screams of the people.

Everywhere, women and children screamed and fled. Men were whipped and pulled by horses or shot. It was a nightmare. Even the Sheriff's horse had to stop and pause to see the horror.

I couldn't pause. I had too much at stake. I thought of my Aunt, Uncle, and Tabitha. Somewhere on the other side of the ranch, they were there in this Hell. The Sheriff's horse refused to go further as if the colt knew that it surely meant death. The Sheriff was as fearless as I was and dismounted to follow, shotgun in hand.

"Mr. Hendricks!" One of the women ran to me. Her dress was torn, and she looked like she'd been beaten. I didn't recognize her, but she was probably one of the ranch hand's wives. "Oh, thank God you're here! Please, you have to go help my husband! These men are monsters!"

"Where are my aunt and uncle?"

"I think they are at the ranch house," she said, losing herself momentarily. "You're gonna help us, ain't ya?"

I wanted to say no, but people needed someone in a nightmare like this. I looked at the Sheriff.

He had a grim expression on his face as though he were losing hope. I sighed and drew my gun. "Show me," I said, regaining my determination.

The woman led us to a nearby home. Green-bandanas were beating a man whose hands they'd tied to a post. He wouldn't last much longer.

I didn't say a word. I leveled my gun and fired three shots. All three hit their mark and sent the men to the ground. The Sheriff drew a knife and cut the man free. He couldn't walk and was missing most of his teeth, but he was thankful that the beating had stopped.

"What are we gonna do, Sheriff?" I asked. He looked back at me.

"We gotta do what we can." He answered grimly, "These devils have brought Hell to your little ranch. These people need you."

"I'm no angel, sheriff," I told him, "I need to help my Aunt and Uncle. I can't save everyone."

"Well, you're the closest thing they have right now. You may not be an angel, but if you have the power to do something and you don't, you may as well have raped and murdered these people yourself. I've known your Uncle since he was a kid, Ace, and I know that ain't what he would want."

I bit my lip. The Sheriff was right. I couldn't stand by and let these people suffer. I knew that he was right about my Uncle, too. That isn't what my mother would want if she was really the woman I knew. I nodded.

"Listen, ma'am," I said, getting the attention of the man's wife. "Get what you can from those bodies. Arm yourself. We need to fight."

She swallowed hard but didn't protest. We would show these demons that they'd come to the wrong ranch. The Hendricks ilk weren't just gonna lie down and die like dogs. If we were going down, we were gonna take as many of Reyes' scum as possible.

The ranch hand's wife scurried off into the backyard of one of the houses, toting all three guns.

There was a potato cellar detached from the building. When she appeared again, two more people followed, an older woman and a young boy about the age of fourteen. Both had determined looks on their faces. They were prepared to fight to defend their homes.

Smoke darkened the sky, blocking the moon and stars, but the orange flames lit up the air with a hellish glow. Our little posse marched down the road of the small ranch village until we saw some of Reyes' green-bandanas trying to drag some women to a wagon.

They saw us, too, armed and ready to fight and dropped what they were doing. They opened fire, but smoke clouded their vision. Bullets rained all around. I hit the dirt.

"Take cover!" The Sheriff yelled. I couldn't see where they ran off to. The bandits were still firing, but they must not have seen me on the ground. I pulled the hammer back and took aim. A loud crack ripped through the air as my gun expelled fire like a great dragon. One of the men dropped. This one-shot inspired many like it, coming from somewhere behind me. One by one, the men all dropped as they tried to fire back. The first woman ran out from cover, nearly stepping on me to make sure the others were ok.

"Aunt Hannah!" One of the girls called out as she saw the ranch hand's wife. The two embraced.

"Kimberly, where are your father and mother."

The girl, Kimberly, looked down at the ground. Her face was covered in ash and soot. She'd been in a fire recently, probably the building up in flames not too far behind her.

"I ain't sure." She finally answered, shrugging. Hannah hugged her.

"We'll find them, baby girl." She consoled the poor lass. "Ain't that right, Mr. Hendricks?"

"I promise you, Kimberly, we will," I answered, unsure if I should approach.

"Young Mr. Hendricks has been riding with a real marshal for the past few months. If anyone can find them, he will."

I was impressed with this woman, Hannah. She was probably around the same age as my mom, in her mid-thirties. She was a natural leader and a strong, courageous woman.

"Let's get going." Sheriff interrupted, "There's still a lot of people unaccounted for."

"You're right, Sheriff." Hannah agreed. "Kimberly, dear, head to the Thompson's house. Behind it, in their potato cellar, there's a few girls taking refuge. You'll be safe there. The rest of you ladies, grab the guns and bullets from those smelly corpses there and come with us!"

We gave them a minute or two to get the guns reloaded and ready. Many of these women, as it turns out, had used guns before to kill raccoons and other varmints while their husbands were away working the fields. Some of them, like Hannah, were crack shots too.

We continued our march through the fiery farm, amassing more boys and women into our group and fighting off the bandits. Many of the men were beaten and whipped so they couldn't fight. Hannah and the Sheriff sent them back to the potato cellar safehouse, and we would continue.

Finally, we made it to the end of the road. There wasn't any home past here besides the large ranch house. That's where my Aunt and Uncle would be since there was no sign of either of them, not even among the fallen. I was relieved that they weren't dead, at least not to our knowledge, but the fact that we hadn't seen Reyes or Fierro didn't calm my nerves.

"Looks like that's all of the snakes. Let's get these fires out!" Hannah ordered her troop of women and boys. "Find every bucket you can, and let's pull water from the wells and river. Move it!"

The militia dispersed every which way, some going to sheds, others dumping slop and hay from the feeding troughs between two of them and using the mangers to fill with water. I was rightly impressed and proud of the women of the ranch.

After barking her commands out like some military sergeant, she turned to me and the Sheriff. "What will you two do?" Hannah asked.

"What do you mean?" The Sheriff said, cocking an eyebrow. "Show me where a bucket is, and I will help put out the flames. It's my job to protect *and* serve, ain't it?"

"Thank you kindly, sheriff." Hannah smiled before turning to me. "A few men rode up to the ranch house before you two got here. You should hurry on up."

"I reckon so." I remarked, looking around, "Any horses ready?" The Sheriff blew a sharp whistle, and his colt came trotting over. He patted it on the head and grabbed the reins. He walked over to me and placed them in my hand.

"Go, son." He nodded. "Save your Aunt and Uncle if you can. If it's too late, put a bullet in those scumbags. For Folklore."

I thanked the Sheriff and Hannah, then mounted up on the old Kentucky horse. I started to reload my gun, but I only had three cartridges left. My heart raced rapidly as I began to gallop down the road.

Three shots didn't leave me with much breathing room. Hannah said she'd seen three men ride up to the ranch; that was one shot for each of them, Reyes, Fierro, and the third man, probably Reyes' second in command, one of the men who was at Boca del Lobo when Reyes shot me. I would have to shoot with absolute confidence that my aim was true and not waste a single shot.

I pushed my nervousness away when the ranch house came into view from the trees.

Chapter 27
Hell on Earth, Part Two

As I approached the house, the smoke didn't clear, and I soon saw why. The large ranch house was entirely up in a blaze, along with the stables next to it and the forest around it. Why burn it all, though?

I rode down the road, nearing the blaze. The Sheriff's colt slowed, not wanting to continue toward the fire. This ended up saving my life because right as he slowed, I saw a man leveling a double-barreled shotgun at my head.

I threw myself off to the colt's side, narrowly avoiding the buckshot that would've taken off my head. I hit the ground hard but was thankful to be uninjured. The second barrel got unloaded into the horse's flank, wounding and frightening the colt. It limped off faster than I could run, leaving me alone with the Bear of a man who was Reyes' second in command. I recognized him from Boca del Lobo.

He'd been the one to pick up my Winchester repeater. There was no sign of the gun, though.

I leveled my pistol at him as he fumbled to open the breech of the shotgun, but I doubted as I was about to take the shot. I couldn't afford to miss it, and with the smoke and ash burning and obscuring my vision, I didn't feel good about my aim. I holstered my pistol and charged the man.

He fumbled around with two of his shotgun shells but saw me approaching fast. Would he try to finish loading the coach gun, or would he fight? He knew, as well as I did, that I would have the upper hand if he made a mistake in choosing the wrong one.

Unfortunately for him, he did indeed choose the wrong one. He continued trying to load the shells, but he hadn't blown out the barrels. Black powder and residue from repeated firing of the gun made the shells challenging to load. As I neared, I grabbed the long gun with one hand and popped him on the chin with the other. He stumbled to the side, dropping the shotgun shells into the grass as he did. His bandolier was empty. He had no choice but to fight me hand to hand.

He closed the breech and swung the shotgun at me like a club. I ducked it and tried to draw my peacemaker again but got hit in the side with a returning backhand swing. The wood cracked against my ribs. Pain shot all up the left side of my body. I stumbled back but couldn't stay out of the fight for long. He had dropped the shotgun, whose stock had shattered against my ribcage, and was now fumbling with the clasp of his military-style field holster. His hands were covered in sweat, and he probably still wasn't entirely conscious after that hard punch I'd given him. I couldn't let him draw his handgun, though. I ran at him wildly. I grabbed his jacket and tried to yank him around.

We were in a grapple now. The Bear grabbed my shoulders and tried to throw me to the side, but my grip held true. I threw a knee up into his gut, and he doubled over. He was strong, though, and when he recovered, he was mad! He pulled me off my feet by my neck and threw me to the ground. I landed on my back, sending the breath from my body.

The Bear had lost his gun in the grapple, though, so he'd have to use the one weapon he had left: a long, sharp bowie knife. He stepped over my body and tried to plunge the weapon down to stab me. I grabbed his wrist with both hands, stopping his attack dead in its tracks. He shoved the hilt of the knife down with his other hand, trying to use his massive size and weight against me. I couldn't hold his blade back for long.

I rapidly swung my leg up and around his, pulling my body back down with it. He plunged his knife into the ground in front of my face, and I bit his hand hard. He shouted and kicked me in the stomach, which sent me rolling a good few yards. I was out of immediate danger, though, so my plan had worked.

He pulled his bowie knife from the ground, but the tip was snapped off. It must've hit a rock that had been buried. His approach felt like being charged by a bull. He was too massive and fast to run from. He slashed the dagger down. I jumped back, barely avoiding being cut. I reached for my own knife but cursed when I realized that I hadn't picked it back up after Leona had killed the man in town with it.

He slashed repeatedly. His long reach, extended even more by the large knife, made it impossible to get any hits in without getting cut, which I wasn't too keen on doing. I had no choice.

I pulled my peacemaker to my hip, knocking the hammer back with my left hand as I did. I saw fear in the Bear's eyes. He threw the knife at me, forcing me to step out of the way. The knife went flying into the blazing woods somewhere.

It hadn't been his intention to hit me with the blade, though. That had just been a distraction. He tackled me in a giant bear hug, sending both of us to the ground. I dropped my gun and ended up underneath his crushing weight.

He postured up, sending both of his giant fists crashing down on my face. After the first few blows, I threw my arms up to defend. He punched my arms with mighty maces for hands.

He paused for a second, trying to catch his breath. I used this pause to my advantage. I pulled myself up and wrapped my arms around his neck. I grabbed his ear with my teeth and bit down viciously, as hard as I possibly could. Metallic-tasting fluid filled my mouth as the man screeched like a wild animal. He grabbed my face with one hand and pushed himself off. A horrendous tearing sound filled the air. More hot blood flew all over my face and chest as I realized I still had his ear in my mouth, but he had pulled himself away. He clutched the side of his head, which was shedding blood in a steady stream. He screamed and cursed and swore. I spit the mangled and torn ear out, feeling a little disgusted. I shook my head, trying to rid myself of the desire to vomit.

The Bear turned to me; his eyes burned with rage. He charged, but his anger was too blinding to him. I ran out of the way at the last minute, and he nearly ran right into the blaze. I knew what to do.

I ran up behind him and sent my boots careening into his back, dropkicking him. I crashed into the dirt, but he went straight into the hellish flames. I heard him cry and scream like a wild beast. His dark silhouette danced and flailed as the fire licked and stuck to him like a predator teasing its prey.

Finally, the screams stopped, and his shadow disappeared to be consumed by the ash.

I sighed loudly, trying to catch my breath. My side ached. My arms ached. Everything, my whole body, was hurting. I staggered over to my pistol and checked to ensure everything was okay. I didn't see any damage. The fact that I still had all three rounds was a good sign, too. I holstered the handgun and started limping up toward the burning ranch house. I had to find Reyes.

I was so focused on Reyes that I didn't notice the wild, sporadic footsteps approaching me from behind. A blazing devil grabbed me in a hug. The flames licked my skin and burned my clothes. The Bear was alive. He wouldn't survive long, but I suppose that when Hell called him, he told the Devil he wouldn't be going without me.

I squirmed and gasped as the flames burned the air around me. The flaming devil threw me around his hips, slamming me to the ground once more. The sclera of his eyes glowed red as though the very hatred in his heart had taken over his mind. He seemed as though he didn't feel his burning clothes consuming his skin and tissues, but I sure did! He wrapped his charred fingers around my neck, determined to finish me.

I kicked and squirmed. The flames were hot. I felt my muscles getting weak. I had to do something, anything. If not, I would lose my life, and my family would lose everything.

My salvation finally came as I felt something hard. I could just barely reach my gun! I drew it up quickly and fired up at his chin. His blood and charred flesh sputtered everywhere. He stopped for a moment, and I feared that he wasn't going to die, but then he fell like a log to the side.

I gasped for air while I beat the flames out of my clothes. I looked over at the ashy corpse lying next to me, fearing that he would stand up again if I moved, but that wasn't the case. The Bear was dead, and no amount of luck or deals with the Devil would change that. I could breathe easily, at least for now.

That is, until I remembered my purpose in being here. I couldn't rest. I had to get up to the farmhouse, even if it killed me at this point. I stood to my feet painfully and made my way up the hill. I didn't even bother holstering my gun this time.

Chapter 28
The King

"Reyes!" I roared as I rounded the corner of the blazing house. All eyes were on me.

Tabitha and Rachel were tied up to a horse post. Iron was tied to it, too, presumably acting as Reyes' mount since I killed his horse in Boca del Lobo. Reyes and Wesley were standing in front of the cellar doors, which were wide open. There was no sign of Fierro. Reyes looked up from my Uncle, whom he had been beating, and smiled at me. He had Selleck's Winchester on his back.

"You're still alive, kid?" He shouted, clearly impressed that I was standing there before him. "I shouldn't be surprised, I guess. You are Caroline's son, after all. At this point, I shouldn't be surprised if the woman herself comes around that corner." He let out a sinister laugh. He threw Wesley to the ground and turned to face me head-on. I raised my gun at him. He raised his hands above his head.

"Where's Fierro?" I growled exhaustedly. Reyes started to chuckle.

"You fought El Oso, didn't you?" He asked, referring to the giant of a man I had just killed, "Is he dead?"

"What do you think?" I spat. "Answer the question. Where is Fierro?"

"Long gone." He remarked with a smile. "He took the money and left when your Uncle finally showed us where it was. We are gonna meet up later."

"Say goodbye then, Reyes."

"Hang on a minute, kid!" He said, fear tinging his voice, "You have to keep me alive."

"I don't have to do nothing." I barked in response.

"If you kill me, Fierro will get away, and you'll never find him again."

I paused for a moment. I wanted to kill Reyes so bad. After all the suffering he'd caused me and others. He'd murdered many people in Refugio and stole all their money. He'd probably slaughtered every citizen of Justicia. He'd destroyed Folklore and burned my Uncle's ranch. He'd killed my mother and shot me. I wanted to send him to Hell, but he was right. I had to spare him if I ever wanted to recover anything and catch Fierro.

I kept my gun trained on him, though. I wasn't an idiot. I knew Reyes was a snake and would do anything possible to escape if he could. His confidence didn't let me shake the feeling that he was planning something.

"Throw your gun belt down. Slowly." I ordered. He smiled and did that. He didn't draw the LeMat revolver, which he had taken from Hernandez. I breathed a little easier, but he was still dangerous and still had the Winchester on his back. He couldn't get it off quickly, so I knew he'd be looking for a way to distract me. I couldn't let my guard down.

"You know why they used to call me 'the King,' kid? Back when I was running with Fierro?"

"No."

"Lotta people think it's cause I have a big ego. Which I do, I won't deny that, but that ain't the reason I started calling myself the King. It's not 'cause of my last name, neither. It's because I am the King of the World. Everyone and everything bows to me and does what I say, one way or another. I utter a word, and the World bends its knee!"

"You're insane." I snapped at him while he spoke.

"Think about it, kid," He continued, ignoring my comment, "Even Fate herself obeys my every word. I have been ahead of you every step of the game. You haven't even gotten close to catching me. *This* is the closest you've gotten, and even now that I am *almost* in your hands, I'm gonna get away. I know it, and I think that you know it."

"How do you figure?" I asked, trying to figure out what he was trying to do. "If you're gonna get away, I should just shoot you now; save me the time of chasing you later."

"You're not going to shoot me, kid." Reyes laughed, "I told you, I am the King. Even if you don't want to obey, you're going to. I should've called myself the God because everyone falls at my command!"

"You're crazy!" Wesley cried out from behind Reyes. He laughed, and that's when I realized what Reyes had been planning.

I hadn't noticed until now that Reyes had slowly been getting closer and closer. I was focused on what he had been saying. It was too late for me to act, though. His plan had already been set in motion. He threw his hat at me, blocking my vision. I fired a shot blindly, but my head was covered now by Reyes' poncho. He used it to pull me to the ground. My head slammed against a rock. I couldn't move, and I started to lose consciousness.

I could hear everything, though. Two men struggled and yelled. They exchanged blows. I tried to force myself up to help whoever was defending me, but my body wouldn't work with my mind's commands. Finally, at the end of the brawl, I heard two gunshots from a LeMat, which finally broke my trance. I tore the poncho off of my head and stood.

Reyes stood over my Uncle, smoking gun in hand. Wesley lay on the ground, clutching his bleeding gut. I pointed my revolver at Reyes, who just smiled and aimed his LeMat at me.

"End of the line, kid." He told me.

"For you, maybe." I spat back. He laughed.

"Let's do this." He started to say, "I want to prove to you that I am the King of the World. Let's holster our weapons and duel. I can show you that even your bullet will obey me."

"What's stopping me from putting a bullet in you right now?" I asked. He smirked.

"The fact that if you don't kill me with the one shot you have left, I will kill every single person you hold dear." He threatened, "I'll start with your Uncle. Then kill your aunt. And finally," He pointed at Tabitha, who had somehow escaped her ropes and was trying to help her father. "I'll take her. I'll let my men have her and finally put her out of her misery when she begs for death and admits that it was your fault." I didn't say anything for a moment. "My spies tell me you took a Mexican girl back in Las Fuentes; a real pretty thing, they say. I think I will take her for myself." My blood boiled.

"If I duel you, you'll leave them alone?" I snarled. I was filled with hate towards this animal who dared call himself The King.

"I swear it to you, Asa Hendricks." He remarked, shoving the revolver in his waistband, "You've earned enough of my respect that I will give you that honor."

I wasn't sure if I could trust him, but he was right. If I hit him and missed, then he would kill me. I only had one shot. He would end me and then go to the only real family I had left in this World, not to mention Leona. I couldn't let him touch even a hair on her head. If there was even a chance he was telling the truth about not taking them, I had to take that risk to keep those I cared about safe. I holstered my pistol and squared up to him.

"*Eso, muchacho.*" He laughed. He took one step forward and squared up. My blood felt hot, and my heart pounded. I forgot about all the pain and soreness I was feeling up until this point.

Everything went silent: my Uncle's moans, Tabitha's cries, even the burning of the house. The elements themselves went quiet to view this duel. A sudden rain started to fall.

Reyes looked like a madman. His clothes were tattered and bloodied, though most of the blood probably wasn't his. His hair was disheveled, and his face was unshaven. He'd nearly grown a beard since I last saw him. His eyes glimmered in an almost catlike way. But his smile was constant. He didn't care if he lived or died; he would go down in history as one of the most notorious and bloodthirsty outlaws of all time: Luis Reyes, the Self-Proclaimed King of the World. Despite this, I saw in his face that The King was confident he would win.

I breathed deeply, trying to calm my nerves. The sudden downpour helped, actually. It cooled and soothed my burned flesh and aching muscles as though God himself were rooting for me in this duel. I silently said a little prayer since it worked so well in the desert. God was supposed to be just and reasonable, so why shouldn't he help me against Reyes, the blasphemer who claimed himself to be a god himself, in control of all things.

Reyes' fingers twitched. I sighed and met his animalistic gaze. That's when I saw it. I couldn't explain how, but I saw into Reyes' very soul. I saw who he was now and who he had been before.

I witnessed fear. I glimpsed, deep down, a boy growing up in the middle of a war-torn country. I suddenly comprehended Reyes in a way that no other man or woman probably ever had. He wasn't a cold, heartless murderer but rather a child who had grown up with no control over his unfortunate and violent situation. He'd been orphaned and displaced by constant wars and rebellions. All he'd ever wanted was control over his own situation, the freedom to live and do as he pleased. Reyes' mind had become so warped and damaged that he'd taken it too far. He'd become a man struggling so desperately for control that he'd lost his mind and, subsequently, himself.

Luis Reyes wasn't insane. He was sick. Reyes had died as a boy, in a manner of speaking, and now all that was left in the shell of the poor kid was 'The King,' a devil of a man who thought himself a deity. Killing Reyes suddenly wasn't about avenging my mom or stopping him from slaughtering and murdering whomever he pleased. It was about eliminating a monster who called himself 'The King' from turning the boy Luis Reyes into his own nightmare.

I now understood who Reyes was and why he was the way he was. I knew it, and I knew from the look on his face that he knew it. His smirk had fallen, and his eyes had lost their fire. He tried to build himself up and make himself believe that he was 'The King,' but he couldn't. That frustrated him. He wasn't divine; he was just a scared child.

"Let's do this!" He roared, trying to sound fearsome. He just seemed pathetic, though. His voice cracked. He was scared. I didn't want to draw anymore. I could've talked him down if I'd had more time and gotten him the help he needed.

Fate forced my hand, though, as I saw Reyes go for his gun. I pulled my peacemaker to my hip and blasted my last shot into his chest. He stood there and looked down at the bloody hole in disbelief. His gun was still leveled at my head, but it was as though his mind no longer registered that his arm was there. He fired a shot, sending a bullet whizzing past my head. The recoil of the gun sent his arm flying back, and his body soon followed. For the first time in his life, Luis Reyes had been beaten in a duel. He started to sob quietly and weakly. I holstered and ran to his side.

"You beat me." He mumbled, looking at me with childlike eyes. They were filled with tears. I cradled the man's head.

"You can rest now, Luis," I responded. He just nodded or tried to, at least.

"Your mom was a good woman." He said, "She tried to raise you right despite her shortcomings. She didn't want you to have the life we lived. I think she'd be happy you turned out the way you did, Ace."

"I know," I told him. "I hope I can see you again, Luis. I genuinely mean that. I don't hate you. In fact, I forgive you for killing her. I'd like to know who Luis Reyes really is, not The King."

"Thanks, kid." He coughed. Blood started to pool in his mouth. "I wish I could've been Uncle Luis to you. Things weren't always like this. I wish I didn't kill your mom. That's my deathbed regret for ya." He let out a weak laugh, unlike any I'd heard from Reyes before. This one felt genuine.

I never got the chance to respond. Luis Reyes passed from this World. He died as he'd lived, violently. Despite all the bad things he'd done, I hoped he understood that I really had forgiven him and no longer hated him. I took one last look into his green eyes, then closed them, sending Luis Reyes, the boy who tried to make himself a King, to his final rest.

I ran over to my aunt, using Reyes' knife to cut her free. She bolted over to Tabitha's side to take control of administering first aid to her husband. I ran over, too.

"Ace." Wesley groaned weakly, clutching my hand with an unexpected strength, especially for a man who had taken two shots to the gut. "You have to go after Fierro."

"I won't leave you, Uncle," I said, holding back tears.

"Go!" He tried to yell. He coughed hard. "He's escaped to the north on his horse, but he wasn't going fast. You can still catch him. If he gets away with that money, my little Tabatha won't have anything in the world if I die. If you want to repay me for bringing you here, you will go now!"

I didn't say another word. It wasn't my place to question a dying man. I just wanted to carry out his wish of keeping his family off the street.

I snatched the Winchester from Reyes' corpse and pulled down the lever to open the bolt. There were two cartridges left in the rifle. If he wouldn't come peacefully, I had two chances to take down Fierro. I took a deep breath and mounted Iron, who seemed more than pleased to have his original rider back.

"Yah!" I yelled as Iron reared back, bolting forward into a full gallop down the hill towards the north. I had to catch Fierro and get the money back. If I wanted to repay my debt to my Uncle, I *had* to stop him, even if I had to kill him.

Chapter 29
The Devil Himself

I didn't have to gallop for too long before finally seeing Fierro trotting Magdalena toward the woods. The horse carried two large duffle bags on her flank, which I assumed was money. I called out to him, drawing the repeater off my back as I did. He turned and smiled his familiar devilish grin. He started galloping towards the woods. I had to get within range of him before he got there. I knew that I wouldn't be able to outride him in the forest.

I had the hill to my advantage, though, not to mention Iron wasn't carrying large bags of gold and money. Magdalena had already come to the part near the woods where the grassland flattened out. I rode hard. Iron snorted and grunted as though he knew what we were trying to do. I was gaining on them, but they were too close to the woods. We wouldn't catch up, even with our advantage of surprise.

I made Iron skid to a stop. I raised the lever gun to my shoulder, carefully aiming right at Fierro's broad back. I hadn't wanted to shoot at him, but I couldn't let him escape. I'd trusted Fierro with everything, so I felt betrayed by him. I sent all that hatred and anger into this one shot.

Magdalena stumbled to one side, probably avoiding a stone or a gopher hole, which caused my shot to miss. It whizzed past Fierro's head but shot a hole right through the Criollo's ear.

She screeched and skidded, throwing the unprepared *gaucho* Martín Fierro forward over her head. I celebrated my assumed victory. I'd been able to get Fierro off his horse.

Fierro flew through the air but didn't let go of the reins. He tumbled and landed on the ground, right on the heels of his boots. Fierro pulled the frightened mare back into his control by the reins before she could bolt off and leave him. He drew his long-barreled dragoon with his free hand and pointed it at me right as I cycled my Winchester.

"It seems we are at an impasse, *muchacho*." He said seriously. "I don't want to kill you. For Caroline."

"I don't want to kill you neither, Fierro." I said, not moving my rifle sights from his chest, "But that's my uncle's money. I can't let you take it."

"The Ranch will recover!" He yelled, "The people of Folklore are good folks. If nothing else, Reyes' attack has united them more than ever."

"I still can't let you walk away, *amigo.*"

Fierro didn't move his aim from me. He didn't even tremble. His hand was steady. He was relatively fresh, whereas I was beaten, burned, and exhausted. My side was aching. My old gunshot wound throbbed. It took all my strength just to keep the repeater level, and even then, it felt like it was getting heavier by the second.

"The only reason you aren't dead in the dirt right now is because of Caroline." Fierro finally said, "You don't understand, Ace."

"I understand plenty." I barked, trying to maintain a strong face. If I didn't back down, perhaps Fierro would give up. "Reyes was the King, and you were the Beast. I hate to admit it, but I think Mom was the Widow. Which means this *whole* time, you've been lying. You lied about how long you've been here and about what you did. I ain't even sure what's true anymore."

"Luis sure has a big mouth." He remarked, chuckling, "Yes, it's true. All of it. Your mother hid it from you. But it's true. I came here to this country seventeen years ago, not long after your birth. Your mother gave me room and board. Even though she had you, I fell in love with her."

"Why, though?" I growled, "Why did you start the gang and keep everything from me? Why didn't she tell me anything?"

"We were tired of living poor, kid! Your mother wasn't like me and Reyes. She just wanted a better life. That's why she left her husband, your father before you were born. That's why she never accepted my marriage proposals. She didn't want *us*, she just wanted you."

"So now you're gonna kill me for it? Or is that why you sent Reyes after her?"

His expression became blank, then distorted into a wild snarl. He bared his fang-like teeth and growled like a wolf.

"You know nothing, *Imbecil!*" He roared. His hand started to shake. I was getting to him. If I could get him to trip up, perhaps I could get a shot off when he was distracted. "Caroline was the love of my life!"

"So why'd you and Reyes cross her then?"

"I... *¡callate!* I didn't kill her. Reyes found me and thought that I had betrayed him to the Marshals. He thought that I was the reason he had been captured. But it was Caroline! She betrayed us.

She wanted out. She *saved* me but let Reyes get captured. I just told Reyes this so he wouldn't kill me! I didn't think that he'd kill her, though!"

"You thought that Luis Reyes, a madman who spent his life seeking freedom, wouldn't go after the woman who had taken his freedom away? Which one of us is the imbecile again?"

"You know nothing!" He yelled. I saw my chance finally. He pointed the barrel of his gun toward the ground as he screamed. I took the shot.

Fierro had realized that he messed up before I fired, so he could narrowly avoid his death, but not the bullet. It struck him in the right shoulder. He pointed his gun from the hip and fired.

It was Iron who saved me this time. The sudden shot from the Winchester frightened the young colt, so he reared up. I hadn't been prepared for this. He threw me off his back and into the grass.

Fierro's shots had missed, but I was starting to feel light-headed. I was exhausted and beaten up. I heard Fierro's boots approaching. He was coming to kill me, that was for sure.

I tried to get up, but my muscles were too exhausted. I turned my head just in time to see him draw his saber. The steel slid across the leather with a frightening hiss. He had a dark expression covering his face, the same expression I'd seen when he killed the rustlers. I was terrified, but I could no longer move.

He jabbed my chin gently with the sword's point, forcing me to raise my head to meet his gaze.

"You're out of options. Probably out of ammo, too." He muttered, "I won't kill you this time, Asa."

"You're a monster," I growled. Fierro just shrugged. "You murdered Selleck's family. You may as well have killed my mother, too. If you spare my life today, I won't stop coming for you, I swear it!"

"That's your choice. Perhaps it's your obligation." He shook his head in disappointment. He was trying to be cordial. I was not. "You will not catch me. You are *exactly* like Caroline was. It is as though she could copy her personality over to you. That's unfortunate for you, though, because it means that no matter what. I will always be ahead of you."

"I'll kill you! I promise!"

"If you want to, you may eventually be able to. When I am old and grey. But as long as I run, you won't catch me. I will always be three steps ahead of you. This is the closest you will ever get unless you descend to where I am. Unless you are willing to forsake all morals, attachments, and even family, you will never catch me. They didn't call me the Beast for no reason. I have killed everyone I ever got close to except Caroline, Reyes, and now, you. Now that you killed Reyes, no one knows me well enough to catch up to me. You will have to become a devil yourself, Ace!"

He sheathed his sword and reached into his coat pocket. He pulled out an envelope and a wad of cash. He flicked them into my face.

"A letter to you from Caroline. And *una recompensa*. Consider it payment for killing that lunatic, Reyes. I was going to end his miserable existence myself after all was said and done, but you have done it for me. You have avenged Caroline for both of us."

He started to walk back to his horse. I finally found the strength to sit up.

"Fierro!" I screamed at him, "Come back here and fight me!" He ignored me and mounted his horse. I grabbed the repeater and tried to shoot him, but there was no ammunition. He raised a hand to me in farewell. *"¡Chau, chico!"* He called out. His voice was free from ire. "I hope to see you again someday!" He spurred his horse and started trotting away.

"Fierro!" I screamed and shouted over and over again. I threw the rifle. I threw rocks. But it was too late. Martín Fierro had disappeared into the forest.

After retrieving the Winchester, I found Iron nearby, trotting back towards me. I mounted up and headed back to the smoldering remains of the house. Fierro's words stuck to my brain like muck. What had he meant when he said that I would have to descend to where he was if I wanted to have any hope of catching him? He'd told me that he had killed everyone he'd gotten close to. Is that what he meant? I would have to fall into the same madness that turns man into a beast?

I shuddered at the thought. I did my best to focus on returning to the house and then to Leona...

Chapter 30
The Road Ahead

When I got back to the house, or rather, the remains of the house, the sun was starting to rise. I was now two days and two nights with no sleep. My whole body ached and burned with every manner of pain. I was sure my ribs were broken. If Tabitha's expression when she saw me in the daylight told me anything, it was that I looked as bad as I felt.

They'd managed to stabilize Wesley, and some farmhands were loading him into a wagon. I needed to head back to Folklore to check on Selleck and Leona, so I offered to drive. Tabitha and Aunt Rachel rode in the back with Wesley, too, but they fell asleep before we even left the ranch.

Everything was burnt, at least in part, but nothing except the farmhouse wouldn't be salvageable. The ranch would recover. I wasn't sure about finances, but it would be recoverable at least. On the way out, we passed Hannah, the ranch hand's wife, who waved as we drove by. She looked exhausted, but she was still helping treat the wounded.

I drove in silence for a good fifteen minutes once we'd left the ranch. I felt tired, but I couldn't sleep. I was too busy thinking about Fierro, my mom, Selleck, and Leona. I was sick with exhaustion. I sighed loudly.

"Everything ok, Asa?" A gruff but weak voice said from the back of the wagon. I turned my head. Wesley was wide awake, with his wife and daughter sleeping on either shoulder.

"I reckon not, no," I admitted sheepishly. "I didn't get your money back. At least not all of it. Fierro gave me this before he escaped." I passed him the cash, which he took, and started counting slowly. "You should keep everything; maybe it can help you get the ranch back in order."

"Don't beat yourself up." After a moment of silence, he told me, " You saved many good people today, your aunt and cousin included. Not to mention you put an end to Luis Reyes, which is no small feat, especially for a sixteen-year-old."

"Seventeen." I corrected. "Pardon?"

"I'm seventeen now. I turned seventeen in July."

"I had no idea."

"How could you have known?"

There was silence for another moment. Wesley finally spoke up again.

"I saw Fierro every single day for the past eight years." He explained, "I trusted him with everything."

"I don't see the point you're trying to make."

"I mean that if I didn't see his betrayal coming, no one could've. You can't blame yourself, son. Nothing good comes from it."

He was right. I was with Fierro every day from when I arrived in Folklore to when I left with Selleck. The only indication I ever saw that he was something other than the ranch's foreman was when he killed the cattle rustlers. Even then, that was no indication that he was a traitor. He seemed content with the life he lived on the ranch.

"What will you do now, Ace?" My uncle asked. "What do you mean?"

"I just noticed that when you talked about getting things at the ranch back in order, you said 'you' and not 'we.' You aren't planning on staying."

I sighed and whipped the reins again.

"I don't reckon I will." I turned my head to look him in the eyes briefly, "I really appreciate everything you've done, Uncle Wesley, but farming just really ain't for me."

"I understand. You're gonna go with the marshal."

"Yes. I think I will."

"I think that's good." He said, taking a deep, painful breath, "Your mom wouldn't have wanted you to be unhappy. That's why she never moved the two of you out to the ranch when I asked her to. You know, after she died, I kept telling myself that maybe if she had just listened to me, she wouldn't have gone. At least, not in the way she did. It's weird to think now that she would've suffered the same fate, no matter what."

I didn't know how to respond to that. I was exhausted and didn't feel talkative. I just grunted in agreement. The ride was silent for a few more minutes.

"I suppose now we'll have to find a new foreman," Wesley said. "Any recommendations?"

"Actually," I answered, "I do. There's a woman on the ranch, a ranch hand's wife, by the name of Hannah. I missed her last name, but she was brave and fought hard for the people on the ranch. Good leader, too. I know she's a woman, but I think it's a good change."

"She can't be any worse than Fierro." Wesley laughed and shrugged, "A woman is a lot better than an insane bandit. Who knows? Maybe a woman in charge is just what we need..."

"I didn't turn out too bad, did I? I never had a man in my life." I said, laughing, "Things will be good. Hannah's smart. She'll learn quick if you give her a chance."

There was no response. Not even a chuckle. I thought my joke must not have landed with him until I turned around. Wesley was lying in the back of the cart, clutching his abdomen and groaning. He needed to get to the doctor now! I whipped the horses, pushing them as fast as they could go. Too many people had died last night. I wasn't going to let Death take another…

When we got to town, some of the men helped the doctor and Rachel unload Wesley from the cart. Tabitha followed her mother and grandpa into the clinic. I went over as well, at least to the steps outside.

Leona was sitting there by herself. She looked exhausted. Her hands were still covered in blood, now dark and dried, from putting pressure on Selleck's wound.

"How is he?" I asked her about Selleck. She looked up at me and gave me a small smile. Her eyes looked so tired.

"Alive. He will live. Just resting now." She said quietly. She was still struggling from last night.

She probably hadn't slept either. I sat beside her, and she laid her head on my shoulder.

"How are you holding up?" I asked. She grabbed my hand, which was just as dirty as hers. "Does killing ever get easy?" She caressed my hand with her thumb, "You kill so many men, but you don't feel bad."

"Leona, you have no reason to feel bad for killing that man last night." I told her, "You *saved* my life. That's what matters."

She looked at me. Her hazel eyes glimmered an amber color in the rising sun's light. "You killed Reyes?" She asked, changing the subject.

"I did." I admitted, "In the end, I didn't want to, but I did. He was sick in the head. All this could've been completely avoided if I had just found a way to get him help." Leona nodded.

We watched the sunrise together in silence. We both needed to sleep, bathe, and eat, but neither had the energy to. Despite my exhaustion, though, I felt whole again with her by my side.

"You can't blame yourself." She told me, "What of Martín Fierro?"

"Got away. Turns out, he turned Reyes on my mom. Didn't mean to, but he did."

"So your mom was *La Viuda?*"

"Yes. Fierro said she killed my dad before I was born and told everyone he went insane and left. After I was born, she met Fierro, and they eventually started their gang."

"I'm sorry."

"Leona," I said after another moment of silence, "why did you come with me? You said your dad wasn't a good man, that he wanted to kill me, and that he beat you, but why did you come with me to the U.S.? You could've just stayed in Las Fuentes and hitched a ride to another part of Mexico."

"I'm sorry, Asa." She said, looking me in the eyes again, "I lie. My father never hit me. He never want to kill you. He wasn't bad. I just wanted to be free. I didn't want to live a horrible life on the farm. I wanted to see the world and have adventures. Find love with a man who could be with me in all those moments."

"It's ok, Leona." I sighed, "I s'pose it don't matter now. I am glad you came with me." I hesitated, unsure if I should tell her what I was about to say, "I feel like, since you came into my life, I found a part of myself that I didn't know I was missing. I think I might be falling in love with you, Leona."

She stared at me, fluttering her eyes. She smiled and squeezed my hand.

"I feel the same way." She confessed. "You make me feel happy and complete." She kissed my dirty, dry lips suddenly. It was pleasant. I felt warm, and for the first time since arriving back in Folklore yesterday, I felt like the future would be bright, like everything would be ok.

"Let's go clean up, huh?" I said, standing up. I reached a hand to help her, and she took it, "After that, we can get a meal and get some rest."

"I'd like that." She smiled, "Remember, *you* owe me a new dress."

"We might be able to make that happen." I laughed. I took her hand in mine, and we walked down the road together. Fierro's words and my mother's death still lived in the back of my mind, but for now, Leona was my focus. The past could wait. The world was at peace, at least at the moment. Selleck was fine. My uncle would be ok.

The road ahead would be difficult, but she made it more effortless. For now, it was just Leona and me, and that made me as happy as I could be.

Epilogue

"Newly Sworn U.S. Marshal Kills Notorious Outlaw in Shootout"

The headline was eye-grabbing, but it wasn't true. Fierro knew that. The kid hadn't been a marshal yet when he killed Reyes. However, Fierro also knew they didn't want Asa to seem like some kind of vigilante, so he understood their creative liberties. Fierro decided to continue with the lead paragraph of the newspaper.

"Newly-Sworn United States Marshal, Asa Hendricks," the article read, "...killed notorious outlaw Luis 'The King' Reyes in a brutal shootout in a small frontier town called Folklore..."

"Hey, Fierro," An older Englishman said, interrupting the reading of the article. Fierro looked up from the newspaper, "Are you gonna play or just read the paper all day. You said you would play when they brought the hot water for your tea or whatever it is. We don't want to make you leave the table."

"Relax, Mr. Weston," Fierro assured him, "I will start now. And, for your information, it is called *yerba mate*. It is tough to get in this country. Expensive, too."

Fierro put down the newspaper on the corner table next to him. He poured the hot water into the herbs and sipped on it through the steel straw. He couldn't help but audibly moan as the freshly brewed *mate* touched his tongue. It had been too long since he tasted it.

"This is what I have been waiting for. It's been too long since I had this. The herb of life! *Madre mia...*"

"What's in the paper?" Mr. Weston asked again as Fierro picked up his cards, "It's about the kid, isn't it?"

"Very astute, Mr. Weston," Fierro remarked with a devilish smile. "I'll call."

"How was he? You met him, didn't you?"

"Indeed. He is brilliant. Picked up riding faster than I've ever seen any American do. He's also a dead-eye."

"Perfect for a lawman then... It's a shame." Mr. Weston sighed.

"Apart from his morals, you'd like the boy a lot." Fierro told the Brit, "He is very similar to his mother."

"Strong-willed and stubborn? Or annoyingly hubristic?"

"The former." Fierro answered, laughing, "His mentor will be a problem, though. Matthew Selleck. Have you heard of him?"

"I'm afraid so. He has been a thorn in my side in the past. Can't be bought either."

"I gathered that."

"Didn't you kill his family?"

"Who can say?" Fierro said with a shrug, "I have killed many families. I wouldn't be surprised if one of them was his."

"You're a snake, you know that, Fierro?"

"I do indeed," Fierro answered the Brit, smiling. He placed his cards down on the table. A royal flush.

"You're cheating!" Isaac Weston yelled, slamming his own cards on the table. Fierro laughed.

"No, Mr. Weston," A dark expression masked Fierro's face, "I am just lucky. Extremely lucky."

If Asa wanted to come after Fierro, then Fierro would let him. He liked the boy, and he loved the chase. He would have so much fun. It was more fun for Fierro, the murder and robbery, if there was someone competent to chase after him. Selleck wasn't that man. He didn't have the will to do what it took to catch Fierro.

On the other hand, Asa would stop at nothing to avenge his mother. Fierro was saddened by her loss, but he had gotten back something better. For the first time in eight years, Fierro felt genuine, raw excitement. He couldn't wait to see what the boy would do.

Elsewhere, far to the south, Maria Montenegro looked at her father in disgust. His favorite daughter, Leona, had left months ago, and he was still a mess. He drank constantly, never did any work anymore, and was letting the farm go into disarray. Leona had been the spitting image of their mother, beautiful and unique, whereas Maria was plain and normal-looking. She was, nevertheless, one of the most beautiful girls in their small community. Still, now that her sister ran away with some American cowboy, no one would ever want to marry Maria for fear that she would do the same one day. Between their father, who had become useless since Leona left, and the rest of the community, who mocked and ridiculed Maria now, Maria's resentment for her sister grew immensely.

Her father had already given Leona special treatment. Maria could tolerate doing the farm chores alone for an hour while Leona cared for her beauty. Maria could take having to do filthy and disgusting tasks while Leona went to the market to sell goods. Maria was used to that because her father had shown Leona favoritism all of Maria's life. She couldn't tolerate the change that had occurred in the last few months since Leona left. She hated Leona now. If Leona left the farm, Maria would, as well, to hunt down her sister and make her pay for this ordeal.

Maria would have her revenge. Her sister had ruined Maria's life by leaving her alone. Maria swore she would kill Leona and the gringo cowboy who had taken her along. First, though, she needed to take care of the *inutil* who dared call himself her father. If he wanted to be her father, he needed to act like one, not sit in the house all day and drink.

It would be so easy, Maria thought. He was passed out drunk right now. All she had to do was take the knife and slide it across his neck. He couldn't fight. He wouldn't be able to struggle. He couldn't scream for help, and even if he could, there would be no one to help him. The nearest neighbor was miles away. It would be easy, and then she would head to Las Fuentes to try and discover where her sister had gone.

So, as she approached her father, who had passed out in his bed, she couldn't help but feel excited. Leona had left her alone and ruined her life. Maria knew this would hurt her because Leona had cared about her father.

Maria felt thrilled as she neared the pathetic drunken man with a blade in her hand. For the first time in her life, Maria, like Martin Fierro, felt genuine, raw excitement.

9 798893 248302